THE RENEGADE MATE

SHIFTERS OF THE THREE RIVERS 2

KIRA NIGHTINGALE

ÉDITIONS SPOTTISWOODE

Book Cover by 100 Covers

Edited by Brigitte Billings

Published by Éditions Spottiswoode

First edition 2024

ISBN (ebook): 978-1-7382838-4-2

ISBN (paperback): 978-1-7382838-3-5

DEDICATION AND TRIGGER WARNINGS

Dedication

To my readers who love these characters as much as I do, this book is for you.

Trigger Warnings

This book contains some adult themes and lots of spice. There are characters dealing with grief in this story as well as references to domestic violence.

CONTENTS

Chapter One

MAI

The sun had barely risen, its rays only just managing to cast an autumnal pale glow over the motel. I remembered when this place opened. It had been the talk of the area, a shiny new motel for travelers and businesses, on the outskirts of our territory, bringing in new money and jobs to our town. Nowadays, its chipped paint and cracked windows highlighted its age and the broken dreams of the hopeful owners. The once vibrant blue sign had its paint peeling, and you could barely see the words "Three Rivers Inn" in the gloomy light.

It was owned by humans, two brothers, if I recalled correctly. The place had opened and swiftly gone downhill when Oliver was the Pack Alpha, but Jem and Hayley hadn't been able to turn things around for the humans in our territory yet. I guess now they never would.

After we checked in, I sat on the edge of the stiff, musty bed, my body aching and covered in bruises. Ryan, my mate—and how weird was it to say that?—stood by the window, his tall, muscular frame tense as he kept watch. He was wounded, too, but stood upright and still. It was only through our bond that I felt pain pulsing through him. Our eyes met for a brief moment, and I could see the same emotions swirling in his—grief and anger.

"I can't believe he's gone, Mai," he whispered. My heart clenched at the mention of my brother, Jem, the Alpha who had been killed by the very person he trusted the most—Hayley, his mate.

"Hayley …" I murmured, and with her name came the image of her cold, ruthless gaze. The betrayal still felt like a knife in my gut, twisting and turning as the reality of her actions sank in.

"Hey," Ryan said gently, walking over and placing a warm hand on my shoulder. His deep blue eyes, usually so full of confidence and strength, now held barely contained rage and determination. "We'll get through this together, okay? We'll find a way to make things right."

"What would 'right' even look like? We can't bring him back."

"Maybe not," he admitted, his grip on my shoulder tightening. "But we'll find a way, Mai. We'll get justice for Jem."

I stared into his eyes, seeking solace in their depths, and I knew we were on the same page—we wouldn't let Hayley's deed go unpunished. We had a responsibility to Jem, to Ryan's brothers, to Sofia and Jase, and to the rest of the Pack.

"I'm going to kill her," I whispered, suddenly feeling calm.

Ryan held me with his gaze. "Whatever you do, we'll do it together."

Before I knew what was happening, he pulled me into his arms. I sank against his muscular chest, the steady rhythm of his heartbeat and the scent of pine on his skin soothing me.

"We'll get through this," he murmured against my hair.

I looked up at him, our faces just inches apart. The air seemed to crackle between us. Slowly, tentatively, Ryan brought his lips to mine in a gentle kiss. I melted into him, the contact igniting a spark of desire that quickly caught flame.

Ryan maneuvered us down onto the bed without breaking the kiss. My hands roamed across the hard planes of his chest as his lips moved to my neck, nipping and sucking in a way that sent jolts of pleasure through me.

"Ryan ..." I moaned, arching into him. I wanted this so badly, something to take away the pain and grief. I wanted to feel Ryan moving inside of me and not have to think about anything else.

He ground his cock against me, the friction delicious even through our clothes. I fumbled with the buttons of his shirt, desperate to feel his bare skin against mine. Sensing my need, he stripped off the shirt and made quick work of my own top and bra.

The lust in Ryan's hooded eyes matched my own. He kissed me hungrily before trailing kisses down my neck. I arched up, needing to feel his lips on my breasts. His tongue did a swirl over one before capturing my nipple in his mouth. I cried out as he sucked and teased the sensitive peak.

Just as his fingers traced the waistband of my jeans, I froze, hearing the sound of footsteps outside the motel room. My heart leaped in my chest; I'd been running and hiding for so long that the slightest noise set me on edge.

"It's okay. It's my brothers," Ryan growled. "Fuck! They always did have shitty timing." He kissed me gently, then handed me my top and walked over to open the door. I pulled my shirt on and stood up, ready to face them.

Mason, the twins—Derek and Sam—plus an unfamiliar girl almost fell into the room. They all looked exhausted.

"Are you guys okay?" I said, taking in their battered appearances.

Sam's arm hung uselessly by his side. Mason was limping, and half his face was swollen, with a black eye and a split lip. The girl had a gash across her cheek, and Derek ... Derek looked like he'd gone through hell and back. His clothes were torn, there were bruises all over his face, his brown hair was matted with blood, and his gray eyes were haunted and distant.

"Are you two alright?" Sam asked, coming straight to me and gathering me up in a one-armed hug. Sam was the Shaw brother who was quick to hug and offer comfort. The complete opposite of his twin, Derek, who had always been serious and stand-off-ish, even before he joined the military. "We were so worried about you, Mai. We should have been better, been quicker, in hunting down Seth. I—"

"Hush, it's okay, Sam. It wasn't your fault," I interrupted. "Besides, Ryan and I dealt with Seth. He can't hurt me anymore."

I felt Sam's chin nod on my shoulder just as Ryan growled, "You wanna let go of my mate?"

I frowned at Ryan. He was staring at Sam, his jaw tight and his arms crossed.

Sam was staring at Ryan, too, and then he glanced at me. "It's fine," he whispered, even though everyone in that room could hear him. "It's the mate bond. It was always going to hit him hard. I'm lucky he hasn't thrown me across the room."

I nodded. I knew that newly mated couples were ridiculously overprotective of their mates, and I knew enough not to get within arm's reach of anyone who was newly mated in case their mate took offense and attacked me, but this was going to take some getting used to.

"Who's the girl?" I asked as Sam stepped back.

The girl was slender, about my height, but looked a hell of a lot better in tight jeans than I could ever pull off. The blood from the gash on her cheek had dried, and she'd put her auburn hair in a ponytail, though some strands had come loose and were stuck to the dried blood on her face.

Mason was staring at her like a lost puppy, but she was avoiding his gaze. Instead, when I asked the question, she turned her eyes to me. "I'm Shya," she said, her voice quiet. "Michael's daughter."

"What?" I bugged my eyes out at Derek, but he remained silent. My best friend Sofia had been on a few dates with Derek about a year ago, but then he started to ghost her. Scared something bad had happened to him, she'd driven over to his house, except on the way there she saw him walk out of a bookshop with Shya and hug her. Derek was not a hands-on kinda guy, and Sofia was convinced something had been going on between Derek and Shya. Since then, Sofia and Derek had barely talked to each other and when they did, they were usually yelling.

I turned to Mason. "Seriously, what the hell is she doing here?" Michael was the Alpha of the Bridgetown Pack. Last I'd heard, Michael was plotting to invade us and start a war. Of course, I'd been out of contact for a few days when my fucking ex, Seth, had kidnapped me, beat me senseless, and kept me locked up in his basement. But even so, it was some turnaround if he was letting his daughter tag along with our renegade Pack.

Mason shrugged. "It's fine, Mai. She's been working as an informant to Derek. Besides, Michael's backed off; he has other things to focus on now. Turns out the murders and the framing of Carson for them were all a plot by Tristan, the Bridgetown Beta, working with none other than our boy Brock to take over both Packs."

Before I'd been taken by Seth, we'd suspected that Brock was up to something, but not this, not killing Jem and taking over the Pack. "How did this happen? How did they get away with it for so long?"

"He must have been planning this for a long time," Mason growled. "We took our eyes off the ball, Mai. I'm sorry."

I shook my head. "It's no one's fault."

Mason looked at me, his eyes haunted. "Hayley killed Jem." His voice was flat, devoid of emotion.

"I know," I whispered, choking back tears. The raw grief threatened to overwhelm me, but I couldn't break down. Not now.

"She did it right in front of us. She didn't even hesitate."

"Tell me," I demanded, needing to know how it happened.

Sam sighed. "We'd gone with Jem to the Alpha House. We knew about Brock's plot, knew he'd started to take out our supporters. We were trying to form a base where our people could come for safety and where we could coordinate everything. Hayley was there. She met us at the door. She hu—" Sam choked off, unable to continue.

"She hugged him, Mai," Mason said. "She hugged him and kissed him, then drove a silver knife into his heart. He never saw it coming. None of us did."

"But why? Why would she do this? It doesn't make sense."

"I don't know. As soon as Jem went down, Brock and his enforcers surrounded us. We barely got away. I think if we'd been any further into the house when she did it, we'd never have escaped. We'd all be dead on that floor alongside Jem."

I could feel the tears rolling down my face. I couldn't stop them. I turned, and Ryan was there, pulling me into him. He held me tight, soothing me, feeling my pain and his as it reverberated back and forth down our bond.

"I'm going to kill her," I repeated, my voice steady and resolute. The others looked at me, and I could see the fire of revenge burning in their eyes. "We're going to make her pay for what she's done."

"Damn right, we will," Ryan growled, his grip on me tightening.

"We need a plan," Derek said, finally breaking his silence. His voice was cold and distant, but his eyes were grim and resolved.

"First, we heal," Ryan replied, his gaze roaming over all the injuries we had. "We're no good to anyone like this. While we recover, we gather intel. Find out what their next move is and how best to counter it."

"Agreed," I said, looking around at my small band of loyal friends. "Our priority is protecting the Pack and each other. Then we get justice."

"Speaking of the Pack," Derek spoke, his voice low and cautious. "We did manage to get some news on the others."

"Sofia?" I asked, knowing my voice betrayed my eagerness to hear about my best friend.

"Sofia and Jase are safe," Derek continued, a hint of relief in his eyes. "They're with Wally and Thomas. They'll protect them."

I breathed out loudly, feeling a weight lift from my chest. Knowing that Sofia and her brother were okay meant a lot.

"It's good that we have friends on the inside," Ryan said, a determined glint in his blue eyes. "We might need their help."

I glanced at Ryan, not sure how I felt about using Sofia and Jase as spies for us. They were my friends; I wanted to protect them, not put them in danger.

"There's one more thing you should know," Derek said, taking a deep breath as if bracing himself. "Jem … He wanted you to take over the Pack. To be the Alpha pair."

My heart hammered in my chest, my hand going to Ryan's.

"You've got to be joking?" I'd only just come back to the Pack. I'd run four years ago, when things got too much. I'd known for years that Ryan was my fated mate, and yet I'd watched him parade around with a collection of girls from the Pack. I'd thought I was okay about it. I was too young, and as my older brother's best friend, Ryan was off-limits until I was of age. But then, at a Regional Pack Meet, Sarah Conley had been all over him, and I'd lost it. I'd marched over to them, dragged Sarah off Ryan, and then declared to the whole fucking Meet that Ryan was my mate.

Ryan and Jem had been appalled. I hadn't realized how delicate our positions were in the Pack. Oliver had been the Alpha then, Jem the Pack Beta. Everyone knew that Jem wanted the top job and that Oliver was searching for ways to weaken Jem. By declaring myself Ryan's mate, I put a huge target on my back—I was the perfect person to take out. It would disable both Jem and his best friend and enforcer, Ryan. Jem and Ryan knew this and had done the only thing they could—Ryan rejected me in front of everyone, claimed I was a delusional little girl with a crush, and Jem had ordered me home.

I'd been so humiliated, so shocked that Ryan, my mate, could deny it that I couldn't breathe. Overwhelmed and heartbroken, I'd run. I left Three Rivers, spent four years dodging any mention of the place. Ended up in Cocrane, where I built up a freelancing website design business. Then Seth had started to take notice of me. He showered me with attention, made me feel like I actually was someone who could be loved, someone who deserved to be loved. It was great, until it wasn't.

It had taken me a while to realize just how controlling Seth was. How quick to anger he was when I didn't do something he wanted. Then, during one argument, he hit me. Broke my arm and two ribs and twisted my knee so badly I had to use crutches. That was it. So I'd run again. Heading back to the only place I knew I would be safe.

I'd just wanted to lie low for a few days. Heal my injuries, make a new plan. But Ryan had found me hiding out in my old apartment in Three Rivers. He told me the truth about why he rejected me and then spent every waking moment trying to convince me to give us a go. Given all that, it was no surprise that I had trust issues. I was just starting to get past that with Ryan, but Jem couldn't possibly have meant for me to take over the whole fucking Pack.

Mason nodded in agreement. "Jem was planning this for a long time. We've been searching for you, Mai. He thought we were close. He was sure that when you came back, you and Ryan would seal your mate bond."

"He can't have known that!" Hell, I'd only known for a few days that I could forgive Ryan and that I wanted to be with him.

Derek walked toward me. "Of course he could. He knew you. He knew how much you loved Ryan and how pig-headedly stubborn Ryan is. He knew Ryan would do anything to win you back. Jem saw it years ago; you two are destined for each other."

"But he didn't know he was going to die. Why would he want to leave the Pack?" I asked. "He loves ..." I gulped down my sorrow, "loved this Pack."

"He knew his relationship with Hayley was destabilizing the Pack," Derek replied. "He thought if you and Ryan took over, the Pack would thrive again. He wanted to take Hayley away, spend time with just her, work out how to make her happy."

I felt a rush of emotions—shock, fear, and an overwhelming sense of responsibility.

I shook my head and glared at Derek, willing him to take back his words. "No. You're wrong. We're not meant to be the Alpha pair. That is never gonna happen."

Chapter Two

MAI

The loud chatter of the crowd faded into a stunned silence as Ryan's words echoed across the packed room. "Mai, you're a fucking kid. We're not mates. We'll never be mates. You don't understand how this works. You will, one day when you grow up, but this is just some little girl's fantasy that's got out of hand."

His blue eyes were cold, cutting into me like shards of ice. Shock and humiliation washed over me in crushing waves. This couldn't be happening, not after I had put my heart on the line and finally told Ryan that he was my mate.

My cheeks burned as hushed whispers broke out among the crowd. I took a small step back. Laughter pierced the air as those in the crowd reacted to my public rejection with cruel delight. I could hear Brock's roaring laughter.

I turned to run but slammed straight into a solid, comforting frame—Jem. I wanted him to put his arms around me, to tell me that everything was going to be okay. Instead, he stared at me with such profound sorrow and disappointment that it stole my breath.

"Why, Mai?" he whispered, voice breaking. "Why did you have to ruin everything?"

Before I could reply, his face twisted in agony. He clutched at his chest as vivid red blood began to drip from his eyes, his ears, his mouth. I cried out, reaching for him, but my hands passed right through his body like smoke.

I startled awake in the pitch-black room, a cold sweat trickling down my spine. The memory of the nightmare clung to me, the heartache of Ryan's rejection, the horror of Jem's face, twisted in a grimace of pain, imprinted in my mind. I swallowed hard, trying to drive the images away.

The room was silent apart from the sound of Ryan's breath, steady and rhythmic beside me, and the low hum of the air con unit. As if drawn by an invisible force, I found myself leaning into him, craving the comfort of his heat. His scent wrapped around me, grounding me in the moment.

Ryan's arms tightened around me, his face relaxed and so beautiful in sleep. I lay there, cradled in his arms, thinking about how far I'd come. The memory of his rejection still ached, but being here with Ryan, maybe I was finally healing. He helped chase away the demons, his love soothing my battered soul. Curled against him right now, I felt safe, cherished even—feelings I thought were lost forever after he rejected me.

Jem's face from my nightmare intruded into my thoughts. Would the pain of losing him lessen in time? It seemed impossible right now that this all-consuming grief would change into something more bearable. Right now, there was only room for the sorrow and thoughts of revenge that wrestled within me, leaving me no room for sleep.

Ryan stirred beside me; his fingers traced an absent pattern on my arm. "Can't sleep?" he whispered, his voice rough.

A choked laugh escaped me, a pitiful sound that seemed to echo through the quiet room. "You could say that."

Ryan's arm tightened around me, pulling me closer to him. "Want to talk about it?"

"I can't believe he's gone," I said. "Hayley … I trusted her, Ryan. We all did."

"I know," he murmured, pressing a kiss to the top of my head. "I feel it too, Mai. The anger, the disbelief … it's like a nightmare that we can't wake up from."

I fell silent, listening to the hum of the air con and the occasional distant sounds of traffic.

After a moment, Ryan broke the silence. "Jem wanted us to be the Alpha pair, Mai. We could use that … we would be able to protect our Pack. Make sure nothing like this happens to the people we care about."

I sat up, turning to face him in the dim light filtering through the thin motel curtains.

"We've been a mated pair for less than a week, Ryan," I said, my voice harsher than I intended. "How are we supposed to lead? How are we supposed to protect the others?" I glanced down at the bruises covering my body courtesy of Seth. "We can barely look after ourselves."

"I'm trying to keep you safe, Mai. Brock and Hayley will come after us. They can't afford to let us live. We're a threat to them. Our best chance is to take the Alpha pair role, build up alliances, and strike back. Otherwise, we'll be on the run for the rest of our lives. I won't be able to keep you safe all the time."

He couldn't be serious. Was he honestly thinking about this? It just seemed too overwhelming, too much right now. Jem had been alive less than twenty-four hours ago.

"I don't need you to keep me safe," I snapped back. "I need you to trust me, to respect my opinions, too."

"I do trust you, Mai. But we need to consider this. For us … for the Pack."

Like hell we did. I didn't want to think about it, not now, not ever. I couldn't fill Jem's shoes, couldn't take the job he fought so hard for when his body was still warm somewhere. "We need to sleep," I said, cutting him off.

I turned over, pulling the covers up to my shoulders despite the heat. It was a long time before I fell back into a fitful sleep.

The light of a new day filtered through the threadbare curtains, and my eyelids fluttered open. Sleep had done little to quell the emotions that stormed inside me. It all rushed back in like a tidal wave. I closed my eyes again, willing away the tears that threatened to spill. No. I wasn't going to cry. Not again.

With Ryan still asleep beside me, I slipped out of bed. I crossed the room, the cool feel of the linoleum beneath my bare feet grounding me to this new world where Jem was dead and we were hunted.

Dressing quickly, I headed outside. I needed air, space to think, to feel. As I sat on the worn-out bench outside the motel, the crisp morning air filling my lungs, the usual calming ritual of watching the sunrise brought little comfort.

I felt Ryan rather than heard him. Turning my head, I saw him leaning against the doorway. He was barefoot and shirtless, wearing just his blue jeans. His dark hair was tousled from sleeping, but his eyes were alert and fixed right on me, like I might disappear at any moment, and he was going to make sure I didn't with the power of his eyes alone. He looked gorgeous in the morning sun, and I felt a such a strong pull toward him. Even in the midst of my grief, even when I was annoyed with him, part of me yearned to get up and walk over to Ryan, to run my hands along his chest, to feel him wrap his arms around me and kiss all my problems away.

I yanked my eyes away from him. I couldn't let myself get caught up in the mate bond right now. I needed time to get my head sorted. Almost like he knew what I was feeling, Ryan didn't move. He didn't come over to the bench. He was giving me space, which I appreciated. Still.

"I'm safe here, you know," I whispered, knowing he could hear me. "I can see anyone coming. You don't need to be on watch."

Ryan didn't reply. Out of the corner of my eye, I saw him cross his arms, his muscles rippling, as he kept staring at me. I hugged my knees to my chest and stared at my feet. I still couldn't believe that Jem was dead. I'd only just got him back. I'd missed him so much when I'd run from here. After our parents died, it used to be just him and me. He'd been the best older brother a werewolf could ask for. He'd loved me and made sure I was okay. Then Hayley came into the picture, and she hated me taking any of Jem's attention away from her.

Jem had seen how bad things were for most of the Pack under Oliver. He and Ryan had put in place a plan to take over the Pack, but that meant he disappeared at all hours and left Hayley to look after me. I'd missed him, missed spending time with him, missed his humor, his wisdom, his awesome hugs. But only a mated pair could challenge for the Alpha spot. That meant it had to be Jem and Hayley.

I'd thought a lot about my brother when I was away. I'd wished that he was happy, that he was doing what was right by our Pack. And when I came back, I got to see first-hand how much he'd done to change the Three Rivers Pack to make life better for all its members.

Then Seth kidnapped me. Ryan had hunted me down, and while we were away, Hayley had made her move. I'd thought that Hayley could never harm Jem, that he was her fated mate. I knew their relationship was difficult. Jem had told me himself that he'd blamed her after I ran away, that he'd neglected and ignored her. It was the last thing she needed.

Hayley had been brought up by an aunt and her family, who had treated Hayley like a modern-day Cinderella. Jem had gotten her out of there as soon as he realized how bad it was, but it affected how Hayley saw the world. She craved Jem's attention, only really felt safe and confident when she had it. She hated being told what to do and was driven by the need to be the one in charge. Jem being angry with her was too much for her to take, and she'd eventually cheated.

Jem had said it was the wake-up call he'd needed to see how dysfunctional their relationship had become. How it had filtered into the Pack bonds and affected everyone in the Pack. People were angrier than usual, on edge all the time. Jem had been trying to mend it, trying to make things right between him and Hayley. But then she allied with

Brock Madden and drove a silver dagger straight into Jem's heart.

I wiped a tear from my cheek. Jem was dead, and I would never again get to cuddle him, to hear him laugh, to have him tell me I had a spot of dirt on my shirt, and then tweak my nose when I looked down.

I stared out over the motel parking lot. There was a faint hint of fog in the air, but it was lifting with the rising sun. I could feel its rays on my face, fighting against the chilly air, and a silent promise echoed in my heart: Hayley would pay. And I would make sure of it.

Chapter Three

Mai

Our half-eaten breakfast sat on the rickety table, the smell of bacon, eggs, and burnt toast lingering in the air, making my stomach churn. Mason and Sam, having brought breakfast for all of us from a local diner, were in deep conversation with Ryan, discussing the Pack, the latest rumors, and our next steps, but their words washed over me.

"... One other thing you need to know. My contacts have confirmed that ripple has made it to Three Rivers. This drug ... Man, Ryan, this drug is bad news. Highly addictive to Shifters and ..."

I frowned. What the hell was ripple? I was going to have to ask Ryan about it later, my mind was all over the place right now and I couldn't concentrate for more than thirty seconds on what they were saying. While the others were occupied, I pulled out my phone and dialed Sofia's number. The connection rang and rang, every tone jolting my nerves. I needed to hear her voice, to know that she and Jase were really safe.

"Sofia's phone," a voice I didn't expect greeted me. Wally, the husband of the Pack doctor, Thomas.

"Wally? What are you doing with Sofia's phone?" I asked, my voice cracking with surprise.

"Sofia's just in the shower. I'm so sorry about Jem, Mai," Wally replied, his voice thick with emotion.

I nodded, knowing he couldn't see me, but there was a lump in my throat stopping me from speaking.

"Girl, if I could take away your hurt, I would in an instant. I can't tell you how glad Thomas and I are that you're okay, glad you got away from Seth."

"Is that Mai?" I heard Sofia's voice in the background.

"Thank you, Wally. I appreciate it. I'm just glad you guys are okay."

"We'll give Jem one hell of a toast tonight, I promise. I intend to get us all so drunk that we'll still be seeing double and walking sideways tomorrow. Hold on, Sofia's right here."

A pause, and then Sofia's voice, familiar and yet somehow distant, came through the line. "Mai? Are you okay? I'm sorry ..." I heard her start to sob.

"Sofia," I coaxed gently. "I needed to call and hear your voice. I had to know if you and Jase are alright."

"We're okay ..." She paused, taking a deep breath. "Jase and I ... I'm so sorry we didn't stop Seth; didn't stop you from being taken."

"It wasn't your fault. Nothing you could have done would have stopped him."

"But if we had, maybe you would have still been here. Ryan wouldn't have left. Maybe you could have stopped Hayley from ... from—"

"You can't think like that." I knew I couldn't. 'What ifs' would drive me crazy with regrets of things I had or hadn't done, and I didn't think

I could cope with anything more right now.

She was silent for a moment, then growled, "If I could bring Seth back to life, I'd turn him into a chew toy for the neighborhood puppies, and then I'd drown him in a puddle."

I smiled. I knew she was going to be okay. She would always be my ride-or-die best friend.

"I know, Sof."

"So, what's next?" she asked, determination replacing her grief. She wanted revenge, just like me.

In the background, I heard Wally call out, "Hell yes! Tell Mai whatever it is, I want in! Just point me in the right direction and I'll bring the sass and the ass-kicking."

I pressed my lips together to stop from laughing. Their support lifted a bit of the cloud that was in my chest. "Hold off for now, both of you. Rest, recover. Sofia, can you and Jase call in sick to work? I want you to lie low until we know more about what Brock and Hayley are up to. Ryan and I will come up with a plan, and we'll let you know."

"Okay, Mai." Sofia's voice was resigned, and I knew she wanted action, not rest. Anything to feel like she was doing something. "We'll wait for your word."

"Take care, chickie."

"You, too."

I ended the call and sat for a moment, my hand still gripping the phone. The motel room felt colder, emptier, as if a part of me had been left on the other end of that call.

The motel room's door creaked open as Derek and Shya strode in.

"We've got news," Derek started, his voice steady and somber.

Ryan shot me a quick look before turning his attention to them.

"What's going on?"

"It's my dad, Michael," Shya said. "He wants to help."

"Michael?" I stammered out, disbelief coloring my voice. The Alpha of the Bridgetown Pack. Extending a hand to us?

"Yeah." Derek nodded, his gaze fixed on Shya, which I took to be a silent form of support. "Michael's got Tristan's rebellion under control. Tristan's done a Houdini and is nowhere to be found. Michael's offering us a safe haven."

The room was silent as we all took this in.

"Are you saying," I began, wanting to be absolutely clear, "that he's offering us sanctuary?"

Shya nodded, her jaw set in a hard line. "He said you, us, we're all welcome."

This was too good to be true. Could we trust another Alpha, another Pack? Especially after the betrayals from our own Pack? I cast a quick glance at Ryan, searching his face for a hint of what he was thinking. His features were unreadable, his gaze locked onto Derek and Shya.

"Why would Michael offer us sanctuary now?" I questioned, suspicion gnawing at me.

Derek shifted uncomfortably. Ryan was quiet beside me, but I could see his mind whirring, weighing the options.

"What's the catch?" I demanded.

Shya was silent. She didn't know or didn't want to say?

"Maybe there isn't one," Mason said.

I slid my gaze to Mason, and he immediately lowered his eyes.

"There's always a catch," I replied.

The room was silent for a moment.

"I think we take the offer," Ryan said finally.

"What the fuck, Ryan?" My patience snapped. "We can't just go marching into a rival Pack and set up home!"

"It's not like we have many other options, Mai," Ryan shot back. "We need a place to regroup, to plan. We're sitting ducks out here."

"So, we just trust some Alpha we barely know? What if it's a trap? What if—"

"Mai," Ryan stepped close to me, his eyes burning into mine, "I'll never let anything happen to you. I know you're scared. But we need to think rationally about this."

Rationally? He did not just say that.

For a moment, I thought my head was about to explode. Although, better yet, I wanted to make Ryan's head explode.

I narrowed my eyes and put my hands on my hips. "Rationally, huh? And exactly how rational is it to just waltz into another Pack's territory? Tell me, Ryan, do you have a master plan hidden in that pretty head of yours? Or are you just hoping they'll have a nice welcoming committee for us with strawberry champagne and scones?"

"Oh, I've got a plan, Mai. It involves us not getting killed out here."

I leaned in closer. "And what if your master plan ends with us in a trap? We escape from Brock and Hayley only to willingly offer ourselves on a plate to Michael and Camille! You think your charming smile will get us out of that?"

He raised an eyebrow. "My charming smile worked on you, didn't it?"

That was it, I was going to punch that smile right off his face.

I don't know if Shya saw what I was planning but she quickly stepped forward. "My father isn't the enemy here. You don't know him, I get it. But I do. He's a good man, a good Alpha. He'd do anything to protect his Pack, and right now, that includes us."

"No offense, Shya," I said, swinging my gaze to her, my voice tight, "but it's a bit hard for me to trust anyone right now."

Shya lowered her eyes. I wasn't sure if it was to keep me calm or because she saw me as a higher rank than her. And that was one hell of a scary thought. The Bridgetown Pack determined their succession through blood lines rather than combat. She was the nearest our kind had to a Pack princess and was next in line to be the Pack Alpha.

"I get it, Mai. I really do. And I can't make you trust my father. But, please, trust me. I've worked for Derek for these last few months. I've never passed bad information. I've always done what is best for both our Packs. I would stake my life on this. My father will help you."

Ryan tilted his head to one side. "He doesn't want Brock and Hayley in charge of the Three Rivers. They worked with Tristan to overthrow him. They are a direct threat to his Pack. It makes sense for him to court us as the alternative Alpha pair. If he offers sanctuary now, we'd owe him. And if we defeat Brock and Hayley, then all of a sudden, he has a friendly neighbor next door. Which only makes it safer for his Pack."

"You're asking me to trust a man I've never met," I said, my voice soft but steady. "To put our renegade Pack ..." I swept my hand around the room. This was our Pack, small though it was, but they were everything to me. "You want me to put their lives in his hands."

"Yes," Ryan replied, meeting my gaze head-on. "Because it's our best shot, Mai, at protecting them."

I glanced around the room. Everyone was looking to me to make this decision. They'd already made Ryan and me the Alpha pair, whether we wanted it or not.

How were they all willing to just trust Michael on this? I'd trusted Ryan to look out for me, and he'd rejected me. I'd trusted Seth, and he'd beaten the shit out of me. I'd trusted Hayley, and she'd killed Jem.

I felt a pulse of concern come down my bond with Ryan. He knew what I was thinking, that I was dredging up these memories.

He stepped close to me and wrapped his arms around my waist. He felt warm, and I eased into the heat. "I won't let anything happen to you, Mai. And we won't let anything happen to them." Ryan nodded to the others. "Michael is our best shot of a safe place to recover while we work out what to do next. If we don't go there, we'll have to go on the run instead. It's your call, Mai. Whatever you want, we'll do it."

I'd run before, when Ryan had rejected me. And I'd run again when Seth hit me. I was done running.

"Alright," I conceded reluctantly. "We'll go to Bridgetown."

Chapter Four

RYAN

I peered out of the car window as Bridgetown unfurled before me, a pulsating hub of urban life nestled in the middle of Shifter territories. Unlike the untouched wilderness of Three Rivers, this was a place where old-world charm met modern sophistication. Two and three-story buildings lined the streets, their modern lines softened by an architectural style that echoed a simpler time.

It wasn't our territory, though, and it set my senses on alert, my wolf pacing inside of me in apprehension. My mind whirled: a storm of worry for Mai, sitting next to me in the back seat while Derek drove; wariness of our new surroundings; and the constant, throbbing undercurrent of our loss of Jem. I couldn't believe he was dead. He wasn't blood, but he was my brother. We'd been through everything together—the death of his parents and my mom, taking care of my brothers when my dad checked out on alcohol, Mai disappearing, challenging Oliver and his enforcers, Jem and Hayley taking over the Pack—we'd done it all together and now he was just gone. I should have seen it. The signs were there, but I'd failed to connect the dots. Hayley's increasing instability, her growing discontent with

Jem and the Pack, the way her eyes would darken with a dangerous glint whenever Jem brushed her off. I'd ignored it, convinced that Jem could handle her, that their bond as mates would keep her in check. But I was wrong.

The guilt gnawed at me, a relentless beast tearing at my insides. If I'd paid more attention, if I'd intervened, maybe Jem would still be alive. But beneath the guilt, beneath the grief that was threatening to consume both me and Mai, there was a simmering rage, a fury that burned white-hot in my veins. Hayley and Brock had taken Jem from us. Hayley had betrayed her mate, but they'd both betrayed their Pack and everything we stood for. And for that, they would pay.

The buildings were closer together now, their facades a mix of old brick and modern glass. The streets were dotted with people going about their business. And elderly couple strolled hand in hand, their steps slow but sure. A young mother pushed a stroller, her eyes flicking down to the babbling infant nestled inside. None of them had any idea of the battles that we'd fought, or the ones that were coming. They didn't know our pain, the depth of the betrayal we had suffered, or the lengths we would go to get justice for Jem, for all of us.

With all these people, we had to be near the heart of Bridgetown. It had taken us most of the day to finalize plans and head over here. Then we took the long way around, making sure we weren't followed. It was almost eight in the evening now, and I knew Mai needed sleep soon. Her ordeals from the last week, plus the grief of losing Jem, had drained her. I could feel her exhaustion through our bond, and my wolf was getting annoyed with me for not finding her a place to rest. As Mai's fingers danced over the screen of her phone, I caught a glimpse of her expression, tight with concern and determination. She was texting

Sofia, filling her in on our decision to go to Bridgetown, and telling her that she and Jase should keep out of sight for the time being.

While Mai was occupied, my thoughts spiraled inward, my wolf unsettled. I was grappling with the responsibility my brothers had sprung on us—challenging for the Alphahood of the Three Rivers Pack. The notion was as electrifying as it was daunting.

Could I really be an Alpha? The word itself seemed too grand, too heavy, for someone like me. But then again, hadn't I been playing a similar role for years? Flashbacks of my childhood rushed back … Mom died when I was ten. After that, Dad had been as useless as he was drunk, and my brothers and I had gone without clean clothes, without food to eat. I'd stolen food, ditched class, and gone hunting each day just to make sure they had enough to eat.

Jem had helped, slipping me food and clothes when he could. Then Jem had made the Beta spot under Oliver. I'd been his number one enforcer, watching his back, making sure we were all safe. It came with a regular paycheck, and life got a bit easier for my brothers. Those years had shaped me, honed my protective instincts, and kicked my Alpha tendencies into high gear.

I glanced at Mai, her face, and that cute frown she got when she was concentrating, illuminated by the phone screen. What would it mean for her, for us, to step into such roles? I couldn't let Mai down. Not again. Being an Alpha pair wasn't just about leading; it was about setting an example, forging a bond that would be looked upon as the epitome of what a partnership could be. Did we have what it took to be that example? Our Pack needed that desperately, especially after the shitshow that Jem and Hayley had descended into.

And then there were the others—our packmates, our friends.

They'd already lost so much. The last thing I wanted was to bring them more pain or uncertainty. But could we bring them something else? Hope, maybe. A fresh start. Justice for Jem.

Mai's phone buzzed, the sound jarring in the silence of the car, and she read the reply, her brow furrowing deeper. "Brock's enforcers were at Thomas and Wally's house," she informed me, her voice barely above a whisper.

Fuck.

"Did they get in?"

She shook her head. "No. Thomas refused to let them enter."

Thank the Goddess for Thomas. "Good. Brock will be reluctant to go against the only Pack doctor. He needs Thomas for now, but it might only buy us a few days. Tell Sofia and Jase to stay hidden for now," I said, my mind racing as I considered our options, "and not to leave Wally and Thomas's house."

Mai nodded, her fingers flying over the keys once again. I could see the strain in her eyes, the worry that was eating at her. I wanted to take it all away, wanted to make sure she never felt like this again. Without thinking, I reached over to hold her hand. As soon as I touched her skin, a bolt of electricity shot through our bond and her eyes widened.

"What was that?" she whispered.

"The mate bond is still new. Until it settles down, it's going to flare up randomly." I trailed a finger up her bare arm, and watched the pulse in her throat quicken. "And sometimes not so randomly."

I could feel my wolf stir, driven by the need to protect and comfort her. The mate bond was powerful, demanding, but it also gave a sense of calm and reassurance. Seeing Mai respond to my touch, the way her tension eased slightly, made my wolf chuff in satisfaction. He loved that we could do this for her. I loved just how responsive she was to my touch. Images of Mai naked in my bed while I explored just how responsive she could be flashed into my mind. I trailed my finger slowly back down her arm to clasp her hand again. It was fucking hard holding myself back. Our bond being this new was driving me on but she needed comfort right now not multiple orgasms.

"We're here," Derek announced as he pulled up in front of the Alpha's residence.

Mason, who was driving the other car with the rest of our little Pack in it, stopped next to us.

"You ready?"

Mai nodded and I got out, looking up at an impressive two-story structure that sprawled across a generous lot near the town center. It was a modern building that had a welcoming air, its walls of glass and steel softened by landscaped gardens. This wasn't the secluded, fortress-like compound of Three Rivers. It was right in the heart of things, a clear message of its importance to the community.

I moved over to Mai and placed my hand on her back.

The grand entrance of the Alpha house swung open, and standing there was Michael, a familiar face in this unfamiliar territory. There was First Nations blood in his heritage, and it showed strongly in Michael with his height, lean frame, and sharp features. Beside him stood a petite woman in a dark, knee-length skirt and navy blouse. She had chestnut hair that was knotted neatly at the nape of her neck, and her lips were set in a thin line. She radiated a silent command that prickled my senses even from a distance.

"Ryan, Mai," Michael began, "this is my mate, Camille."

She nodded at us, her gaze unflinching, appraising. "It's

unfortunate we meet under these circumstances," she said, her voice carrying a hint of steel.

"Indeed," I replied, "but we appreciate your hospitality."

A sudden flurry of movement stole my focus. Two figures, one a towering beanpole of a teen and the other a whirlwind of energy, bounded into view from behind Michael and Camille. The taller boy couldn't be more than seventeen, a spitting image of Michael, but with watchful eyes that were a reflection of his mother. The other boy looked about seven years old and wore a happy, playful smile.

"This is Henry," Michael said, his rough voice turning unexpectedly tender. "And this vivacious firecracker," he gestured to the younger boy, "is Tucker."

Henry offered a polite nod in response, his eyes never still, taking in everything. Tucker, on the other hand, flashed us a brilliant, cheeky grin that showed he was missing his two front teeth.

Henry and Tucker's eyes darted toward the two cars behind us. A gasp escaped Tucker's lips as he saw the last passenger get out of the car.

"Shya!" he whooped, his voice cracking with youthful delight. He took off, sprinting across the lawn and cannonballing into his older sister. Shya, surprised by the little human missile, staggered back a step, then laughed, her worry lines softening for a moment. Henry hung back, his gaze watchful and protective, before walking over to join the reunion. His greeting was more restrained, a warm hug and soft words exchanged between siblings.

As Tucker disentangled himself from Shya, his eyes danced with mischief. He turned to his parents, his grin growing wider. "Dad, did you know wolves run faster than cars?" he blurted out. Michael chuckled, a soft rumbling sound, his eyes twinkling with amusement. Camille, suppressing a smile, quickly feigned a stern look. "Tucker, manners."

"What?" He frowned. "It's true! Can I prove it, Dad? Can I? We can race now. You Shift, and I'll drive the car!"

Michael laughed out loud, turning to us. "He's been trying to drive a car for the last six months, ever since he saw a Formula One race on the TV. He keeps coming up with new ways for us to allow it."

"It hasn't worked yet," Camille said sternly. "And this one isn't going to work, either."

"Aw, Mom!" Tucker whined, still in Shya's arms.

"Aw, Mom, nothing. It's time for your bed. I said you could stay up to see your sister. Now, scoot, young man."

Henry stepped forward and held out his arms to his sister. "Here, let me. I'll put him to bed. You get caught up with Mom and Dad."

Shya smiled at Henry, passing the struggling Tucker over to him.

"I'll come and read you a story in a bit, okay, Tucker? Promise."

Tucker stopped struggling, but stuck his tongue out at his older brother.

Camille sighed as they walked past. "I don't know what we're going to do with that one."

"Go-karting," I said. "Lots of fun and works a charm for kids who want to drive. I did it with my younger brother Sam, and it shut him up about driving a car for years."

Camille tilted her head to one side. "Good idea. I'll try it."

Behind Camille, a tall, wiry woman with frizzy brown hair stepped forward. Her sharp, foxlike features softened in a polite smile. "I'm Danni, the new Beta here in Bridgetown," she introduced herself, extending a hand to me. Her grip was firm—a fighter's grip.

"Nice to meet you, Danni."

Then came two others, a pair who could only be the enforcers. The man was broad, with a deep-set scar running down his cheek. The woman next to him had a lean, almost wolfish figure, her eyes alert and wary.

"This is Ivan," Michael introduced the man. He offered a curt nod, but didn't say anything. "And Elise," he continued, gesturing toward the woman.

"Hello, pleased to meet you all," Elise said, her gaze sharp and assessing.

Mai was silent, taking it all in. I couldn't put my finger on it, but I felt a faint current of tension running beneath the polite introductions and forced smiles. I guessed not everyone was happy we were here.

"Please," Camille nodded at the entrance, "follow me. Mai, Ryan, we would appreciate it if you would join us in the study. Danni will show the others to their rooms. They are all adjoining. Shya, of course," and here Camille's voice went from polite to iron firm, a mother making it clear to her child who was in charge, "will have her old room."

Derek shot a glance at me. I nodded, telling him to follow Danni, then I took Mai's hand as we followed Camille into the wolf's den.

CHAPTER FIVE

RYAN

We walked through the door and into a spacious hallway. The interior design was interesting, a modern minimalism accentuated by high ceilings and a sense of open space. Warm lights glowed softly, highlighting the rich dark wood of the floor and the contrasting white of the walls. Modern artwork hung on the walls, while potted plants gave the impression that this was a home where nature was welcome.

Camille led us further, guiding us through a series of rooms, each clean, tidy, meticulously designed and furnished. It felt like a maze of sleek architecture and elegance. The others peeled off and up a beech staircase while Mai and I followed Camille into the study. It was a long room with floor-to-ceiling bookshelves lining two of the walls. The dark mahogany shelves were packed with leather-bound books and artifacts that were definitely not local. In the center of the room sat an enormous antique desk, its surface neatly organized. A high-backed leather chair stood behind the desk, with two smaller guest chairs opposite it.

On the far side of the room, tucked between two large windows, was a cozy sitting area. Two chocolate-colored leather couches faced each other across a glass coffee table. Behind them, the windows offered a picturesque view of the sprawling gardens outside. The last of the evening sunlight filtered in, bathing the room in a warm glow.

"You have a lovely home," Mai said to Camille.

"Thank you, Mai. We like it here."

Michael cleared his throat. "Ryan," he began, his voice tight. "I was wrong about Jem. About the Three Rivers. I let myself get taken in by Tristan's lies. I owe you an apology."

I wasn't expecting that, not from an Alpha who, rumor had it, accepted no challenge to his authority.

He must have guessed my thoughts, as he continued, "I'm trying to accept my mistakes. Tristan and Shya have taught me no good comes from always being stubborn."

"Really?" Mai smiled beside me, her voice teasing. "Perhaps you can give Ryan lessons?"

I knew she was trying to put our hosts at ease. I was guessing that she had picked up on the subtle currents of unhappiness, too, and was trying to show that we weren't a threat.

Camille's lips curled up, but the smile did not reach her eyes. "I appreciate you trying to move on from our apology, but it is important to us that we explain. Tristan ... he was convincing," Camille said, her voice filled with anger. "However, we should've trusted our instincts instead of his words. We won't make that mistake again."

I wasn't the only one who caught the note of threat in her words.

"And what do your instincts say about us?" Mai asked, getting right to the heart of it.

Camille studied Mai, then glanced at me. "I'm not sure yet. I won't deny that I took some convincing to offer sanctuary, but I do believe it is the right thing to do. Our daughter trusts and respects you. Enough to feed you information about our Pack and seek help when we didn't listen to her warnings about Tristan."

"We're not here to make trouble for your Pack," Mai assured her.

Camille shook her head. "Trouble was already here. We are going to have to work together if we want to undo the damage that's been caused and ensure both our Packs are safe."

There was a knock at the door before I could reply, and Mason strode in. His presence had an immediate effect on me as always; a familiar warmth washing over me taking the edge off my nerves. Mason had a quiet strength about him that never failed to make me feel more grounded, more secure. He was wearing his usual stern expression, his dark eyes scrutinizing the room, instantly alert and ready for anything.

"Sorry to interrupt," he said in his deep, gravelly voice, his gaze briefly meeting mine before scanning the room once again. "I have a message for Ryan, but it can wait."

I caught the way Mason's eyes flickered to Mai, a silent check-in. He wasn't here with a message. He was checking on us, ensuring we were okay.

"Not at all, Mason," Michael responded with a gracious nod. "We're glad you're here."

Mason gave me a slight nod, telling me he was there, ready to lend a hand, ready to fight if needed. I gave my head the slightest shake, indicating that there was no need. Not yet, anyway.

"Do you have any news from Three Rivers?" I asked.

Michael shot a look to his mate, one I couldn't decipher. Whatever passed between them, Camille was the one to answer.

"They have killed some of your enforcers and rounded up the rest. Brock and Hayley have claimed control and announced themselves to be the Alpha pair."

I saw Mai freeze at the news. "How can that be?" she whispered. "Jem was Hayley's mate."

Camille sighed. "She's claiming that Jem tricked her in some way, but she realized the truth in the last couple of months when Brock told her that he was actually her real fated mate. Hayley has said that she knew he was right and has been trying to separate from Jem ever since."

"That's bullshit!"

Camille shrugged. "I will have to take your word on that, but it is what they are saying. Brock and Hayley have called a regional Pack Meet in five days. There, they will declare themselves the new Alpha pair of the Three Rivers Pack, and their power and reign will be cemented. You have until then to challenge them with the support of the other Packs. After that, the Wolf Council laws come into force. As such, other Alphas cannot interfere, and no challenges can be made on the Alpha pair for at least one year."

I looked at Mai. There was no way we could go against the Wolf Council. It was our ruling authority. They made and enforced all our laws. Come to think of it, this year, it was the turn of the Three Rivers Pack to nominate someone to serve on the Council. It was not an easy job, and the werewolf chosen would have to give up their bond to our Pack. But you didn't refuse the Council. They were known to be ruthless and protected the peace between the humans and werewolves with deadly efficiency. We no longer had time to work this out at our own pace. The clock had just started ticking. We needed to decide if we were going to put ourselves forward as an Alpha pair, and soon.

"In the meantime," Camille continued, "we're here with whatever you need. A safe haven, a place to rest and recover, a base of operations—"

"Thank you," Mai injected quickly. "We don't have any plans yet, but having somewhere safe to rest and where we can work out our next steps is appreciated."

I looked at Mai as she stood there, processing this information. Her wavy dark hair was windswept but silky, and her scent, of honeysuckle, mint and aspen leaves, was aflame with anger at Camille's news. As she bit her lip in concentration, I felt a flare of determination course through me.

Goddess, she was beautiful. And mine. All mine. I had finally been able to claim her as my mate, even if it had taken me four long years of searching for her so I could fix the damage I caused when I rejected her. Part of me wanted to take her away from here, from all of this pain and danger. I wanted to take her somewhere she'd be safe, somewhere she could be happy. But another part knew that there was no running away. Our place was here, fighting for our territory and our Pack.

Camille nodded. "Of course. This is a safe place. They've been stopped for now."

"They?" I queried, thinking back to the intel on Bridgetown. They'd been expanding their Pack, both humans and Shifters, for the last few months, recruiting from out of the area. "Was it just Tristan, or did he take other members of your Pack with him?"

Michael exchanged an uneasy glance with Camille. "We were preparing for a war with the Three Rivers. The bad intel that Tristan and others were providing us all pointed to Jem being an unstable Alpha and for the troubles in your Pack to spill over into ours. We needed to be ready for any contingency. It is apparent now, though, that Tristan was not working on his own. Some of the new recruits were loyal to him, not to our Pack, not to us. They have since disappeared and are probably with Tristan, plotting their next moves."

"You think he'll try again?"

"The trouble with Tristan," Michael's voice hardened as he spoke Tristan's name, "is that he really does believe that Shya is his mate. I have no doubt that he will return for her."

My gaze moved to Mason, the usually composed wolf now looking anything but. His fists were clenched, his knuckles white, and his eyes had a wild look to them. Something had struck a nerve.

Protectiveness over someone in danger or something more?

I felt a pit opening in my stomach as I watched Mason, a sense of realization washing over me. Could Shya be Mason's fated mate? The thought added an entirely new layer of complexity to an already tense situation. If that was the case, then we were heading into even murkier waters.

Chapter Six

MAI

As I settled into the overstuffed chair in the study, my mind kept drifting back to breakfast. I'd slept badly, nightmares waking me often in the night, only to be lulled back to sleep in Ryan's warm arms as he pulled me close and stroked my back until my heart rate had slowed and sleep claimed me once more.

We'd woken early and headed downstairs. The tension that hung in the kitchen was thicker than the syrup on Ivan's pancakes. Danni, Ivan, Elise, and Camille had all been there. They tried to make us feel welcome, but I could see their exchanged glances, and the strained conversation was awful. Who the hell wanted to talk about what color sofa Elise should buy? Even Sam, who usually had a sarcastic comment for everything, was uncharacteristically quiet.

We were strangers in this Pack. Yes, we were guests, but we were outsiders, all the same. We couldn't afford to be strangers for long, though. We needed to bridge the gap, make them see us as allies, not threats. But how?

A pang of anxiety twisted in my stomach. I'd never been good with diplomacy, with the smooth words and calculated gestures that soothed doubts and fears. I was straightforward, to the point. No sugar-coating, no empty promises. But I had to figure it out, for all our sakes. We needed to be accepted by the Bridgetown Pack, to be truly welcomed, not merely tolerated.

A deep voice pulled me back to the present. "Mai," Derek called, a frown creasing his forehead. "You listening?" He leaned forward, resting his elbows on his knees.

I offered a weak smile, brushing my wavy hair back from my face. "Yeah, Derek. Sorry, I was just thinking."

"We're not just your Pack, Mai," Sam chimed in. "We're your family. And we've got your back, no matter what."

I looked at each of them in turn, their words echoing in my mind. My gaze finally landed on Ryan, the only one who would meet my eyes. He was watching me intently. They were all acting like we were already the Alpha pair, and it was pissing me off.

"I know, Sam," I replied. And I did know. They were my family, and I was so fucking grateful to have each and every one of them. But I didn't want such a momentous decision to be forced on me.

"I was saying we need a plan," Derek said.

Ryan ran a hand through his dark hair, leaning back in his chair. His blue eyes were thoughtful as he regarded his brothers. "Alright, lay it out for us."

"We've been thinking," Mason began, his voice steady, his blue eyes serious. "We all know what Brock and Hayley have done, and if we don't step up, who knows what they could do next. We need leaders who can stand against them."

Derek nodded. "And not just any leaders. Alpha leaders."

The words hung in the air like a heavy curtain. Alpha leaders. The thought was absurd. Me, an Alpha?

Sam caught my eye, giving me a reassuring smile. "You and Ryan are it. You're the best shot we have, Mai. You're strong, both of you."

"And it's not just about strength," Derek added. "You two have the loyalty of our new renegade Pack. That's a powerful thing. I have no doubt that when you make it known that you are challenging Brock and Hayley, there will be plenty of others from the Three Rivers who will support you."

Ryan looked at me, the question clear in his gaze. Would I consider this?

The room seemed to tilt on its axis at their words. I blinked, my heart pounding against my rib cage. I was no leader. I was just Mai Parker, a girl still grappling with the loss of her brother and the unraveling world around her.

"But us? As an Alpha Pair? We've only just got together. We've had no time to bond properly. I was taken by Seth and then Jem ... With everything that's happened, you can't honestly think we'd do any good?" I could hardly swallow the lump forming in my throat. This was so much more than I felt capable of handling.

"Look, I get it," Derek started. "This is ... overwhelming, to say the least." I had the feeling he was using his military training to keep his composure, but I could see a flicker of worry in his gray eyes.

"But," he continued, "you need to understand why we're saying this, Mai. I don't know how much Ryan told you about our father or how much you remember, but he was a dickhead supreme. After Mom died, he lost it. Lost himself in the bottle. Didn't work, didn't really eat, didn't give a fuck about the four boys he still had left. Ryan didn't have a choice; his childhood ended when our mom died. He stepped up, not just because he had to, but because he loved us. Ryan raised us. You have no idea the sacrifices he made to keep us alive, to keep us safe. Yes, it turned him into an Alpha asshole, but he was born to be an Alpha. You and Ryan, you were always meant to be, and together, you're the strongest pair I know, stronger than you give yourselves credit for."

Sam chimed in next, his usually jovial demeanor replaced by a serious, almost pleading expression. "We know you can do this. You're not just strong, you're smart, you're fair, you're … you're what this Pack needs, especially now."

Mason, normally the silent observer, added his voice, his words measured and calculated. "We wouldn't be here, pushing this on you, if we didn't believe you two could pull it off. And, if you're worried about screwing up … Well, we're here. We won't let you fall."

They threw their words at me like lifelines, desperate for me to grab hold and believe. They believed in something bigger, a hope for a better future for our Pack. But it was hard to see past the storm of fear and doubt that was raging within me.

"Think about it, Mai," Sam pleaded, his eyes reflecting a strange mix of desperation and faith as he stood up to leave. Mason and Derek had matching expressions. "You and Ryan are the only hope for the Three Rivers Pack."

The room felt heavier, emptier once Derek, Sam, and Mason left. I sat beside Ryan, my thoughts a whirlpool of doubt and fear.

"The only hope? That was very Star Warsy, even for Sam." Sam had always been a big *Star Wars* fan, but he was laying it on thick, even for him. "How long do you think he's been waiting for an opportunity to say that?" I asked.

Ryan laughed. "Years, probably. He's not wrong, though. You'd be amazing, Mai." He took my hands in his; they were warm and comforting. "We can do this."

The words hung in the air between us. A promise. A challenge. A beacon of hope. I wanted to believe him. I wanted to believe in us.

But could I? Could I ever trust Ryan the way I'd need to for us to be the Alpha pair? I'd seen what a lack of trust did to Jem and Hayley. It affected the whole Pack, even before she'd allied with Brock and murdered my brother. I couldn't do that to them. The Pack needed a pair who were in sync, who knew each other inside and out, who trusted each other, and who worked as a team to make things better for everyone.

"I ..." I started, my voice faltering.

My phone buzzed on the table beside me. I grabbed it; anything for a distraction from this conversation. The display read "Jem," and my heart froze.

Oh, my God! Was he...? Could he have survived?

"Jem?" My voice was a whisper, full of hope and need.

I heard crying at the other end. "Mai, I'm so sorry."

Hayley.

Rage blossomed. Ryan was by my side in an instant and gestured for me to give him the phone. I shook my head; I needed to be the one who talked to her.

I growled, "How could you? He loved you. How could you do this?" Suddenly, I had to know, had to understand.

"Mai, I ... You can't understand what it was like. Brock, he promised me it would be different, that what I felt meant Jem couldn't be my fated mate, but I didn't know ... I'm so sorry. I need him to come back,

Mai. I need him. I don't know what to do, Mai!"

She was rambling. Was it regret? Was it the death of her mate and the effects that had on the mate bond? She had to have felt his death, had to have suffered horrendously when the bond was shattered.

"Hayley, he's not coming back. You killed him. Stabbed a knife into his heart, remember?"

She started sobbing again. "Mai …you can't come back here. He'll kill you."

Trying to protect me? Or trying to keep me from challenging her for the Alpha spot? "I'm not scared of Brock."

For a moment, there was silence before I heard her take two deep breaths. Then her voice changed. It was calmer. Not completely calm, but like the steadiness you get after you are all cried out. "Don't come back here, Mai. There's nothing for you here."

Then she hung up before I could reply.

I stood there for a moment, not sure what I was feeling. Rage, pity, frustration?

All of it swirling through me. Then a tidal wave of grief came out of nowhere and crashed over me, threatening to pull me under. Hearing Hayley's voice had cracked open the wound of losing Jem, raw and bleeding once more. I sank to my knees, sobs tearing through my chest as all the sorrows I'd been holding back broke free.

My big brother, my protector, my family—gone forever. The pain was unbearable, an endless abyss of anguish that I saw no way out of. It clouded my vision, stole my breath, consumed every part of me until I didn't know how I could take another breath in a world where such vital light had been extinguished.

And then Ryan was there, his strong arms surrounding me, holding the shattered pieces of me together. Through our bond, I felt his love envelop me in a soothing embrace. He couldn't take away my pain, but he eased it, his presence giving me the strength to ride the storm of grief.

I clung to him as the sorrow crested and finally began to recede, leaving me weary but intact. Ryan had anchored me through the worst of it, promising with his silent comfort that I would never have to face such darkness alone. Not anymore.

I clung to that, to the love pulsing through our bond. I didn't know how I was going to move on without Jem. How we were going to keep on living when he didn't get to. There was a lot right now that I didn't know. But I knew one thing for certain, and I grasped onto it. I couldn't let Hayley lead the Three Rivers Pack.

I took a deep breath, steeling myself, then looked at Ryan. "It's okay. I'm alright now."

"It's going to take time, Mai. Grief is going to hit you unexpectedly, but I'll always be here when it does. I promise." He ran his fingers through my hair and kissed the tip of my nose.

"I know. But we can only make it work if we do this together. As a team."

A small smile tugged at the corners of his mouth. He nodded, his grip around my waist tightening slightly. "I wouldn't have it any other way."

"Really? Well, I want to tear my hair out sometimes, you make me so mad. That or kick you in the head to get you to see how stubborn and unreasonable you're being."

"I'll admit I can be overbearing and obnoxious sometimes."

"*Sometimes?*"

"I'm not used to having a mate. I've been alone, knowing you're out there and thinking I'd rejected you for four years, Mai. I've had to learn how to deal with that. I'm used to making decisions by myself and them being obeyed without question. You coming back, us sealing our bond, that changed everything. But it's going to be a learning curve for both of us."

I nodded. He was right. This was something we were going to have to work out as we went along. "I just wish we could do that in our own time."

"Me too. But we don't have a choice anymore. Brock and Hayley will be coming for us. They are in charge of the Three Rivers now, and I can't even begin to imagine the damage they can cause to our Pack. They'll take us back to the bad days when Oliver was in charge. They'll undo all the good that Jem did. We can't let that happen, Mai."

His expression turned playful. "Plus, I'll let you kick me in the head anytime I cross the line."

I narrowed my eyes at him. "You'll *let* me?"

His grin widened. "I'll probably enjoy it."

I shook my head, a small laugh escaping me. Maybe, just maybe, we could do this. And if he did start to get too bossy ... Well, I knew how to throw a kick that Ryan would most definitely not enjoy.

I turned as the study door creaked open. Elise, one of the Bridgetown Pack's enforcers we'd been introduced to earlier, stepped in with a tray of food. I looked at her, and her eyes, which had seemed alert and wary before, now had a different kind of intensity.

"Thought you two might be hungry," she said, her voice oozing casual friendliness. She placed the tray filled with sandwiches and drinks on the table near us.

"Thank you, Elise. That's thoughtful of you," Ryan said, his eyes meeting mine for a brief moment.

Something didn't sit right. Her scent was off—it was tinged with a sharp note that set my inner wolf on edge. Before I could give a warning, Elise's hand shot under the tray and pulled out a knife. Then, with one swift movement, she dove toward Ryan.

CHAPTER SEVEN

MAI

The gleam of Elise's blade sent a chill down my spine. Before I could even register the danger, Ryan had pushed me back and leaped toward Elise, using his body as a shield to protect me. I stumbled back into the arm of the sofa seat and flipped over it onto my ass.

Fucking brilliant.

Ryan and I were going to have to work on fighting as a team. I jumped up just as Elise slashed her knife across Ryan's chest. My wolf erupted in fury, a snarl tearing through my lips. We had to end this, but we had to keep Elise alive. The consequences of us arriving here and killing one of their enforcers were not lost on me. If we had any hope of fitting in here, we couldn't kill her; we needed her alive so she could be questioned, and there would be no doubts about our motives for this fight.

I wasted no time. I aimed a roundhouse kick at Elise's head. She managed to duck, but the motion put her off-balance. Ryan took advantage and dove at her, tackling her to the ground. She bucked underneath him, using her legs to kick up and throw Ryan off her.

As he staggered back, she jumped to her feet, her eyes zeroing in on me. My heart raced as she lunged, blade aimed directly at my throat. I sidestepped, but her blade caught my arm, slicing through the skin. The sharp sting of pain was instantaneous, but it only fueled my adrenaline.

Ryan moved like lightning, his arms wrapping around Elise's neck from behind. I darted in, grabbed her wrist, and twisted. The knife fell, and it skittered across the floor. Elise aimed a powerful front kick at me. I danced back out of range. Elise was strong. If her kick had connected, it would have broken my leg. Ryan's grip around her neck was iron-clad, and I could see Elise's face redden as she gasped for air. Desperation filled her eyes, and for a moment, I thought she might relent. Then she drove her elbow into Ryan's ribs. Once, then twice. He grunted, but his hold didn't falter.

The study door burst open with a bang that resonated through the room like a gunshot. Camille rushed in first. "Let her go."

Ryan released Elise, and the enforcer slumped forward, gasping for breath.

"What is the meaning of this?" Camille's voice was harsh.

"She attacked us," I replied, pointing to the knife on the floor.

"Liar," spat Elise. "They came at me when I brought them food."

Sam charged into the room, took one look around, and, his eyes blazing with anger, positioned himself between us and the two Bridgetown wolves, his posture unmistakably protective.

Camille picked up the knife and then walked back to Elise, who was kneeling on the carpet.

"This is your knife, Elise. Why? Tell me that, at least," she said softly.

Elise knew she was out of options. "I take my orders from the true Alpha of the Bridgetown Pack. Not you," she growled, and then lunged toward Camille. I threw myself between them and took the brunt of Elise's tackle. I hit the ground hard as Elise leaped up, aiming for Camille again. She was ready, though. Camille jabbed the heel of her hand into Elise's jaw and, with her other hand, drove the knife into the enforcer's stomach.

Elise fell to the floor just as Ivan and Danni sprinted into the room.

"Take her to the med bay. Sedate her and keep her under guard."

Ivan, shock flashing across his face, bowed his head and moved quickly to pick up Elise.

Camille turned to me. "I'll find out what orders Tristan gave her, and afterward, Elise will be dealt with; I promise you that. We gave you sanctuary here, and that has been breached. I can only offer my sincere apologies and assure you that we will be looking into and interviewing each and every member of this Pack to weed out any other Tristan supporters."

"Are you fucking kidding?" Sam stepped forward. "They were attacked in your study! You promised us they would be safe here. If you can't even offer safety in your own home, then what the fuc—"

"Enough, Sam!" Ryan interjected. "We dealt with it. The message will be loud and clear: Mai and I are not easy targets. This might even help us in the long run. Discourage other half-hearted attempts to curry favor by taking us out."

Sam's whole body was taut, simmering with barely contained rage.

"Stand down, Sam," Ryan said softly but firmly.

It took him some effort, but Sam's body slowly relaxed, and he bent his head toward us both. "I should have been here."

"No," I said. "If we are going to challenge for the Alpha pair, we need to fight our own battles."

"You decided?"

I nodded.

His whole demeanor changed in an instant, and he grinned as he swept me up in a hug. "You won't regret this!"

"Yeah, but you might if you don't let go of my mate right fucking now," Ryan growled.

Chapter Eight

Mai

My chest heaved as Sam stepped back. Adrenaline still coursed through my veins from the fight, setting every nerve on edge. I became aware of stinging on my arm and looked down to see blood seeping from a gash.

Ryan was at my side in an instant, his eyes with concern. "You're hurt."

"It's just a scratch," I said, though now that the haze of the fight was fading, it was throbbing painfully.

"What about you?" I placed my hands on his chest, searching for a wound. His shirt had a slash in it, but I couldn't see or smell any blood.

"She missed. It's just my favorite shirt that got attacked."

Ryan led me over to a chair. I sat down, and he crouched before me, inspecting the wound with gentle fingers. His touch sent little sparks dancing across my skin, despite the circumstances.

"We'll need to clean this properly, but for now ..." Ryan trailed off as he tore a strip of fabric from his already tattered shirt.

I had to fight the instinct to pull away and insist I could handle it myself. Letting someone care for me went against every self-reliant instinct life had ingrained in me. I forced myself to stay still.

This was new territory for me—letting my guard down, allowing vulnerability instead of pushing it away. Ryan had broken through those walls, his devotion enabling me to unlearn the belief carved into me during four years on the run that accepting help was dangerous.

I sucked in a breath, arousal swirling as his muscular chest and arms were exposed. He gently wrapped the makeshift bandage around the gash, his fingers lingering on my skin.

Our eyes locked, the air suddenly charged between us. Still gripping my arm, he leaned in, bringing his lips to the sensitive spot just below my ear. I shivered as his tongue traced delicate patterns on my skin.

"Ryan ..." I gasped as I felt heat pooling between my legs.

His stubble scraped my neck as he made his way to my mouth, capturing my lips in a kiss. My fingers tangled in his hair, holding him against me as our tongues danced.

He pulled back just far enough to meet my gaze, his eyes burning with lust. "You know, I can't just take your word for it. Thomas would be furious with me if I didn't check you over for other injuries. Thoroughly check you over."

"I wouldn't want you to get into any trouble with Thomas," I whispered back, my voice husky with need.

Ryan grinned wickedly. "Let's get you somewhere more private then."

We made our excuses, and as Ryan led me toward our room, I watched his muscles ripple under his torn shirt. I couldn't tear my eyes away from him. After fighting together, with all the adrenaline still bouncing around in me, my body burned for him.

The mate bond seemed to ignite something primal within me. I wanted him to claim me, possess me, remind me that I was his. I yearned to feel him unleashed on my willing body. I didn't want him to hold anything back. The mate bond was like a drug, heightening my senses, my lust, my need for his touch. I shuddered just thinking about having his muscular frame pinned on top of me, utterly under his control as he took me with unrestrained desire.

Ryan opened the door, and we stepped into our bedroom. It was a large space decorated in soft blues and off-whites. A king-sized bed sat in the middle of the floor, a bedside table with a funky steel lamp, and an antique wardrobe to the side. An open door opposite the bed opened into an adjoining bathroom.

Ryan locked the door behind us, his eyes hooded with desire. A smirk played across his lips. "Why don't you lie back and relax?"

He walked me back until my knees hit the edge of the bed, then Ryan lowered himself onto me, bracing himself with one hand as he slowly peeled my top over my head and tossed it aside. I trembled as his fingers trailed down my stomach, my body craving more of his touch. Ryan leaned over me, his hot breath tickling my neck as his lips trailed down to my collarbone. I let out a soft moan as his hands slowly roamed over my body, kneading and teasing my skin.

My nerve endings sizzled as our bare chests brushed together.

"You're incredible," he said, his voice a low growl.

I arched my hips into his, my hands sliding across his back, feeling his broad shoulders bunch and flex as he pressed into me.

Every ounce of him was pure muscle, hard and rippling. I followed the lines of his biceps, his broad shoulders, marveling at the warrior's body that would be claiming mine tonight.

He ground against me, the rigid length of him hot even through our clothes. I whimpered, arching into him again, desperate for that connection.

My head felt light, as if I were floating on air, and all the while, heat pooled between my thighs, wetness seeping through my panties with every movement.

I inhaled his scent, of pine needles and musk and something uniquely Ryan.

He pulled away and lifted me to my feet to shimmy me out of my jeans and panties. He let out a predatory growl at the sight of my wet panties.

"Perfect," he murmured. Eager hands quickly rid us both of the last of our clothing.

"Hurry," I breathed. I needed him. The ache was building, the throbbing between my legs begging to be satisfied by him.

His hands circled my ass, giving it a playful squeeze just long enough to make me gasp, then they slid around and higher to cup my breasts. The feel of his erect cock pressing against my stomach made my breath hitch in anticipation.

He pushed me back onto the bed. "Don't move," he ordered as he knelt down. Then his tongue met my aching clit. I cried out, drowning in the intense bolts of pleasure.

He lapped at my pussy like a man starved, eager moans vibrating against me. My hips rocked desperately, needing more friction to relieve the building tension.

Ryan's strong hands gripped my thighs, holding me open wide for his devouring mouth. His tongue flicked, licking from my entrance up to my swollen clit.

I lost all control, writhing and panting as he sucked me between his lips. The wet sounds of his mouth on me echoed in the room, punctuated by my choked moans.

My fingers twisted in his hair, urging him on as my climax rushed up to meet me. He slid two fingers inside, pumping them in time with each flick of his tongue.

"Ryan!" I cried, shattering under the intense stimulation. My pussy spasmed around his fingers, inner muscles clenching desperately.

He didn't stop, pushing me through a chain of orgasms as his lips and tongue and fingers continued their sweet torture. All my nerves were on fire. I couldn't think about anything except the sensations coursing through my entire body.

When he finally gave me a reprieve, I was spent and trembling. But the glint in his blue eyes promised he was far from done with me.

"I told you not to move, Mai. That's something we're going to have to work on. Turn over," Ryan ordered. "On your knees."

I scooted around until my back was facing him. Ryan traced his fingertips along my outer thighs as he stood behind me. I tried to speak, but all that came out was a soft moan as he teased open my legs with his hands. I could feel the heat radiating from his body against my exposed wetness. He kissed my back tenderly before digging his fingers into the soft flesh of my ass. A small whimper of pleasure escaped me, and I buried my face in the sheets to muffle my moan.

I felt his fingers sliding between my legs, through my slick folds, then into me. His touch at this angle sent a jolt through my body, and I gasped with delight, willing him to keep pressing deeper even as he began to slowly slide his finger in and out.

I reached forward for the bedpost as he slowly began to work a second finger into me, stretching me. My breathing became ragged with the overwhelming sensations. Every touch made fire run through me, searing every nerve ending so that soon I was vibrating with need for him to be inside me.

"Ready?" Ryan whispered against my neck, the warmth of his breath sending shivers down my spine where it brushed against my sensitive skin.

I nodded, reaching back to guide him into me as I arched even more, offering myself up for his pleasure and mine. Heat suffused my face as the head of his cock brushed my drenched folds, and then our bodies gave way, and he slid deep into me.

"Mine," he growled as he thrust into me with a fierceness that left me breathless. "Mine," he repeated, setting a relentless pace that had the bed creaking.

"Yours," I gasped. I could only clutch the bed and take it as he claimed me over and over.

He growled as he thrust faster, his pace fierce in a way that pushed my legs wider apart to open me completely for him. His hands wrapped around my hips driving me back into him as his thrusts grew more frenzied and his breath came in sharp gasps.

I could feel his desire for me, our bond humming with the intensity of his love and his need to protect me. It wrapped around me like a golden blanket, making me feel safe and loved.

"Yes!" I gasped, my voice barely a whisper. His sculpted body was all coiled power, and I urged him on greedily. He was losing all control, and I loved it. Harder, faster, more—I was an animal in heat for him.

We moved together furiously, all wolfish passion and primal need. I surrendered completely, until nothing existed but the bliss of his body possessing mine.

Our bodies were slick with sweat, the pleasure building and building each time his cock drove into me.

Then all the sensations collided together until I thought I might faint from the bliss.

"I can't wait … any longer." My heart pounded in my chest, beating out the frantic wails as I moaned. My orgasm shattered through me, a tidal wave that stole my breath and left me weak in its wake.

Ryan didn't let me rest. As soon as it was over, he flipped us, lying down so I was on top, facing away from him but straddling his hips in the reverse cowgirl position. His hands gripped my waist, urging me on as I slid down on his cock.

I ground my hips against his, chasing the pulses of pleasure radiating through me. It was all I could do; there was no thinking, no analyzing, no doubt. Just me and Ryan and the feel of his massive cock moving inside of me. Ryan met my rhythm, thrust for thrust, his fingers reaching around and tweaking my nipples.

Using my arms to balance, I rose up even higher this time until just the tip of his cock remained inside me. Then I slammed back down, moaning in satisfaction as the walls of my pussy clenched around him.

I repeated the movement, and the steady build-up of tension reached explosive levels. I was going to come again. Ryan must have felt it. I was trembling, exhaustion and pleasure pulsing through me. He surged up and around to capture my mouth in a searing kiss, rolling us again so I was on my back. He lifted one of my legs over his shoulder and began to pound into me. The headboard banged against the wall with the force of his thrusts.

I was drowning in him. This was what I'd always dreamed of. Ryan's scent, his taste, the feel of his body against and inside mine. All coalescing into a maelstrom of pleasure and love and connection.

"Faster," I groaned. Ryan sped up, the friction of his huge cock against my inner walls driving me mad. I tilted my hips up, giving him more access. I was coming apart. Our bond was on fire, and I knew he was close. The thought of Ryan coming inside of me, of his hot liquid squirting into the depths of me, sent me over the edge again.

I could feel my muscles contract in waves against his cock, milking it, drawing out his orgasm. Ryan groaned into my mouth as he came, his release triggering another shattering orgasm within me. We clutched at each other, our harsh breaths and pounding hearts slowing and syncing as we came down from the high together.

Chapter Nine

Mai

The table was laden with an array of dishes, colors, and fragrances that danced in the midday sun filtering through the dining room window. Tucker's eyes sparkled with mischief as he reached for a drumstick. Food was important to werewolves. We needed a lot of calories to fuel our Shifts. The Bridgetown Pack was no different, and this lunch would have been a feast on a human's table.

I wanted us to fit in and knew we had to start as soon as possible. I had to get them to engage with us. "I'm curious about the name Bridgetown. Why is your Pack called that?"

"Ah, it's the story behind this place, a history that defines us," Michael said, his voice filled with warmth, cutting through the jovial chatter.

"Don't get him started," said Camille. "Once he gets going on our history, it's hard to shut him up."

"It's okay, I'm interested. Really."

"Well, don't say I didn't warn you." Camille smiled at her mate.

"It all began with an Alpha pair called Richmond and Isona," Michael continued, winking at Camille. "There was war between two local wolf Packs, not unlike our recent past, but in their time, they emerged as a beacon of unity. Richmond and Isona were from opposing Packs, you see. Their kin were killing each other, yet those two fell in love. They fought their own Packs so they could be together. Eventually, they persuaded their families to stop the war and insisted on building a new town between the two territories," Michael explained, his voice tinged with reverence. "They believed that a place of common ground, that belonged to neither one Pack nor the other, could be a place where werewolves from both sides could come together to heal the wounds of the past, and having this as a meeting place for disputes between the two would stop any future wars."

"What happened to the original Packs?" There were only the Three Rivers and Bridgetown in this area now.

"Oh, they both got subsumed into Bridgetown eventually—though that is another story altogether—then Three Rivers was established sometime after that."

"So, none of the original Packs remain?"

"Well, I suppose we are all descended from them, so in a way, yes, their blood runs through ours."

"I didn't know." I glanced at Ryan. He shook his head. He hadn't known, either. Was it Oliver who had a lot to answer for? When he was the Alpha, a lot of our history had been forgotten. Or had this been buried even before Oliver came along?

"Bridgetown," I murmured, the name now holding a deeper meaning for me.

"Yes," Michael affirmed, his gaze meeting mine. "We were founded on unity and hope for a peaceful future, and it's a legacy we strive to uphold every day. It's more than a name; it's our way of life."

Ryan crossed his arms. "You're talking about the human tourists who come here?"

Camille leaned forward. "Yes. When we took over as Alphas, Bridgetown was dying. Three Rivers was the main town in this area. All roads lead there, all shipping and trade go through your territory. We had to do something, or within a generation, Bridgetown would be lost. So, we took the principles of why we were founded and applied them to the human world. What we offer here is a chance for humans to interact with us. To see that we are not the scary big bad wolves that some parts of the media and government portray us as. The Wolf Council supports our aims here. We draw in tourists, who spend their money here, which supports our community and means our young people don't have to leave to find work. The tourists spend time alongside werewolves; they are served coffee and beer by us, taken on hikes or canoeing trips by us, they party with our kind, and then go home and tell their friends that we're not so scary and the rumors they've heard about us are bullshit."

Michael nodded. "There are hardline factions in the government that want werewolves to be contained in camps. They don't believe we are a 'safe species,' as they like to call us, and have been calling for laws that will regulate our everyday existence."

"That is why Bridgetown is so important. We're not big enough to be an official conclave city where humans and werewolves live side by side. But we are a vital place in the northeast for humans and werewolves to interact. We'll need human allies if we want to stop these factions in government from wielding power over us. We need to show the world we are united, that there is peace and prosperity when humans and werewolves mix.”

I was silent, trying to take it all in. I'd not heard about these different factions in government; I'd been too busy just living day to day. But this affected us all.

Tucker, unable to contain himself for long, broke the silence with a triumphant grin.

“And that's why we have the Bridgetown festival every year, to celebrate unity! You should see the games and races,” he exclaimed, eyes gleaming, his excitement spilling over.

Henry cast a knowing glance at Tucker. “You only like it for the food; admit it.”

Tucker's cheeks flushed, but he grinned unabashedly. “Well, duh!”

I glanced at Ryan, sensing the connection between these people and what they were trying to achieve for all werewolves.

Danni, her previous stern demeanor now softened by the family gathering, chimed in. “And we mustn't forget the dance. Even Tucker doesn't dare miss the chance to dance with his sister.”

Tucker rolled his eyes but didn't argue.

“You'll join us, won't you?” Tucker asked, turning to us with an eager grin. “The festival is the highlight of the year, and it's at the end of fall, just a few weeks away.”

I glanced at Ryan. There was something more to Tucker's question; it was a chance to fully engage with this community. And yet, I couldn't help but desperately hope we'd be attending as a visiting Alpha pair, not because we were still living here.

“We'd be honored,” Ryan said, his voice strong and sincere.

Ivan, who had been quietly watching our conversation until now, finally spoke, his voice carrying a hint of skepticism. “It's not all games and dances, you know. The festival is a tradition, a symbol of what we stand for. It's important."

"We understand," Ryan replied, his tone matching Ivan's seriousness. "We respect what Bridgetown stands for, and we want to be part of it, even if just for a short while."

Tucker's excitement seemed to dim for a moment, catching the undercurrents at play here. But his optimism was undeterred.

"You'll see," he said, his voice softer now, a warm smile spreading across his face. "The festival will make you feel like part of the family. And who knows, maybe you'll even decide to stay!"

Ryan laughed. "Maybe!" he replied as he squeezed my hand under the table. We both knew we were grateful for the offer of sanctuary here, but we had no intention of making this our permanent home.

"With these human and werewolf events, do you have any issues with the out-of-towners bringing in drugs?" Derek asked.

Michael's face turned serious. "You mean ripple?"

I frowned, remembering Ryan's conversation with Mason and Sam in the hotel room. "What exactly is ripple?"

"Theriothiamine, or 'ripple' on the streets, is a new drug that is reported to be highly addictive for Shifters. It's popular in the conclave cities and is now spreading into the Shifter communities."

Derek nodded. "We've been hearing rumors about the drug. It was all down south, but I have reason to believe it's here now. I was wondering if you had drug issues before in your human community and the tourists who visit? If so, the supply lines would already be there, and the dealers could use those to start shipping ripple into the northern Packs."

"There is recreational drug use here, but we keep an eye on it. We know who the dealers are, and if they try to move in the hard stuff, we shut it down. This ripple, though," Michael paused, glancing at Camille, "it's concerning. The side effects are nasty for Shifters, and I have a contact down south who told me they're hearing rumors that the dealers down there are planning to flood the north with this stuff."

Derek and Ryan exchanged a look, and I remembered what Sam had said about it.

"You think ripple is already in Three Rivers?"

"You remember the two Bridgetown humans killed?" Ryan replied. "The ones Carson was framed for?"

"They were low-level drug dealers, no?"

Ryan nodded. "When Derek and I went to see Eddie Keller—the witness who was forced to say he saw Carson at the scene—he said the humans had been dealing in ripple."

"Why wasn't I told about this?" Michael did not sound happy.

Ryan shrugged. "We weren't exactly sharing information at that point. And since then, we've all been somewhat distracted."

Michael glared down the table at his Beta.

"I'll look into it," Danni said, keeping her gaze on the table.

As the conversation drifted to other topics, my attention began to slide toward Shya. She was seated across from me, a smile occasionally playing on her lips. With Tucker, her warmth was unmistakable. Their interactions were full of playful glances and teasing remarks. Tucker's youthful energy found a kindred spirit in Shya, and their connection was the spark that often ignited the room's laughter. But it was her interactions with her brother Henry that revealed a deeper layer of her character. She listened to him carefully, her eyes softening with genuine affection whenever he spoke. There was a mutual respect between them, a shared understanding.

But I noticed the tension in Shya's posture when her parents spoke. Her mother's gentle reminders and her father's proud glances seemed to chafe at her, an invisible tether that pulled her back to a role she seemed desperate to outgrow.

"I hope you'll join us for the traditional Baka dance, Shya," her mother said, a note of expectation in her voice. "It's always been a favorite part of the festival for you."

Shya's eyes flickered, a momentary shadow crossing her face. "I'll think about it, Mother," she replied, her voice holding a hint of defiance. "I might have other plans."

Her mother's eyes widened, and her father's fork paused in mid-air. Around the table, conversations stilled, and I could feel the unspoken tension rising.

"You know how much it means to your father and me," her mother began, but Shya cut her off.

"I know, Mother, but I'm not a little girl anymore. The Baka dance is for the Pack's children. I know we stretched the rule these last few years as I wanted to do it with Tucker and Henry, but I'm getting too old for it now."

I caught the disappointed look on Camille's face before she turned away. "Of course. Perhaps you're right."

Mason wasn't taking his eyes off of Shya. He was going to have to be more subtle. It wouldn't be long before Michael and Camille noticed, and I didn't know how they would feel about Mason and Shya getting together—that is, if Shya even accepted him. If they objected, would they ask Mason to leave? I couldn't let us be split up. If Mason left, we would all need to go. Out of the corner of my eye, I saw Ryan kick his brother under the table. Mason grunted, quickly turning it into a cough when everyone at the table looked at him. I guess I wasn't the only one who saw him brooding over Shya.

The differences between the two Packs became more noticeable as the meal wore on. The Bridgetown wolves seemed to have specific rituals about the passing of dishes and the order in which food was served. Each action was measured and deliberate, contrasting with our more casual dig-in-and-eat-what-you-can ways.

Ryan caught me watching and whispered, "They follow the Alpha's lead in everything, even in eating. Did you notice how no one started until Michael and Camille took their first bite?"

I nodded, feeling the distinction. I'd not been in a Pack that followed this custom before.

"Before the festival, there is a Pack hunt. We take most of the Pack up to our western hunting ground for a week. Tell me, Ryan, I've always been curious: how does the Three Rivers organize its hunts?" Ivan asked, a polite smile on his face. I had the feeling he was testing our suitability to fit in with his Pack.

"We generally rely on individual strengths and dynamic planning. Everyone has a say; the Alpha decides on the best course, and then we adapt as the situation demands."

I could see Ivan weighing our words, his brows furrowing slightly. "That's quite different from how we operate," he finally said, choosing his words with care. "Bridgetown believes in a strict hierarchy and detailed planning. Each wolf knows their role and follows the Alpha's directives without question."

Danni chimed in, her tone echoing Ivan's reservation. "It ensures a smooth execution and minimizes risks. We have always done it this way. Sometimes tradition has its value."

Ryan nodded. "Tradition certainly does, but so does innovation."

I smiled, thinking it was funny that Ryan was trying to be diplomatic. It was not usually his forte.

Ivan's eyes turned to his Alpha as he said, "Do you remember that hunt last winter? With the elk stag?"

"Of course! That was quite the day!" replied Michael.

Ivan nodded, a knowing smile on his face. "Indeed, the way you led us, the tactics we employed. It was an extraordinary hunt."

Uh-huh. The message was clear. This was Ivan's not-too-subtle attempt to remind us that Michael was a formidable leader. In case we got any ideas about trying to destabilize, or even take over, the Bridgetown Pack.

Danni's laughter rang around the table, her words directed at the Bridgetown wolves. "And Tucker falling into the river! I don't think I stopped laughing for the rest of that week."

The room erupted in laughter, but it wasn't a memory our renegade Pack was privy to.

I glanced at Ryan, feeling the separation. We were guests and outsiders, our connection to our own Pack pulling us back, and our understanding of Bridgetown limited to the surface. We had a lot of work to do if we wanted this to truly be the safe haven we needed it to be.

Chapter Ten

RYAN

"Can I go for a run?" Tucker jumped up from the table, dashed to the full-length window, looking out into the woods, and pressed his face up against the glass.

Camille laughed. "He always does this after a meal. It's like he can't stand being in human form longer than a couple of hours." She turned to her son. "Yes—"

"Whoop whoo—"

"*After*, Tucker! After you have helped your brother and sister clear away the dishes."

Tucker grinned at me, then came to take the plates to the kitchen, following his brother. I had a feeling he would be out the kitchen door and into those woods before Henry had the time to come back and get the rest of the dishes. Mason and Sam stood up and helped clear the table, Mason hovering close to Shya as she moved plates into the kitchen.

I looked out of the window into the woods, and my wolf stirred inside me. Tucker was not wrong. A run right now would be good for all of us. I glanced at Mai. Her leg was bouncing under the table.

Derek was staring out the window, his fingers tapping against the tabletop. Mason and Sam came back from the kitchen, having a very stilted conversation, their voices devoid of their usual cheerfulness. We needed something familiar and untamed.

"Why don't we go for a run as well?" I suggested. Derek, Mason, and Sam immediately perked up.

Mai grinned, a spark igniting in her eyes.

"There is good running ground in the east woods," Michael said. "Just head into the forest and turn left when you reach the first stream."

We said our thanks to Michael and Camille and headed outside. The scent of earth and pine welcomed me, my body responding instinctively to the call of the wild.

I closed my eyes for a moment, feeling the connection to my inner wolf, the fierce and free spirit that resided within me.

I set off toward the woods. I didn't want us to Shift out here, not until we got to the safety of the trees.

Mai sprinted past me, yelling, "Race ya!"

I broke into a run just as Derek zipped past me.

I don't think so.

I sped up, overtaking Derek and then gaining on Mai. My heartbeat quickened from the anticipation of what was to come. The forest was getting closer, its familiar embrace calling out to us, promising freedom, even if it was only for a short time. Mai kicked harder and nipped ahead just as we reached the shelter of the trees. I slowed down, allowing the others to catch up. My wolf was wagging his tail. This might not be our territory, our Pack lands, but the forest was our domain, our connection to something primal and untamed.

We headed deeper into the woods, the terrain changing as we went further in. Tall pine trees stood like guardians, their needles carpeting the ground, releasing a rich, earthy scent with every footfall. The undergrowth was a mosaic of greens punctuated by wildflowers that added a dash of color to the dense foliage. Birds serenaded us from the canopy, their melodies intertwining with the whispering of the wind through the leaves. Occasionally, the rustle of a small creature in the underbrush reached our ears, hinting at the life that surrounded us. Old animal tracks crisscrossed our path, each one telling a story of the forest's other inhabitants. The sharp tang of a fox's trail mingled with the musky odor of a deer's recent passage.

The further we went, the more the forest embraced us. The constraints of the human world seemed to peel away, layer by layer.

Mai glanced back at me, her big brown eyes sparkling with delight, her wavy dark hair catching the light as she moved. I stayed close to her. My wolf didn't want to lose sight of Mai.

I stopped when we reached a small clearing, and looked around, scenting. No one else was here. "This'll do."

I stripped and focused inward, feeling the power of my wolf stir. It was a sensation I'd never grow tired of, that moment when human and animal merged into one.

With a deep breath, my body contorted and reshaped, the sensation both painful and exhilarating. Bones cracked and rearranged, fur sprouted from my skin, my face elongated into a snout. My senses expanded, and the world took on new dimensions.

I let out a joyous howl, now fully in my wolf form. By unspoken agreement, I'd Shifted first while Derek kept watch over us. Now it was my turn to make sure they could all Shift in safety. One by one, the others followed, their Shifts a raw dance of transformation. Mai was the last, her dark fur shimmering in the dappled sunlight as she changed. I stood between them and Mai while she Shifted, but as soon as she was done, my brothers' wolves surrounded Mai, all wanting to greet her. Sam rubbed his muzzle against Mai's cheek. It was his way of saying "hello," but it was too much for my wolf. I growled, low and serious. My brothers bounded back away from my mate.

Better.

With a wag of my tail, I led the way, my paws thundering against the earth as I ran. The wind rustled through our fur, the scent of the forest filling our nostrils. I snarled at my brothers when they got too close to Mai. Part of me knew it was the effect of the mating bond, but I didn't care. Mai was mine and mine alone.

We ran together, darting between trees and along old tracks, enjoying the pure joy of movement, and I knew this was exactly what we all needed.

We were crossing another stream when I caught a whiff of something on the wind. The scent that was familiar yet tinged with alarm. It made my fur stand on end.

Tucker.

My ears perked up, and I slowed, signaling to the others.

Mai came to my side, her eyes questioning and concerned. She had picked it up, too. Derek, Mason, and Sam gathered around, their bodies tense, alert to the change in our dynamic.

There.

I sprinted forward, leading them in the direction of Tucker's scent, my instincts screaming that something was wrong. I picked up speed, the joy of our run replaced by a sense of urgency.

We ran for what felt like forever, but must have only been ten minutes or so. Jumping over fallen logs, zipping through the underbrush, ignoring the thorns and spikes that jabbed into my fur. As Tucker's scent got stronger, I slowed. We couldn't afford to go rushing in. Then I picked up another scent, and all thoughts of slowing down fled.

I dashed forward, Mai at my heels. I rounded an oak tree and saw Tucker, his small wolf form backed against a rock, his body quivering, blood dripping from a wound on his flank. The fear in his eyes was unmistakable, and his whimpers reached into my very soul.

Between him and me stood a male grizzly bear. He was bigger than any bear I'd seen before, with a torn ear and scars across his back. His mouth dripped drool and blood, and a gash down his face told me that plucky little Tucker had fought back. As he turned his head to me, I saw his eyes were filled with madness. This was not a normal bear. The bear growled, the sound resonating through the forest, a deep, angry rumble. My eyes caught Sam and Mason's, then flicked to Tucker.

They would protect him.

I snarled at the bear, warning him away. He charged forward quicker than I would have thought possible. I barely had time to react as his massive body slammed into me, knocking me sideways. I tumbled across the forest floor, leaves and dirt swirling around me in a blur. Pain radiated through my body as I struggled to regain my footing.

The bear loomed over me, his paw poised for another blow, just as Mai leaped forward, fangs bared and claws extended. The bear swiped at her. She danced to the side, but not before his massive paw swatted at her side. Mai went flying through the air. I scrambled to my feet, ignoring the pain pulsing through my body.

With a deep growl of rage, I lunged. The bear met me head-on, and we rolled and tumbled across the forest floor, each trying to gain the upper hand. His claws raked against my fur, tearing through flesh and muscle. Blood sprayed across the leaves as I fought back. I could hear Tucker's whimpers nearby, but I couldn't spare him a glance.

My jaws clamped down on the bear's throat, feeling the warm gush of blood filling my mouth. He shook me off and staggered back. I couldn't let him regroup. I charged. Mai and Derek flanked me, their eyes locked on the bear, their movements synchronized with mine. Mason and Sam circled, keeping themselves between the fight and Tucker, but ready to provide support.

The bear reared, his paws slashing the air, his teeth bared in a fearsome snarl. He veered left, swiping at Sam, who dove out of his way. Mai went right, and Derek leaped in front of the bear, Derek's body taking the brunt of his weight. Mason launched himself forward, hitting the bear with the full force of his mass as the bear's teeth tore through Derek's shoulder and back.

The bear's ferocious attack on Derek sent a new wave of fury coursing through me. The sight of my brother's torn flesh, the scent of his blood mingling with Tucker's, added fuel to the inferno of my anger.

I lunged at the bear again, my fangs sinking into his hind leg, tearing flesh and muscle. The bear roared in pain and frustration, his paw swinging at me, but I darted away.

Mai charged back into the fray, her dark fur a blur of motion as she leaped at the bear's face, her teeth snapping at his eyes. The bear shook his head, trying to dislodge her, but she was relentless, driven by a primal fury that matched my own.

There was something very wrong with this bear. He didn't smell like a normal grizzly.

Derek and Mason rammed into the bear from opposite sides, their jaws trying to break through his thick hide. The bear struggled against them, his movements growing more frantic, more desperate. Sam darted in and out, nipping at his flanks, distracting him, keeping him off balance. The bear stumbled, fell, then scrambled to his feet. He roared in anger, the noise deafening. Then he turned and lumbered away into the trees.

Chapter Eleven

RYAN

I turned to go to Tucker when two familiar scents announced the arrival of Ivan and Danni. Good, we could do with the help.

They bounded into the clearing, powerful and alert. Ivan, large and imposing even as a wolf, and Danni's wolf, lean and sharp, every movement calculated and precise.

Their snarls filled the air, aggressive and challenging. I glanced between them, trying to work out what was going on. Then, realization made my stomach sink. They hadn't seen the bear, only the aftermath. Their noses were filled with the mingling scents of our battle, Tucker's fear, the bear's blood.

In their eyes, we were the transgressors. They saw Tucker, young and inexperienced, bloodied and frightened. They saw us, the renegade Three Rivers wolves, on their territory, reeking of violence. They must have thought we had gone for a run with Tucker after lunch and had led him into danger. If it was one of my Pack, I'd be pissed too.

I had no time to explain. No way to communicate what had happened. They saw us as a threat to one of their most vulnerable, and they were responding to it. In that moment, their aggressive posture made sense, and I knew we were on the brink of a confrontation.

The tension in the clearing snapped like a frayed rope, and all hell broke loose. With powerful leaps, Danni and Ivan launched themselves at us. Their eyes were aflame with a fury, driven by their instincts to shield Tucker from harm. The harm they believed we'd brought. I growled at Mai, warning her to stay out of this, then twisted and dodged, claws and fangs a blur, every muscle in my body straining to fend off their attacks. Mai ignored me and was beside me in an instant, her movements a mirror of my own, our bodies working in harmony even in this chaos. We couldn't let them win. But we couldn't really fight back, either.

My mind raced, torn between the need to protect my own Pack and the knowledge of what this fight could cost us. Every bite I held back, every claw I pulled, was a decision. A choice to keep this fight from turning deadly. We weren't their enemies, but if we responded in kind, we could really hurt them. I wasn't sure how Camille and Michael would feel about us seriously injuring their enforcers, but if it was me, I would throw us out of their territory.

Tucker's terrified whimpers pierced the chaos, a reminder of what was at stake. We were fighting ourselves, fighting our friends, all because of a fucking misunderstanding.

I needed to Shift back to human form, tell them what had happened, but it was too dangerous. I'd be vulnerable. Out of the corner of my eye, I saw Mason begin to Shift. He must have come to the same conclusion as me, and we needed to protect him while he went through the change.

Tucker's desperate cries escalated into a piercing scream, slicing through the turmoil like a blade. He'd beaten Mason to it and Shifted into his human form. Time seemed to freeze as Tucker jumped between us, his arms flung wide, his face twisted with terror and determination. The danger he was in was absolute; any misjudged swipe of claws or teeth would seriously injure the boy or worse. My heart lurched into my throat, and I skidded to a halt behind him.

Mai was beside me, her body trembling with the effort to stop, her eyes wide with fear. Ivan and Danni were frozen, too, their snarls dying in their throats as they recognized the peril Tucker had placed himself in.

"No!" he yelled, tears streaming down his face. "Stop it! All of you, stop it! They didn't hurt me; they saved me! There was a bear, a huge bear, and they saved me from it! They're not the enemy! STOP!"

Danni and Ivan, both panting heavily, seemed confused for a moment. Danni swung her head to look at me as if searching for confirmation. She must have seen something to relax her, as she moved back out of range and started to lick a gash on her flank. The fight drained out of me, replaced by relief.

Tucker continued to stand between us.

"It's over," he whispered. "It's over." Then he collapsed to the ground, unconscious.

Chapter Twelve

MAI

The veranda of the Alpha House creaked under our weight as Ryan, Sam, Mason, and I sat in silence. Derek was sleeping. He and Tucker had been taken to the Bridgetown medical wing as soon as we got back. Sam had gone with them and returned about an hour later, saying Derek's wounds were superficial, and he was sleeping it off. Tucker was another story. We were waiting, hoping for good news about his condition. The recent battle kept replaying in my mind. Could we have done anything differently? It had been a chaotic dance of claws, teeth, and desperation.

Ryan reached out, gently inspecting my wounds.

"No more arguing. I need to clean these." He picked up a tube of salve that Shya had brought out earlier. She'd apologized and said the Pack doctor was seeing Tucker and Derek, but she'd be out afterward to check over our injuries. Ryan had wanted to clean my scratches right away, but I'd refused. I wanted to hear about Derek first. Thanks to our werewolf DNA, we healed pretty quickly, so I wasn't too worried about the state we were in. I was more concerned about Tucker right now.

Ryan's touch was tender but firm as he wiped a cloth across the cut from Elise on my arm that had reopened in the fight. I could feel his need to take care of me through our bond. He wanted this; his wolf needed this, to touch me, to make sure I was okay.

"Despite my warning that you should stay out of it, you should have seen yourself out there," Ryan said. "You were incredible, Mai."

"I was never going to listen to that when you were in danger," I replied. "I did what I had to. We all did."

Ryan didn't respond as he gently applied the salve across my skin. The world narrowed down to just the two of us.

"Yeah," he finally said, his voice heavy with something unspoken. "That's something we're going to have to work on. But it doesn't mean it wasn't extraordinary."

I looked at him, and for a brief moment, I felt the pulse of love that throbbed through our bond. I knew we had our differences, knew we hadn't agreed on our roles or about what kind of Alpha pair we should be, but in that moment, I caught a flash of how it could be. If we'd just get out of our own ways and let the bond guide us.

"Tucker was brave," I said, my voice muted. The memory of his little body, all cut up from the bear attack, yet still standing between us and Ivan and Danni, yelling at us to stop fighting, brought a smile to my face.

Ryan's eyes sparkled with agreement. "He didn't hesitate for a second. He's a little warrior."

My thoughts swirled from Tucker's bravery to the complex tightrope of trust and acceptance that our being here demanded. Ryan must have sensed my turmoil because he reached out and held my hand in his.

"We'll find our way through this, Mai," he said.

We were in a tough situation, facing challenges that seemed insurmountable, but Ryan's belief in us, in our ability to lead and protect ... it made me feel like maybe, just maybe, it was possible.

I squeezed his hand as the afternoon sun dipped lower, casting long shadows over the Alpha House.

Half an hour later, and there was still no news. Ryan and Sam were talking in low whispers on the edge of the veranda. Mason was staring out at the view, a grim look on his face.

I had to get him out of whatever place he was in his head.

"Hey," I said, nudging his knee with mine. "You okay?"

Mason blinked, focusing on me. "Yeah, I'm good. Just taking it all in, you know?"

I nodded, though something told me there was more going on beneath the surface.

"So ..." I began, leaning back against the chair. "Shya seems nice."

Mason's eyes darted to mine, his expression snapping into neutral. "Sure," he said, his voice strained. "I guess."

I bit back a smile. Clearly, I had hit a nerve. Time to poke it a little more. "She's Michael's daughter, though. That could be ... complicated."

Mason crossed his arms, his jaw tightening almost imperceptibly. "It's not complicated. She's the Alpha's daughter, nothing more."

"Doesn't seem that way to me," I pressed. "I see how you look at her."

Mason sighed, running a hand through his hair. "It doesn't matter how I look at her. She's off limits, end of story."

"Because she's Michael's daughter?"

"Partly, yes," Mason admitted. "But also because nothing can happen. We're guests here until we figure things out back home. Getting involved with someone, especially Michael's daughter, would be a bad idea."

He wasn't wrong—our situation here was temporary at best, and it was a bad fucking idea to rock the boat. We needed the Bridgetown Pack right now. They were open to offering us sanctuary, but the rift between our Packs went back decades. I wasn't convinced they'd be so open to one of us being involved with their equivalent of a Pack princess. Still, I'd seen the way Mason looked at her. If Shya was really Mason's mate, I knew first-hand the damage running from that bond could cause.

"What if she's your mate?" I asked, point blank.

Mason froze, his eyes widening fractionally. "She's not."

"But what if—"

"No," he cut me off sharply. "Don't even go there."

I held up my hands in surrender. "Hey, just looking out for you. Can't have our best fighter distracted, right?"

The corner of Mason's mouth quirked up in a reluctant half-smile. "Nice try. I know you're playing matchmaker."

"Maybe." I laughed. "But seriously, Mason. Promise me you won't shut this down just because it seems complicated. If she's really your mate, the bond won't let you ignore it forever. That never ends well."

Mason's expression turned thoughtful. "It's just attraction. Really, really strong attraction." He shook his head. "It's too risky to pursue anything here and now. Like I said, she's off limits."

I frowned, annoyed with the Shaw stubbornness. He was just like his brother, but I knew I couldn't push further. "Just don't write it off completely. Who knows what the future holds?"

"Maybe," he conceded. "For now, though, don't go planning the wedding just yet."

I laughed, holding up my hands in mock surrender. "Fine, fine. I'll stay out of it."

But privately, I hoped Mason would keep an open mind. Because from the way Shya had glanced his way when she thought no one was looking, the attraction was clearly not one-sided.

Ten minutes later, Michael strode out of the double doors. He came directly to Ryan and held out his hand. "Thank you, all of you, for saving my son. He would have died if you had not jumped in to protect him."

"It's what anyone would have done," Ryan replied.

"How is Tucker doing?" I asked.

Michael turned to face me, his eyes haunted and drawn. It had been a close call with his son, and he knew it. "He'll be fine."

Relief flooded my body as Michael's words washed over me. Tucker was okay. My heart, which had been pounding with worry, slowed to a more normal rhythm.

"Tucker's a tough one," Michael continued, his voice tinged with pride. "Camille and Shya are looking after him. Knowing him, he'll probably try to escape within the hour."

A laugh escaped my lips, the tension breaking. "That sounds like Tucker."

"We're glad he's all right," Ryan said, his voice sincere.

"Thank you again," Michael said, his eyes meeting mine. The gratitude was genuine, and I could see the weight of worry lifting from his shoulders.

Ryan's brow furrowed. "What about the bear? Do you have an issue with them around here? Have there been any reports about this one before?"

Michael shook his head. "No, most bears don't like how we smell. They keep clear of our territory or pass through quickly. We haven't had a bear attack in over twenty years."

"It didn't smell or act like a normal grizzly," Ryan said. "You got any bear Shifters in the area?"

"You think it might be a Shifter?"

Ryan nodded. "It would explain his scent and why he attacked and didn't retreat when he was confronted with four werewolves."

Michael's face turned thoughtful. "I've not heard about any bear Shifters passing through recently. But I know Tristan had contacts with some of them up north. It's possible this bear has allied with Tristan and was sent here to test our defenses." Michael looked out at the woods beyond the Alpha House. "I'll organize a hunting party. See if we can track this bear down and find some answers."

The rustling of leaves caught my attention, and I turned to see Ivan emerging from the side of the house. His face was drawn, eyes narrowed, his body language screaming tension. My heart lurched; I knew what was coming.

Ryan's body stiffened next to me, his eyes locked on Ivan. Controlled anger emanated from him.

"Ivan," Ryan growled, his voice low and threatening. "What the fuck was that? You realize you injured my mate with your pig-headed impulsiveness."

Ivan marched up to Ryan, getting way too close for my liking. It was a show of dominance, and I wasn't sure Ryan would hold it together.

"Yeah, well, considering, at the time, I thought you and she had lured Tucker into the woods and put him in danger, you all got off lightly."

"Is that right?" Ryan replied, his voice suddenly calm. *Uh-oh.* This was not a good sign. "Coz to me, it looked like you rushed into a situation you didn't understand. Instead of evaluating, you saw Tucker hurt and jumped to conclusions. We all got hurt, and you put Tucker in further danger by starting a fight. You need to be aware of what's happening, Ivan. You need to use your head, even in wolf form. If you don't learn this, and fast, you're going to continue to put your Pack in danger, and next time, maybe you—or Tucker—won't be so lucky."

Ivan's jaw clenched, his eyes darkening with defiance. "I did what I thought was necessary. I protected my Pack."

"Your Pack did not need protecting," Ryan snapped, his voice sharp as a blade. "You acted without thinking."

"I acted without trust," Ivan shot back, his voice filled with bitterness. "We don't just trust outsiders here, you know. It's something you need to earn."

Ryan's eyes bore into Ivan, a challenge and a warning all in one. "We saved Tucker."

"And for that, I'm grateful," Ivan replied grudgingly, his voice softer but still edged with steel.

I could see the struggle in Ryan's eyes, the battle between anger and understanding. I knew he wanted to lash out, to make Ivan see reason, but he also knew that anger wouldn't solve anything.

"We will earn your trust," Ryan finally said, his voice steady and resolute. "We will prove that we are friends to the Bridgetown Pack, but you need to fight smarter, Ivan, before you get someone killed."

With a final, lingering glance at Michael, whose silence spoke volumes, Ivan turned and walked away.

"I'll have a word with Ivan," Michael said, watching his enforcer leave. "He is fiercely protective of his Pack, which is an attribute I highly value, but he can make mistakes, like today. He joined our Pack five years ago. His birth Pack was killed by a werewolf gang who infiltrated it, wanting the territory for their own. The gang injured one of their own, and he claimed sanctuary from Ivan's old Alpha. It was granted, but it was all a ruse. As soon as the werewolf was fit enough, he opened all the gates and let his gang in. Ivan was one of the few survivors. He is fantastically loyal to this Pack, but he doesn't trust easily, and he sees plots where there aren't any. And now, with what has happened with Tristan and Elise, Ivan is even more paranoid than usual."

I looked over at Ryan. Trust. Ivan was right. It was a fragile thing, easily broken, hard to rebuild. But it was vital. It was the foundation of everything we were trying to achieve.

And if I wanted this to work, we would have to build it, stone by stone, no matter how long it took.

Chapter Thirteen

Mai

Ryan grinned as he slid the saltshaker just an inch away from my reach, eyes sparkling with mischief. "You want this?"

"Seriously?" I laughed, stretching over to snag it back, but not before my other hand darted out, snatching a piece of his bacon.

He looked at his plate, then back at me, feigning betrayal. "That was my last piece!"

I chuckled as I salted my eggs. "Well, you're lucky you're cute, or you'd never get away with keeping the salt hostage."

"You're one to talk about being cute while committing bacon theft."

Just as I was starting to think mornings could always be this easy, this good, our cozy bubble burst. Michael and Danni walked in. I didn't need wolf senses to know something was up.

"Morning, Mai, Ryan," Michael greeted. "Mind if we interrupt?"

"Not at all," I replied. "It will keep Ryan from stealing the salt."

Michael smiled but got straight to the point. "We've got something on ripple. A werewolf named Noreen Hunting has reached out to us about her sister. Apparently, the sister is hooked on ripple. We're just headed out to go and see them. Interested?"

I exchanged a quick glance with Ryan, seeing my own curiosity mirrored in his eyes.

"We're in," Ryan said.

We pulled up in front of an apartment building. The area lacked the gleam of affluence—no doormen, no flashy cars parked along the curb—but it was far from rundown. Neat rows of modest homes and small businesses lined the streets, telling the story of a middle-class neighborhood that took pride in its appearance. The apartment building itself was well-kept, with cute flower boxes on the balconies, their blooms lending splashes of color to the otherwise nondescript structure.

Danni led us inside. The lobby was clean, its walls freshly painted in a soft, welcoming green, and there was a small table near the entrance with a vase of fresh lilies, their petals still vibrant. A community bulletin board hung on one wall, its cork surface covered with neatly arranged announcements for neighborhood events, lost pets, and local services. Every detail—from the polished floor to the lack of clutter—spoke to a building well cared for by its residents.

Danni pressed the button on the elevator for the fifth floor.

"We're here to see Arabella Hunting," Danni said as the doors opened, and we stepped inside. "She's nineteen, works in advertising, and lives here with her sister Noreen. Noreen contacted me this morning. She's really worried—says Arabella has been on ripple for about two weeks now."

The elevator gave a soft "ding," its doors gliding open on the fifth floor. The hallway was narrow, the carpet a muted shade of gray that had clearly been vacuumed recently. Framed prints decorated the walls at regular intervals, giving a homely touch.

"We're almost there. Brace yourselves; this could be rough," Danni warned as she led the way.

Danni stopped in front of number 365. She knocked, the sound echoing a soft thud-thud against the wood. After a moment, the door swung open to reveal a young woman, mid-twenties at most, who looked like she hadn't slept in days. Her eyes were tired, dark circles marring her otherwise pretty face. Her dark blond hair was tied in a hurried braid, loose strands framing her face.

"Hey, Danni," she said, her voice tinged with both relief and apprehension.

"Noreen, good to see you," Danni replied. She gestured to us. "This is Mai and Ryan; they're from the Three Rivers Pack. Mai, Ryan, this is Noreen, Arabella's sister."

Noreen extended a hand, first to me and then to Ryan. "Nice to meet you," she said, although her body language suggested "nice" was not currently in her vocabulary.

"Likewise," I replied.

Noreen's eyes then landed on Michael, and her posture shifted almost imperceptibly, back straightening as her gaze dropped to the floor. "Alpha Michael," she greeted, a note of deference lacing her voice.

Michael nodded in acknowledgment, his own expression softening. "I know this was difficult, but you've done the right thing by reaching out to us, Noreen."

She lifted her eyes just enough to meet his gaze before lowering them again, a flicker of relief crossing her face. "Thank you, Alpha."

"May we come in? We have a lot to discuss, and time may not be on our side."

"Of course. Please..." Noreen stepped back, opening the door wide for us to enter, and led us into a cozy living room. A floral-patterned rug anchored a matching set of furniture—nothing fancy, but each piece looked loved, lived in. On the wall, there were photos of Noreen, an older couple I presumed were her parents, and a girl who looked like a younger version of Noreen but with vibrant black hair. The girl was pictured in different places: canoeing, at the top of a mountain, in a park surrounded by three other girls, all of them laughing. She looked happy, full of life.

"Please, have a seat." Noreen gestured toward the couch.

Michael took the armchair while Ryan and I settled onto the couch. Danni stood by the door, eyes scanning the room.

"Noreen," Michael began, "why don't you tell us what's been going on with Arabella?"

Taking a deep breath, Noreen clasped her hands tightly in her lap. "Two weeks ago, Arabella started using this drug. It's called ripple, I think. You have to understand, Arabella is not a druggie. She has never taken drugs before. They're not supposed to work on Shifters. But she works hard. She wants a promotion at work. She's been there two years, and she's still on basic pay. They've brought in three new people, all male Shifters, since she started, and all have been promoted. She works her ass off—late nights, early mornings, almost every weekend—and gets nothing in return. Then, two weeks ago, she pulled an all-nighter trying to prepare her boss for an important meeting with a client. At the last minute, she was asked to sit in on the meeting. She thought this was her chance to show them what she could do. One of her colleagues, one of the men who'd been promoted above her, offered her something to keep her awake and alert for the meeting. She ..." Noreen's voice wavered, "she took it."

Noreen paused, looking out of the window. "I didn't know. Not then. It wasn't until later that week. After the first dose wore off, Arabella thought that was it. It had been a one-time thing. But then she said it was all she could think about. Just one more hit. Something to take the edge off. She went back to the guy and asked for more. I only noticed something was off when she stopped going to work. She was ambitious, she was determined to get that promotion, and in the space of a week, she suddenly doesn't give a shit. That's not right. She stopped eating; she's lost over five pounds in two weeks. And she hasn't Shifted. Not even once, Danni. You know how bad that is for one of us."

Noreen's whole body screamed of a mix of desperation and hopelessness. "I don't know what to do. She's not just my sister; she's my best friend. She's all I have. I can't lose her."

I looked over at Ryan, his eyes tight with concern, and then back to Noreen. "Noreen, where is Arabella now?" I asked, my voice as gentle as I could muster.

"In her room," Noreen replied, pointing down a short hallway. "I tried to get her to come out, but she won't listen to me. She won't listen to anyone."

"Can we see her?"

Noreen got up and led the way down the hallway. She pushed open a door, allowing us a glimpse into a room that was disarrayed and chaotic. It was a medium-sized space that was probably cozy in better days. An oak dresser stood to one side, its mirror cracked, and several drawers hung open, spilling their contents like a wound. A matching nightstand held a purple lamp with a lopsided shade. In the middle of it all was a double bed, its linen twisted. Clothes—some folded, most not—were scattered on the bed and the floor, mingling with loose papers and makeup items. A vanity table on the other side of the room was cluttered with beauty products, some of which had toppled over, the liquid contents slowly dripping down onto the carpet.

Den is dirty.

My wolf didn't like it in here. I couldn't say I blamed her.

Then my eyes fell on Arabella. She was perched on the edge of the bed, rocking gently back and forth. Her dark eyes were sunken, and the once-lustrous hair from the photos in the living room was now dull and lifeless. She looked like a wisp of her former self, fragile and hauntingly empty. I couldn't believe this wreckage happened in just two weeks.

"Holy shit," Ryan muttered under his breath.

Danni stepped forward, locking eyes with Arabella. "Arabella, hi. I'm Danni. We're here to help you."

"I don't need help. I need ripple," Arabella snapped, her eyes not even looking at us as she continued rocking.

Danni looked at us and shook her head. "I've heard about cases where werewolves decline slowly on regular, small doses. To get to this stage should take a few months. But what we're seeing here? This isn't that. Arabella," Danni squatted down in front of the girl, "have you been taking large doses?"

"Who the fuck cares about doses? I feel alive when I'm on it, okay?

I'm pure, finally pure."

I stepped over some discarded clothes and crouched down next to Danni so Arabella and I were on the same eye level. "You're not living; you're dying. Look at yourself, Arabella. Look at this room. You need help. You need to get off ripple. It's making things worse, not better."

Arabella's eyes finally focused on me. "And what would you know about it? Actually, who the fuck are you?" Arabella glared at me.

"I—"

"Enough, Arabella." Michael stepped in, his voice full of the kind of authority only someone who'd been an Alpha for a long time could muster. He turned to Noreen. "I've seen enough. I'm taking her back to the Alpha House. We'll get her set up in the med wing. She's going to detox, whether she likes it or not."

Arabella surged up off the bed. "The fuck I am! I don't want to detox. I like ripple. I need ripple!" She grabbed onto her sister, her voice switching from anger to whining in an instant. "Just one hit, and everything will be okay, Noreen. You'll see. Just one hit and that's it. It'll be different this time. I promise."

Noreen's face had turned even whiter. With tears in her eyes, she silently shook her head.

"You fucking bitch! You can't let them take me. I'm your sister. How can you do this to me?"

Noreen was openly crying now. "Arabella, please!"

I turned and grabbed Noreen, pulling her out of the room and back to the living room. She didn't need to see this. "It's the drugs talking. It's not her; it's not what she really thinks."

Noreen sobbed in my arms. I felt so helpless.

Michael appeared a few moments later, carrying Arabella in his arms. She was quiet and still, staring dully ahead. The Alpha of a Pack could quiet even the loudest demons inside us. I had to learn how to do that if Ryan and I wanted to be effective Alphas.

"I'll take her to the car and will wait for you there," Michael said, then carried Arabella out.

Ryan walked back into the living room. "Danni's getting clothes for Arabella to take. Noreen, do you want to help pick some things out?"

Noreen straightened up. "Yes, of course," she whispered.

Ryan waited until she disappeared down the hallway before asking, "You okay?"

"What the hell is this drug? Shifters are not supposed to react like this. If this takes a hold in the north, it'll devastate our Packs."

"I've got Derek and Mason on it. They're trying to track the suppliers. We need to get the Three Rivers back, and then we'll shut this thing down."

"If this is the damage it can cause in two weeks, we don't have much time."

"No," Ryan agreed, "we don't."

Chapter Fourteen

RYAN

My brothers and I sat under the dappled shade of a large oak tree, the town green stretching out before us. On it, Shya and some of the other Bridgetown Pack members were training in the open. Some had brought weights out and were doing sets. Michael had a group off to the side and was drilling them hard. I wasn't sure if this was usual or a reaction to Tristan's attempted takeover.

Tucker was trying his best to keep up with Michael's group, but only seemed to be getting in their way. I'd already seen Ivan trip over the boy and curse him out. Tucker had taken it, eyes downcast, looking remorseful, then jumped up and continued doing exactly what he was doing before Ivan had told him off.

The Alpha House, the symbolic heart of the Pack, loomed as a reassuring presence in the background. A cool breeze was trying to whisk away the late-summer heat, but it couldn't soothe the unease bubbling within me.

Arabella hadn't said a word on the way back here, just stared out of the window. Michael had taken her straight to their medical wing. He'd assured us the staff there had all experienced humans detoxing before, so they knew what to expect. I wasn't convinced a Shifter detox would follow the same pattern as a human's would, but I didn't have any experience of either. Arabella wouldn't be able to get out or take another hit of ripple; that was the main thing. We had no idea how long it would take for her to detox, but I was pretty sure that she and her carers were in for a rough time.

Michael was not happy about this new development of ripple in his territory. After he got back from the medical wing, he'd ordered Danni to find out who was supplying it and put them out of business. It wasn't going to be easy. There was too much of it down south and in the conclave cities. The dealers were established in those places and searching for ways to expand north. It looked like they'd found some. We needed to get back to Three Rivers; we needed to see if this drug had already spread there. But first, we had to take care of Brock and Hayley.

"As Alpha, I ..." I began, my voice trailing off. It was a title I was still getting used to. My brothers knew me too well.

"You'll get used to it, bro," Sam teased.

I wasn't so sure. "Look, we can't make plans blindly. We need information on what's happening in our Pack."

Derek, his brow furrowed, nodded in agreement. "I've already activated my network, and I've been in touch with some of our enforcers who managed to evade Brock's men. They're in hiding, but they're going to put out feelers. We should know soon who we can rely on and just how many of our people Brock and Hayley have locked up."

Mason and Sam exchanged a glance.

"Our PI agency could be of some use here, too," Mason said. "We've had to relocate everyone out of the territory—they were too much of a target for Brock and Hayley. But they're getting set up, and then we can pull some strings, dig deeper into Brock and Hayley's connections and alliances. See what the wider implications might be."

I nodded, smelling Mai before she came into view. Mai, her dark hair catching the rays of the setting sun, making her glow like a beacon, walked toward us, a fierceness in her stride. I felt a pang of pride. My mate, so strong and resilient, ready to face whatever the world threw at her.

As Mai sat down next to me, I noticed Mason's eyes were on Shya, tracking her every movement. I was going to have to talk to him, and soon. If she was his fated mate, I didn't know how Shya felt about it, how Michael and Camille would react, or how this might complicate our stay here. A part of me liked the thought, though. That even amidst our current situation, Mason could find his mate. He deserved it. He'd spent too many years having all of our backs. It was time something good happened for him.

Mai took a seat next to me, her eyes glancing between Shya and Mason, and I knew she'd picked up on it, too. Her gaze shifted to me, and I smiled. She was so fucking beautiful, and I was going to make sure she knew that when I fucked her later.

"Mai," I began, brushing my leg against hers. My wolf needed to touch her. "We've been talking about getting more information. Do you think you could contact Sofia? See what she can find out?"

At my words, Mai stiffened, her eyes narrowing as she stared at me.

Out of the corner of my eye, I saw Derek do the same.

"You want me to involve Sofia and Jase?"

"Yes," I said simply.

Mai folded her arms across her chest. "I don't want Sofia and Jase involved. They've been through enough."

I understood her fear, her need to protect her friends. But I also knew that we needed all the help we could get. We couldn't do this alone. I'd learned that the hard way when I was young. I'd raised my brothers and had to make some tough decisions to make sure they were safe. I couldn't have done it without Jem's help. He had taught me that we are all bigger than a single person. Alone, we were weak. We had to rely on others and let others rely on us. It was how a Pack was supposed to work, and this renegade Pack was more than just Mai and me.

"We need them. They're part of this Pack, part of this fight. It's not like they're the kind to sit on the sidelines."

She glared at me, saying nothing.

"And you don't know them as well as you think if you believe they'll just let us fight this alone," I continued. "You know they'll do their own thing, probably get it wrong, and end up getting hurt."

I could see the gears turning in her head, wrestling with the idea of putting her friends in danger and how to keep them safe.

"Alright," she conceded after a long pause, sighing heavily. "I'll contact Sofia. I don't like it, but you're right. She and Jase will just go off and do something stupid, like get themselves killed."

I reached out, squeezing her hand in reassurance. I didn't like this any more than she did, and knew Derek was biting back his objections as well, but it was necessary.

"I can check on Sofia," Derek said, his tone casual. "I can sneak in. Make sure she's okay."

I knew what Sofia meant to him. But it was a risk too great. One that I, his brother and Alpha, could not afford to take.

"No," I stated firmly. "It's too dangerous. We can't afford to lose you or give them any idea of our plans."

His face twisted with frustration. He looked as if he wanted to argue more. With a heavy sigh, he ran a hand through his hair, nodding reluctantly.

"Alright, Ryan," he muttered. "But if anything happens to Sofia…"

"I know, Derek," I assured him, clapping a firm hand on his shoulder. We all had someone we would go to hell and back for. For Derek, it was Sofia. And for me, it was the fiery woman next to me.

A loud crash echoed through the air, drawing my attention. I turned to see some of the Bridgetown Pack clanging their weights back on the racks with aggressive grunts and determined looks on their faces as they glared across at us.

Okay, then.

One of them, a hulking brute of a werewolf with a closely shaved head, locked eyes with me across the lawn. His piercing gaze was full of defiance. I felt a growl rumble in my chest, my wolf bristling at the challenge.

Just then, Tucker ran up to the werewolf, jumped up, and grabbed onto his arm. "Can I do weights now, Ethan? Can I?" Tucker yelled, swinging from the man's biceps like it was a tree branch.

The man reluctantly tore his gaze away from mine. He looked down at Tucker, then grinned.

"Sure, kid. Come on."

I couldn't help it; I laughed. Tucker had everyone wrapped around his little finger.

Chapter Fifteen

Mai

I stood at the edge of the training field, arms crossed, eyes narrowed. I'd seen the guy, Ethan, and Ivan glare at Ryan on and off for half an hour now. My wolf was not happy. It didn't feel safe here. She wanted to bound over there and rip Ethan's head off for daring to look at our mate that way. She was always the more bloodthirsty of us. I knew she was overreacting, but there was too much mistrust between us and the Pack here.

The Bridgetown wolves were practicing their one-on-one fighting in human form, moving in calculated patterns, like pieces on a chessboard. Ivan and Danni were calling the shots. They were good, I'd give them that. But the atmosphere was thick with something I couldn't put my finger on—like walking into a room where your name's just been spoken in a hushed tone.

The scent of sweat and dirt filled the air. The sound of feet pounding against the earth reverberated through my bones.

Ivan's gaze flicked to me, a quick scan up and down. Assessing. Danni caught his glance and turned her eyes my way, too.

"Care to join us, Mai?" Danni grinned, a mix of challenge and curiosity.

I hesitated.

Everyone had stopped. Their eyes were on me, waiting to see what I'd do.

Screw it. If I wanted to be an Alpha, I had to be a fighter, not a wallflower. I uncrossed my arms, and with a last glance toward the sky—as if asking for an ounce of favor from the Goddess—I stepped into the field.

As soon as I moved, I felt Ryan by my side.

How the hell did he move so fast?

"Not thinking of having all the fun without me, are you?"

I glanced at him, then shrugged. "You can join in if you think you're tough enough."

Every step toward the center of that makeshift arena felt like a declaration. We were in it now, no turning back.

The ground was uneven under my feet, pointing to the countless training sessions that they had held here. They all watched us, and I could almost taste their collective breath of anticipation.

Ivan and Danni stood at the center, a soft sheen of sweat on both of their faces.

"This should be interesting," Ryan murmured, just loud enough for me to hear.

"Fun," I replied. "It's going to be fun."

I wasn't kidding. I needed to blow off some steam, and this was the perfect way for me to let loose.

Ivan finally broke the silence. "You sure you're both up for this?" Ivan's eyes shifted from me to Ryan as if sizing us up, measuring our worth in a single glance.

I met his gaze and smirked. "That sounds like you're backing out. Don't tell me you're scared, Ivan," I said, glancing at Ryan for a brief second. His eyes met mine, a spark of agreement flickering between us. We had to prove our worth to this Pack. Show them we could handle ourselves, that we didn't need their Pack to risk their lives to protect us.

For a heartbeat, the world stilled. Then Ivan nodded, and it was like a dam breaking. The tension inside me vanished, replaced by a wave of adrenaline. It was go time.

Ivan gestured to a young wolf standing off to the side. She looked to be in her late teens, her eyes bright with a mix of eagerness and youthful bravado. Her physique was lean and muscular, but it had that youthful softness to it that suggested there was potential to develop even more. She was still a warrior in the making. "How about a little one-on-one, Jalal?"

The werewolf stepped forward, her chest puffing up ever so slightly. Her eyes flicked toward Danni, as if her approval was the prize she sought even more than beating me.

My nerves flared up, electric and edgy. I had to shine, but not too bright—I couldn't afford to look like a threat. It was a fine line to walk.

From the corner of my eye, I saw Ryan watching. I could see the coiled tension in his posture. Him holding back and not jumping in to fight for me was killing him. I reached out, placing my hand on his chest. "I have to do this. You can't fight every battle for me."

"I know," he grunted, clearly not happy.

It was the best I was going to get.

The moment Ivan gave the signal, Jalal came at me. I met her charge with a smile, feeling the rush of adrenaline course through my veins. My wolf growled in excitement, egging me on to take her down. I snapped my arms up in a defensive stance, but she was too predictable. She threw a punch that I easily dodged, then followed up with a kick that never made it past my thigh. I could see the frustration in her eyes as she realized she wasn't going to take me down easily. I countered with a few quick jabs and an uppercut that sent her stumbling backward. She recovered quickly, though, lunging back at me.

I took a step back, using her momentum against her, and sent her flying with a well-timed sweep at her legs.

Jalal hit the ground with a thud, looking up at me in surprise. Ivan's eyebrows shot up; Danni's lips twitched into a reluctant smile. They exchanged a glance, and I knew I had their attention now. Round one, and I'd left my mark. The walls between us had cracks now, even if they were just hairline fractures. I held out my hand to help Jalal up, but she pushed it away and got back on her feet by herself. She didn't look too happy about losing to an outsider.

"That was good," I said, nodding at her. "You're getting there."

Jalal grunted. "You got lucky."

I shrugged. "Maybe. You wanna go again?"

"I think it's my turn," a voice said off to the side. I glanced that way and saw Ethan, the hulking werewolf who had been staring daggers at Ryan, walking toward me. Tucker was following, skipping behind him.

I grinned. This was more like it. Ethan was someone I could really go to town on. Ethan stopped a foot from me and looked me up and down with a sneer on his face. He didn't think much of little old me, and I was going to enjoy showing him otherwise.

"Time for you to work out with a real werewolf," he said with a knowing glint in his eyes.

Chapter Sixteen

Mai

Before I could reply, Ryan was beside me, flashing his teeth at Ethan, with a green sheen flaring in his eyes. His Shifter magic only changed his eyes from blue to green when he was really pissed, and I wasn't the only one who could feel the angry vibes streaming off Ryan, his body radiating a controlled sort of power. Ethan took a small step back. It was a tiny step, but it spoke volumes.

"Mind if I take the next round?" Ryan said.

Ivan looked him up and down. "You up for a spar?"

"Absolutely." Ryan stared at Ethan, cracking his knuckles. "I've been itching for some real action."

I walked to the side, giving them room. I knew it was important for Ryan to fight Ethan. Ethan had been pushing at Ryan's boundaries all afternoon, and Ryan needed to show him that we wouldn't tolerate it, but I was disappointed that I wouldn't get a chance to take Ethan down. I still had excess energy I needed to work off.

I watched as they squared off, my heart doing a weird flip. This was Ryan's moment to make an impression, and knowing him, he'd go big or go home.

I glanced around, looking for the Shaw brothers. Derek was talking in a low voice to a tall, slender woman from the Bridgetown Pack. Mason and Sam were walking toward me.

"You did good," Sam whispered.

I smiled at him. "Yeah, it'll be your butt I'm kicking next time."

Sam grinned back at me. "You're on!"

Derek said a final something to the woman and then came to stand by us. "I've been doing some digging. Ethan is not someone to mess with. His brother died a month ago in a trucking accident. He's grieving and angry and will be looking to pummel something or someone."

And Ryan had just offered himself up on a platter.

Great.

I heard some of the other werewolves calling for their friends to come and watch. The air grew thick with tension, like the calm before a storm. It was charged, electrical, setting my nerves on edge and heightening my senses. Even the distant calls of birds seemed to hush as if they, too, were waiting for the clash.

The moment Ivan nodded, Ethan barreled toward Ryan. Ryan waited until the last second, then danced to the left. Ethan grunted in annoyance and went for Ryan again. Ryan sidestepped and landed a swift kick to Ethan's leg as he went past. It was like watching a dance, a brutal ballet of force and finesse. Ethan was methodical; he had obviously been trained, but he had no initiative. It was like he was following a rule book on how to fight. In contrast, Ryan was a wildfire, bobbing and weaving, unpredictable and all-consuming.

Ethan seemed to embody the Bridgetown way—disciplined, hierarchical. Ryan was pure Three Rivers—raw and effective. Two worlds colliding in a tangle of fists and will.

Ryan was letting Ethan tire himself out. Ryan leaned back, avoiding a punch from Ethan, then countered with a swift jab that Ethan barely dodged.

I found myself holding my breath as they circled each other.

The sound of their boots scuffling against the dirt became a rhythmic soundtrack to their dance. Dust kicked up, swirling in the fading sunlight like miniature tornadoes. The sharp tang of sweat cut through the air, mingling with the earthy scent of the training field.

"What? That all you got?" Ryan taunted.

Ethan lunged forward, aiming a kick at Ryan's midsection. It was a textbook move, clean and precise.

But Ryan was anything but textbook. He sidestepped, twisted, and slammed his fist into Ethan's side. Ryan then feinted a punch, drawing Ethan's guard up. It was a ruse. With a quick change of direction, Ryan snapped a low kick at Ethan's knee. Ethan jumped straight up, so Ryan's leg went under him, but frustration flickered across Ethan's face. He lunged forward suddenly, his fist flying toward Ryan's face at breakneck speed, the weight of all his muscles behind it. If it connected, Ryan would be out. Ryan ducked under the punch and rammed his shoulder into Ethan's stomach.

My heart was in my throat. Ryan had to walk the same line that I did; we had to show that we did not need their protection, that we could hold our own, but we couldn't really hurt them, either. We needed their respect; we needed them on our side, and we couldn't do that if we broke one of them in a training session.

Ethan started to kick and punch randomly. He was getting angry and losing control. Ryan darted left, leaped, and twisted in mid-air, driving his fist down hard on Ethan's jaw, snapping his head back. Ethan staggered but didn't fall. He regained his balance, shaking his head as if to clear it, and then, surprisingly, he chuckled.

I let out the breath I'd been holding and my shoulders relaxed. This was it; the unspoken questions had been answered. We could stand toe-to-toe with them, and they knew it.

Ryan turned to look at me, his eyes glowing with exhilaration. He gave me a small wink as if to say, "We did it."

"Well, you don't suck," Ethan said as Tucker came running up to Ryan and jumped on his back. "That was awesome!" Tucker yelled into Ryan's ear. "You have to teach me, Ryan. Will you?"

Ryan reached over his shoulder, grabbed Tucker, and pulled him around to his front, tickling the boy.

"Hey," Tucker giggled, "no fair, I wasn't ready!"

A group of the younger wolves started to make their way toward us. Their faces were open, their eyes less guarded than before.

One of them, a girl with a braid down her back, spoke up first. "You did alright there, you know."

I looked at her and smiled. "Thanks."

"I'm Due-Lah. Think you can show me that leg-sweeping move?"

"Sure. Let's do this," I said, striding back onto the field.

"Don't hold back, Due-Lah," Ivan called. "Let's see what you've really got."

Due-Lah came at me fast, aiming a kick at my ribs. I dodged, the breeze from her boot brushing my skin. She followed up with a flurry of punches aimed at my chest and face. Damn, she was quick.

I waited for an opening, then slammed my fist into her shoulder. Due-Lah staggered back.

"I don't know what you're talking about!" Shya's angry voice broke my concentration. I turned to see her arguing with Mason. He growled something I couldn't hear. I spun back just as Due-Lah swept my legs out from under me. I hit the dirt with a painful thud.

I looked up into her worried face.

"Like that?" she asked, her voice uncertain.

"Uh-huh. That was good," I replied.

I jumped to my feet. Due-Lah grinned.

When she aimed another kick, I grabbed her leg and flipped her onto her back. Before she could react, I pinned her down, my forearm across her throat.

"Or you could do something like that," I said.

Her eyes widened. "That was super cool! Do it again!"

I laughed and helped her up.

"Due-Lah," Camille called from the edge of the veranda wrapping around the Alpha house. "You're on kitchen duties this week because of that stunt you pulled in training yesterday."

Due-Lah looked down, a meek, contrite expression on her face. "Of course, Camille. Apologies, Mai. I better go. I'll see you all later." She gave a small wave and ran back to the house.

Off to the side, I saw Shya arguing with Mason. She wasn't yelling at him anymore, which was an improvement.

Ivan walked toward us and clapped Ryan on the back—a silent but powerful gesture. "You've got skills," he said, locking eyes with both of us.

Some of the younger wolves, who had been so guarded earlier, were now chatting with Derek and Sam. The icy barriers had thawed, at least a little.

Ryan slipped his arm around my waist. "Not a bad start, huh?"

I smiled up at him. "Not bad at all."

Chapter Seventeen

Mai

Half an hour later, the adrenaline from the fight was still buzzing through me as I grabbed a towel and water bottle from a rack next to the weights, glancing around for Shya. The other wolves were leaving after the training session, but I spotted her sitting under the same oak tree that our renegade Pack had been sitting under earlier, shooting quick glances at Mason.

I went over and sat down next to her, the shade welcome.

"That was fun," I remarked, taking a swig of water.

Shya let out a short laugh. "You're telling me. You did good. The others are starting to respect your little Pack."

"We're that obvious?"

She shrugged. "It's what I would have done in your situation. You don't need there to be tensions between our Packs. You need us right now, and if you can get on side with the majority of us, you'll be safer here for longer."

"You don't mind us being here?"

Shya glanced again at Mason, then quickly looked away. "As a family, as a Pack, we don't turn away those who need help. Plus, you guys helped me convince my dad that Tristan is a scheming motherfucker, and my dad is no longer pushing me to mate with him. So, I owe you."

"What about you?" I asked, curious. "Did you ever think Tristan was your mate?"

She nodded slowly. "He had me convinced me for a while. He seemed so sure that I was destined to be his mate. He ... he was very good at playing with my emotions, at making me doubt myself," she said, her voice shaking with emotion. "I fell for it. For a long time, I thought he was right, and we were meant to be together."

"I'm sorry."

"Don't be. I worked it out. When Dad wouldn't listen, I went to Derek. I told him what was happening here. It wasn't easy, but being his informant meant I could do something about it. It took a while to find out what Tristan and Brock were planning, but we stopped them; that's the important thing."

"I think what you did was brave, you know. No one believed you here. You worked undercover and did something that you knew your family would be furious about—all because you wanted to stand up for what was right to protect your Pack."

She looked at me, then smiled softly. "Maybe. Can I ask you something?"

"Sure."

"I've heard that you've had some dealings with questionable characters before. How do you know who you can and can't trust?"

I considered the question. "I'm not really the right person to ask. I have huge trust issues. I'm sure you heard that Ryan rejected me years ago. In front of not just our Pack but at the regional Pack meeting."

She winced. "Ouch."

"Yeah. Then there was Seth. He hit me, and when I ran, he kidnapped me and tried to break my bond with the Three Rivers Pack."

She tilted her head to one side. "Is that even possible? I thought only Alphas could break the bond."

I shrugged. "He was working with a witch. I don't know if it would have worked, but it felt like it might have."

"That's fucked up."

"You're telling me. Then there's Hayley. I always knew she had no love for me, but she adored Jem. I don't know what changed. What could drive her to kill him? It makes no sense to me."

"I'm sorry about your brother."

I swiped my hand across my face. It came away wet. "I can't imagine ever getting over this. The grief; it's so painful. How do people do this? How do they cope when they lose a loved one?"

"I don't know," she replied softly.

I looked across the lawn to my Pack. Ryan, Mason, Derek, and Sam were huddled together, chatting with Ivan and Ethan.

"Well, I don't, either. So, I'm going to have to try different things. The first one being revenge."

I felt her studying me before she said, "If there is anything I can do to help, just say the word."

I took a deep breath, trying to push down the grief that was threatening to boil over. The last thing I needed was to start sobbing here. "So, yeah, probably not the best person to ask about trust."

Shya sighed and looked over at Mason again. The Shaw brothers looked so alike. You could see the family resemblance in the set of their jaws, the shape of their noses, the way they all glared when they were angry, like the rest of the world better watch out because they were coming to destroy it.

"Of course, if you mean can you trust Mason, then the answer is one hundred percent yes. He's a good guy, Shya. He wouldn't gaslight you, wouldn't try to trick you. He loves his family, loves his Pack, and will do anything to protect the people he cares about."

I paused, considering how much I wanted to open up. Letting my guard down did not come naturally after everything I'd been through. But something in Shya's uncertain expression resonated with me. I recognized that quest to understand yourself amidst outside influences trying to twist your reality.

"Trust is hard for me, but I'm trying to be more vulnerable, little by little. To heal from old wounds so I can build new bonds."

Confiding in Shya felt like a small step on that journey. If I expected others to lower their walls, I had to lead by example. I couldn't expect to find meaningful connections if I wasn't willing to reveal my true self.

"That's the thing, though. Mason loves his Pack. I love mine. There is no future there."

I shrugged one shoulder. "Who's talking about the future? Why don't you just have a bit of fun, see where it goes? Though, do me a favor and don't tell your parents just yet?"

Shya laughed. "I can just imagine my dad's face if I told him I wanted to date someone from another Pack. From your renegade Pack, no less! No offense, but currently Mason has no job, no home, and is being hunted by another Pack."

I smiled; she had a point. "None taken. Just, I ran from my bond. I ran for four years, and I was miserable every moment." I reached out and touched her arm. "I don't want that to happen to you or Mason."

"I'm not ready."

"For the fated mate bond? No one ever is."

Ryan strode over to us and held out his hand to pull me up. "I'm heading in for a shower. Want to join me?"

Hell, yes. I still have some energy to burn off.

Shya must have seen my expression. She laughed and said, "See you guys later."

Chapter Eighteen

RYAN

I shut the door and strode over to where Mai had stopped in the middle of our room. I didn't say anything, just captured her sweet lips in mine. I could kiss her all day. Kissing Mai was like a drug, one taste and I couldn't stop with just her lips, I wanted to spend the whole day marking every inch of her body with my lips. I broke the kiss to peel her top off her and tossed it aside.

"You're undressing me."

"That is the plan," I replied, then stepped back from her. "Or is this me being overbearing and obnoxious?"

She glared at me.

"I can stop. Just say the word, Mai."

"Ryan," she growled.

"I wouldn't want to get a kick in the head—"

"Which is exactly what you'll get if you don't fucking continue what you started!"

I grinned at her. "And you call *me* overbearing and obnoxious?"

I could see her thinking about kicking me, but before she could move, I unclipped her bra and swept my hands under the cups to grasp her breasts. They were full, and the nipples were already pert, just waiting for me. I felt her shiver under my hands. Our bond flared to life, and I could feel her need for me and the throbbing ache in her core. I couldn't help but smile. I fucking loved that I could make her feel this way.

Her pants came off next, and then she was standing in front of me in just her panties. I stripped then leaned in and kissed her hipbone, moving along her toned stomach. She sucked in a breath as I kissed lower, my mouth closing over her clit through her panties.

"Ryan," she moaned, and my cock went rock hard at the way she said my name. I wanted her to say it again when I was driving into her.

I looked up at her, knowing she could see my desire. "You want me to stop?"

She shook her head, biting down on her lower lip in a way that drove me wild as I continued exploring every inch of her perfect body.

I dragged my tongue up to the column of her throat, nipping at her delicate skin. She shivered, tilting her head to give me access. My teeth grazed the skin on her neck, teasing whimpers from her lips as my fingers pulled on her nipples. Mai's back arched, pushing her breasts into me. I ducked my head, taking her soft flesh into my mouth, and sucked until she was writhing in pleasure.

"More," she begged.

Okay, then.

I dragged her panties down and threw them on the floor. My fingers trailed lower, finding her slick and ready for me. My nostrils flared, taking in her scent; it was intoxicating, rich with arousal. I slid a finger between her wet folds, growling at how drenched she was.

Mai rocked her hips as I stroked her.

"Feeling impatient, are we?"

"Yes," she breathed, rocking her hips faster.

I curled another finger inside of her, pumping them slowly inside her tight heat. Her arousal soaked my hand, and I knew she was getting close.

"Please, Ryan," she pleaded.

"So impatient," I scolded.

I lifted her up, marveling at how light she was, positioning her so that my cock was pressed right against her entrance. She wrapped her legs around me as I walked us backward, pinning Mai against the wall. My wolf was close to the surface, desperate to take her hard and fast.

No, I wanted to tease Mai, to draw this out.

I looked at her, not breaking eye contact as I slid in an inch and then pulled out, raising one eyebrow. In response, she scratched her nails down my back, hair wild, eyes burning. Her scent enveloped me, rich and earthy with arousal. I knew exactly what she wanted. She'd get it, just not yet.

I teased her again. Pushing my cock in another inch, then back out again. Her hips rolled, and I felt her drenched pussy inviting me in.

"Please," she begged again. "I need you."

I inched in slowly, watching her face as I slowly filled her up. Her eyes opened wide, and her breath hitched. Before I was all the way in, I withdrew, positioning my cock against her entrance.

"You want this?" I asked.

"Goddess, yes!"

"Say my name, Mai. Beg me again."

She didn't hesitate. "Please, Ryan, please fuck me."

With a single thrust, I was inside her. Mai gasped.

I groaned. I was never going to get used to this incredible feeling of being inside her, of feeling her so hot and wet for me. Mai bucked her hips, taking me deeper. I pulled out before plunging back into her.

"Please, Ryan,"

"Please, what?" I wanted to hear her say it.

"Please, I want to feel you fucking me senseless."

"As you wish."

I pounded into her, bracing my hand on the wall. Each slap of our bodies fueling the frenzy building between us.

Mai bit down on my shoulder, moaning. I could feel her pussy clenching around my cock as I drove into her again and again.

She bucked her hips against mine, letting me know with no uncertainty what she wanted.

"Harder," she breathed, throwing her head back as her eyes fluttered shut.

And that was all it took for me to lose it. With a barely controlled urgency, I drove into her over and over again, focusing all of my energy on giving her what she craved.

The sensation of her on me was incredible, and I moved faster, thrusting deeper and harder until she felt as though she was on fire, burning just for me.

She arched her back, letting out a low moan that urged me on as I pumped in and out of her.

Fuck, she was so wet. I could feel it dripping down my legs, and I loved it. Loved that I could make her this way, so fucking wet and wild.

"Say my name, Mai," I ordered. "I want to hear my name when you come."

"Ryan," she breathed. "Oh, fuck, yes, Ryan!"

I felt her inner walls start to flutter around me. Then it was like an explosion. Her pussy clamped around my cock as she threw her head back.

"Ryan!" she screamed again as her orgasm crashed through her. Her body jerked and jolted, so fucking wild. I growled as I pumped my cum into her.

Mai collapsed against me. I gave her a moment as I stroked her hair and kissed her neck. Then I lifted her off of me and set her on her feet. She wobbled, and I snaked my arm around her waist to keep her from falling. She smiled up at me, her face relaxed and sated. She was in for a surprise if she thought I was done with her. I intended to explore every inch of her gorgeous body, to learn all the ways I could give her pleasure. Her nightmares were going to end tonight. I was going to make sure there was no room left in her head for bad thoughts, that she could only think about what I was doing to her. I was going to fuck her until she was so exhausted, she wouldn't be able to think straight.

Chapter Nineteen

Mai

Our bedroom was dim, the only light coming from a lone bedside lamp. It cast long shadows across the room, flickering every now and then like a shy firefly. I was wrapped up in a soft robe. Ryan, naked, his muscular form sprawled across the bed, was watching me.

Ryan had fucked me again in the shower. It had been hot and delicious, and I had the feeling that we still weren't done. There was something I had to do first, though.

I pulled out my phone. My fingers danced across the screen, bringing up Sofia's number. With a deep breath, I pressed "call."

The familiar ringtone echoed around the room until Sofia's warm voice filled the air. "Hey, you." Her tone was light, playful, the same Sofia I had known for years.

"Hey, Sofia," I responded, my voice mirroring her own. "How are you, girl?"

"Oh, you know me. I bounce back quick."

"I'm so sorry. I didn't mean for this to hap—"

"Don't be silly, Mai," Sofia interrupted. "This wasn't your fault.

This was Seth, and I gotta say, me and Jase were over the fucking moon when Derek told us you and Ryan killed him. He deserved what he got."

I paused, a swirl of emotions in my chest. I hadn't realized how guilty I'd felt that Sofia and Jase got injured by my ex-boyfriend.

"How's the Alpha life treating you?" she asked, and I could almost see the impish grin that was likely on her face.

"Derek told you."

"Yeah, Derek told me. You're doing the right thing, Mai. You gotta know I have your back. So, how's it been?"

"Challenging, so far. I'm not sure when it gets to be all spa days and massages, but I can't wait."

Sofia giggled. She knew as well as I did that being the Pack Alpha left little time for treats like that.

"Well, when it does happen, I'm your spa buddy. Deal?"

"Deal. So, how is the patient life treating you? Has Jase morphed into a nurse yet?"

"Jase? A nurse? More like a clumsy bull in a glass factory. He got sacked when he dropped my soup twice. Once all over my knees!"

I laughed. "Tell him I said to get his act together," I said, my voice lighter than it had been in days.

"I will. He needs a little scolding from his Alpha."

I smiled at her way of telling me that Jase was backing me and Ryan, too.

"Mai, have you heard anything over there about a drug called ripple?"

My stomach sank. It was too much to hope that it hadn't reached Three Rivers.

"What happened?" I asked.

"A werewolf was brought into Thomas's surgery today. It was … it was bad, Mai. He was hooked on ripple. Thomas doesn't know if he's going to make it."

"It's here in Bridgetown, too. We need to shut the suppliers down, but we don't know how it's getting in yet. It's all too new."

"Mai, the man, from what he was saying, I think ripple's been here for a while."

"What do you mean?"

"He said he first tried it six months ago. Has been taking it ever since. Small doses at first but building up as he stopped hitting the highs. He made it sound like there's an underground network that was getting set up, and now that they are, they're really starting to push this drug."

That was not good. If the network was already set up, it made our job of dismantling it all much harder. Whoever was running this must have known the Packs would push back as soon as we found out ripple was infiltrating our territory. They would have planned for it. I wondered what the Packs in the conclave cities had done. Whatever they'd tried, it obviously hadn't worked.

"Derek and Mason are looking into it. I'll pass the information along. Don't do anything stupid, alright? Don't try to track down the suppliers. These people will be dangerous and well organized."

Sofia laughed. "Don't worry. I have no delusions of being a renegade drugbuster. Not yet, anyway."

"How about a renegade spymaster?"

"A what now?"

"I need your help."

"Who do we need to kill? Just tell me, and I'll be there."

Goddess, did I love this girl.

"I said spymaster, not expert assassin!" I laughed.

"Yeah, well, close enough! What do you need?"

"Do you think you can use your contacts? You know a lot of people from Bottley Bar. They come in and chat with you. They trust you. Can you try to quietly get in touch with some of them? Find out what Brock and Hayley are up to? What they might be planning?"

"Hell yeah, I'm in! Jase, too. He's just itching to get some action, and he knows a lot of folk from his delivery job."

"Thank you. I can't tell you how much it means to me. Just be careful, okay? Don't take any unnecessary risks. Information, that's all," I said, a warning tinge to my words.

"I'm always careful, Mai. You just make sure that hunk of a werewolf has your back, too, alright?" she replied, her tone equally serious.

"Thank you, Sofia." My voice was whisper soft. I'd really missed Sofia when I disappeared from Three Rivers. Now that I was back, I wanted to spend more time with her. But fuckheads like Seth and Brock kept getting in the way. As soon as we got the Three Rivers back, I needed to make time for my best friend.

"Everything okay?" Ryan asked as I ended the call.

I knew with his werewolf hearing that he had heard every word, but it was sweet of him to ask.

I nodded. "Have you heard anything more about Arabella?"

"No, but I'm sure she's being taken care of."

"I know; it's just I can't stop thinking about her. Did you see the photos of her on the apartment walls? She looked so happy, so carefree.

Full of life. Now, she's just a shell who can only think about her next hit."

Ryan reached out and traced his fingers along the palm of my hand. "It'll be okay. If she doesn't start to improve, I'll get in touch with my contacts down south who have seen this before. We'll find a way to help her."

"I just don't want to see any of our friends or family in that state."

"You won't. We'll shut it down."

"Promise?"

"I promise. How's the pain in your arm?"

"Why?" I asked.

"Just wondering if you need a distraction."

Mmm. "What sort of distraction?"

Ryan, his eyes dark, leaned over me, then brought his lips down to meet mine. The kiss was electric, sending pulses of desire shooting through me. I wrapped my arms around him, drawing him even closer.

"I definitely need distracting," I murmured against his mouth.

"Good, coz I'm not nearly done with you."

Chapter Twenty

RYAN

My wolf woke me. The scent of Derek, a mix of pine and moss, hit first, before he started banging on my door. Mai stirred beside me.

I glanced at the clock. Eight in the morning. We'd slept late. I slipped out of bed and pulled on a pair of sweatpants before padding over to the door. My hand lingered on the cold handle, and I took a deep breath, bracing myself for whatever was on the other side.

"What is it, Derek?" I whispered, not wanting to wake Mai. His familiar figure was framed in the dim hallway light.

"You need to hear this, bro," he said, his voice tight.

My stomach dropped. More bad news. I nodded, stepping back to let him in.

Mai had sat up, her beautiful brown eyes wide and alert, her dark hair a wild tangle around her shoulders. She pulled the sheet closer to her as Derek stepped inside, the chill from the open door cutting through the warm room.

"Sorry to barge in on you guys like this, but it couldn't wait," Derek said, his gaze flicking between the two of us. "I've been in contact with

Evelyn. She was one of our enforcers who escaped the sweep by Brock's men. She's staying in an empty house of her cousin's for now, still inside the Three Rivers territory."

"She's got news for us?" I asked.

"Yeah, and we've got a problem."

"The problem being?" Mai questioned, her voice sleep-roughened yet alert.

"Tristan," Derek said simply, letting the name hang in the air. "I sent the photos of him to all our contacts. Evelyn's seen him. Says he's walking around Three Rivers like he's the Alpha there. That he's all tight with Brock's enforcers."

"Fuck!"

"Yeah. It was too much to hope that he'd crawl into a ditch somewhere."

"We need to warn Michael," Mai said. "If Tristan is back working with Brock, then their plans aren't finished. Tristan is still aiming to take over the Bridgetown Pack, and Brock will be helping him."

I nodded. "We'll get dressed and meet you downstairs."

Ten minutes later, we walked into Michael's study. He sat at his desk, his head buried in some paperwork. Shya was reading a book near the fireplace and picking at a plate of breakfast food. Michael looked up at our arrival, his calm exterior barely hiding the worry in his eyes.

"You have news?" he asked, pushing aside the pile of papers to give us his full attention.

"Is Camille around? She needs to hear this too," Mai said.

Michael shook his head. "She's dealing with Henry and Tucker. There was some dispute over a favorite book of Henry's found covered in mud and ice cream stains."

I smiled and made a mental note to buy Henry a book and Tucker some ice cream.

"How is Arabella doing?" I knew Mai couldn't stop thinking about her, how much she had changed from the fun, happy girl in the photos to the shell of a person she was when we found her.

Michael shook his head. "It's not going well. The detox is having some unforeseen effects. Our doctor believes that if she Shifts, we'd have a better chance of purging ripple from her system, but she is unable to Shift. We don't know why, but it's like she's lost that ability."

"Because of the drug?"

"Perhaps. She may be able to Shift when it's all out of her system, and the withdrawal has passed. But if she doesn't Shift, we're not sure she will survive that long."

"Do you have contacts in the southern Packs? They might have some ideas; they've been dealing with ripple for longer than we have. I know some people if you want me to call them."

Michael inclined his head. "Thank you, but no need. We're waiting for someone I trust to send me information. Is that what you wanted to see me about?"

I shook my head. "It's Tristan. He's been seen in Three Rivers. It looks like he's working with Brock again. Openly this time."

"That dickhead," Shya spat out, her anger erupting as she jumped out of her chair. "I knew he wouldn't just disappear. That utter cockroach! He must have had this as a backup plan all along."

"Perhaps," Michael replied. He leaned back in his chair, his gaze fixed on a point in the distance, as if he could see the unfolding future. "But we couldn't do anything until we confirmed where he was first." Michael looked at me. "You need to up your timetable. Strike now while they are all together."

I stared at Michael, his words sinking in slowly. "Up our timetable?" I echoed. "Just barge into Three Rivers without any clear plan?" I was a fighter, yes, but I also knew the importance of strategy.

"We don't have the luxury of time, Ryan," Michael said, his gaze never wavering. "If Tristan is in Three Rivers, it means they're preparing for something big. We need to take them by surprise."

"Michael, they have enforcers everywhere. They have all the entrances monitored. This would be suicide."

"I get it, Ryan." Michael's voice softened. "I really do. But if we wait too long, they will attack us here, and it will be war between our Packs. The loss of life will be enormous."

I looked at Mai, and when she spoke, her voice was calm and steady. "Ryan's right. We can't just go in without a plan. That's how we lose. We need to know what they're planning, how many fighters they have, where they are likely to strike, and where they are vulnerable."

"I have an idea," Shya chimed in.

"Yes?" I said, glancing at Shya. Her fingers played idly with a pendant around her neck.

"I know someone who might be able to help us," she began. "He's a bit of a shadowy character, but he deals in information. And he's had dealings with both Brock and Tristan in the past. There's no love lost between them. If anyone knows what's going on and what Brock and Tristan are up to, he'll know."

"You trust this man?"

"I trust him to honor a deal. If we can offer something he wants, he'll stick to it. Plus, he's absolutely dedicated to protecting his own skin," Shya replied. "It won't go well for him if Brock and Tristan are in charge in these parts. If he thinks we have a shot at taking them down, he'll help us."

I felt my jaw clench. We were treading on thin ice, but Shya's plan felt like the only viable option. I turned to Michael, our eyes meeting across the room. "We have to try," I said. "We need more information. Then we decide."

Chapter Twenty-One

MAI

Danni led Ryan and me down the sterile white hallway, the rhythmic beeping of machines echoing off the walls. The air smelled strongly of harsh cleaning products, barely masking the stale undertones of illness and suffering. The fluorescent lights lent everything a cold, clinical feel. We were deep in the medical wing of the Alpha House, where both Shifters and humans in Bridgetown were treated, heading to see Arabella. Shya was currently setting up a meeting with her contact, and I wanted to see how Arabella was doing before we left.

"How's Noreen doing?" I asked.

Danni paused outside a door labeled 217B.

She sighed. "Not good. This is difficult for everyone involved. I've sent Noreen home to get some sleep. She was exhausted, and we're going to need her later on when Arabella might be more cooperative. I have to warn you that Arabella has deteriorated since you saw her."

Ryan gave my hand a reassuring squeeze as Danni opened the door. The scent hit me first—the sharp sting of antiseptics poorly masking the stale odor of sweat and sickness. Then I saw her.

Arabella was strapped to a hospital bed, her wrists and ankles bound. Her skin was sallow, dark circles ringing her sunken eyes. She was rail-thin, her hospital gown hanging loosely off her frame.

As we walked in, her head lolled to the side, glassy eyes struggling to focus. Recognition sparked, and she let out an anguished wail, her body contorting against the restraints. My heart broke at the sight of her wild-eyed despair.

"Ripple," she rasped. "I need it. Please, please ..."

I moved to Arabella's side, taking her clammy hand in mine. "Arabella, it's me, Mai. We met at your apartment. Do you remember?"

Her eyes finally focused on me, filled with confusion and torment. "Mai?" she croaked.

"Yes, I'm here with Ryan. We want to help." I kept my voice low, hoping some part could reach her.

"Help ... me?" Her words came out slurred, almost unintelligible.

"We want to help you and your sister get through this." I squeezed her hand.

She thrashed against her bonds, face contorting. "I don't want your fucking help. I need ripple ... I need it! It's the only thing that will make the pain stop." Fresh tears leaked down her hollowed cheeks.

Danni hurried to her side, speaking in low, soothing tones and checking the IV drips. After a moment, Arabella's pleas quieted to a whimper.

"The withdrawal is intense," Danni said. "We're trying to keep her sedated most of the time, but her wolf keeps fighting it."

As if on cue, Arabella's back arched, muscles straining. A grating scream tore from her lips. Ryan rushed to help hold her down as she thrashed.

"Make it stop!" she shrieked. "It burns!"

A nurse hurried into the room. He was male, Latino, and looked to be in his early 30s. He had short black hair and warm brown eyes. His name tag read "Rico" in neat block letters.

Rico moved with quick efficiency, his muscular arms helping to hold down Arabella's limbs thrashing against her restraints. His voice was soothing as he spoke gently to her in Spanish, trying to calm her distressed cries. I didn't understand his words, but his tone was calm and comforting.

With Ryan and Rico both holding Arabella, Danni stepped back, pulling out her phone.

"Camille? We need you down here. Yes ... No ... Okay."

At Danni's words, Arabella's cries went from frantic to desperate.

"Please, you don't understand. None of you do. Please, I just need one more hit. That will make this all go away. Please ..."

My heart ached, knowing there was little I could do to ease her suffering. Rico injected Arabella with something, and almost immediately, her body relaxed, and her eyes closed.

"The Galloway Pack is sending one of their doctors," Danni said as she turned to us. "She has some experience with this. She'll be here tomorrow."

"It is just Arabella so far?" I asked. "No other reports of Shifters addicted to ripple in Bridgetown?"

"Not yet, but it won't stay that way. I've been making calls. In the five Packs that I've managed to speak to, they've had twenty-one overdoses and sixty-six Shifters who are addicted. We know it's here. It's only a matter of time before we get reports of others. We're going to have to be prepared."

I looked at Arabella. She was asleep but had a grimace on her face. "Any idea who supplied Arabella?"

"I've got enforcers making house calls on Arabella's work colleagues. We should know soon, and then we'll start to trace the route back to get to the dealer. They'll give up their contacts—both their bosses and who they've been supplying. I've no doubt about that. Michael and Camille will make sure of it."

"That'll get the intelligence on how ripple is getting into the Bridgetown Pack, but if you're going to shut this down, you'll need to go to the source. They must be powerful to have gotten ripple into so many Packs. If you get me the information, I can put Mason and Sam on it. Their agency has experience with running informants and infiltrating the top ranks of shady operations," said Ryan.

Danni nodded. "I'll run it by Michael and Camille, but I don't see it being a problem. We're going to need all the help we can get on this. In the meantime, we're trying to get more rooms ready as we're going to detox anyone who has taken this stuff."

"What then?" I asked. "How are you going to stop them getting out of here and trying to find more ripple as soon as they've detoxed?"

Danni looked at me. "Honestly? I've no idea. I don't know; we haven't seen a Shifter addicted to drugs before. We're going to have to take this one step at a time and hope the southern doctor has more information."

Just then, Arabella arched up with a scream. I turned to help her as Camille swept into the room. Her presence instantly calmed Arabella's cries. Camille grasped Arabella's face between both hands, staring deep into her eyes.

"Shhh now, child. You are safe here."

A wave of energy pulsed around the room. Relief swept over Arabella's features as Camille's Alpha power flowed into her. The lines of pain eased, her facial muscles relaxing one by one, her breathing evened out, her whimpers quieting. I'd heard of Alphas having the ability to temporarily take pain away from their Pack members, but had never seen it in action. Was this something that Ryan and I would be able to do for our Pack?

It wasn't the only power that Alphas had that other Shifters did not. Alphas could also do a partial Shift, only turning their hands into claws or their heads into wolf heads. I'd only seen it done once, and it was freaky as fuck, but all Alphas were supposed to have that ability, drawing on their Pack bonds to give them the control needed. How the hell would I even learn how to do these things?

Danni nodded at me, and Ryan and I followed her out to give Camille and Arabella some privacy, Camille's soothing voice following us into the hall.

I knew then, without a doubt, that ripple had to be stopped. It was here now, in Bridgetown. According to Sofia, it was in Three Rivers. It would destroy Packs, destroy our communities. The dealers peddling this poison had to be eradicated, no matter what it took.

"We have to stop this drug any way we can," I said.

Beside me, Ryan nodded.

Chapter Twenty-Two

Mai

The rumble of the car's engine filled the silence as we drove, leaving the territory of the Bridgetown Pack behind. Ryan's eyes were firmly on the winding road ahead. Mason sat in the passenger seat, his gaze alternating between the side-view mirror and the road. Sam, Shya, and I were squeezed in the back, an awkward silence hanging in the air. I stared out of the window, thinking about Arabella. I couldn't get the image of her yanking against her restraints, pleading with us to give her more ripple, out of my head.

"We're nearly at Ronnie's," Shya finally broke the silence.

Ronnie Bishop was Shya's contact and the man we were hoping was going to help us. "Tell me again what you know about him," I turned to look at her. Shya had already given us a run down of everything she knew about Ronnie but I wanted to make sure we hadn't missed something.

"Ronnie's human. He's smart and ruthless. It's a good combination and it has gotten him far. I know serious people who are afraid of Ronnie. His gang runs out of Haxton but he has sources all across the northeast. Ronnie deals in information and … other things," she said, her tone hinting at the illicit nature of these "other things."

"Some of the men in our agency have dealt with Ronnie before. His reputation is definitely interesting," chipped in Sam.

Shya laughed, a low, throaty sound that seemed out of place in the tense atmosphere of the car. "Yeah, you could say that. He straddles the line between legal and illegal. But he's trustworthy, for a price. And that's all we need right now."

A bad feeling settled in my gut as I thought about what meeting this Ronnie Bishop would mean for us and what he'd want in exchange for the information we needed. But given Brock and Tristan were so friendly these days, we didn't have much choice. We were stepping into a world far removed from our own, into a realm solely controlled by humans, where the rules we were used to no longer applied. I just hoped we were ready for whatever lay ahead.

Out of the corner of my eye, I saw Shya sneaking glances at Mason.

"You know him; what do you think Tristan will do next?" I asked Shya.

She shrugged. "I know what his end goal is—to be the Alpha of Bridgetown and to run the humans out of our Pack lands."

"Tristan as Alpha and you as his mate?" I prodded.

Shya drew a deep breath, her gaze focusing on the darkened horizon ahead. "Tristan's good at manipulating people," she began, her voice low and heavy. "He always has been. It's just now he thinks I'm his ace in his hand."

"Why?"

"As the Alpha's daughter, having me by his side would give him the legitimacy he needs to rule the Pack. My parents have fostered a core of extremely loyal supporters. With my parents dead, my being his mate would appease a lot of the Pack and make his succession much smoother, more secure."

"We won't let him have you, you know. Even if anything happens to your parents. I know we're nothing to look at right now, but we're going to get the Three Rivers back, and I promise you will always be welcome there. No matter what happens."

She smiled. "Thank you. That means a lot. Of course, I fully intend to see Tristan dead and buried, but I appreciate you thinking of me."

I grinned. I liked this girl. She had spunk.

"I haven't heard the story of how you met Derek." I was curious, but I also wanted to know the truth behind Shya and Derek so I could let Sofia know if she had been wrong when she thought there was something between them.

Shya's expression softened, a flicker of something close to fondness crossing her features. "That's a whole other story," she chuckled. "I was in a human bar in Tillotin, trying to drown my sorrows; you know, typical heartbroken stuff." She rolled her eyes at her own melodrama.

"Why a human bar?" I asked. In the front, Mason had gone still. He was facing forward, staring ahead at the road, but I knew he was straining to hear every word of what Shya was saying.

Shya shrugged. "I just wanted to be someplace where no one knew me, where I wouldn't have to pretend to be strong or brave, or an Alpha's daughter, where I could just be ... Shya."

There was something incredibly raw and vulnerable about her confession. It was the kind of honesty that only comes from pain, from knowing what it feels like to be stripped of everything you thought you knew about yourself. I was beginning to realize that Shya, like me, had her own scars.

"Anyway, I'd just found out that Tristan had been gaslighting me. I'd tried to go to my parents to warn them, but they'd shrugged it off as a lover's tiff. They were close to Tristan and liked the idea of me with him. Derek was there on business. He knew who I was. He came over and asked if I was okay. We got to talking, and he gave me his card, said if I needed anything, I just had to call. I didn't think too much about it at the time. But then, a few weeks later, I'd done some digging into Tristan and what he was up to. I knew he was meeting with people in the Three Rivers Pack, but I didn't know who. I suspected there might be a plot between the Packs to take over, but I had no proof. So, I called Derek. He didn't believe me. But he didn't shut me down, either. He needed proof and said he'd help me get it."

A silence hung in the air as we all digested her words. "And that's how you ended up working for him?" I asked.

She nodded. "Yeah, he made me feel useful. I wasn't a traitor to my Pack; I was protecting them. Derek saw that."

I glanced at Shya, her profile illuminated by the passing streetlights. There was a certain fierceness in her eyes, a kind of strength that came from overcoming hardships. There was a lot more to her than just being a Pack princess, and I had the feeling Mason would be in for one hell of a ride if he ever decided to make a move.

Chapter Twenty-Three

Mai

The scene in front of me was straight out of a rugged urban tale—a biker repair workshop nestled in the heart of bustling Haxton. Packed between an old hardware store and a graffiti-adorned brick building, it was a world of its own. Worn-out motorcycles and greasy parts cluttered the limited yard, while men marked by ink were either lost in mechanical work or passing time. They were all human, but the glint of metal—guns, knives, brass knuckles—made it clear that we were in a den of wolves, albeit of a different breed. I knew if it came to it, it would be tough going trying to fight our way out of this.

Ryan parked our car amidst the buzz of power tools and the metallic symphony of hammers and wrenches. The air was heavy with the smell of oil, gasoline, and heated metal. The workshop's noises dimmed as we stepped out, replaced by an unnerving silence as every eye turned our way. Ryan moved to my side and placed a warm hand on my back. He was making a statement to everyone here, and my wolf sighed in contentment.

A man emerged from the crowd—a vision of raw strength and easy charisma. He had broad shoulders that rippled with muscularity, capped by a head of thick, tousled chestnut hair. Blue eyes, electric under the workshop lights, appraised us with measured curiosity. His biceps, where a snake tattoo coiled in a captivating dance, bulged as he crossed his arms. He was wearing a fitted black T-shirt that outlined his powerful torso, and a leather wristband around a strong wrist. This had to be Ronnie—even though he was young for a gang leader.

"Shya," he greeted, his voice gravelly but not unkind. He barely glanced at the rest of us, his eyes only for her.

Mason was on alert. Only those who knew him best would see it, but while his body was casual, underneath his relaxed posture, I knew he was coiled and ready.

"Ronnie. Good to see you," Shya replied, walking forward and shaking his hand. "These are my associates." She introduced us one by one, Ronnie giving us all a curt nod.

"Come on," Ronnie said, "we can talk in the office."

He led us through the workshop. Men stepped aside, their hard gazes watching us.

Ronnie's office was tidy, almost clinical, with clean countertops and a polished oak desk. A large window overlooked the workshop, giving a clear view of everything outside. There were no biker gang posters or naked-women decorations. Instead, it was clean, sleek, and modern with framed pictures of motorcycles, a corkboard neatly pinned with maps and notes, and a single black-and-white photograph of a teenage Ronnie with a beautiful woman and two young kids. It was the kind of office that reflected a man who valued order amidst chaos.

Ronnie sat down in the chair behind the desk and leaned back. "So, what brings you all the way out to Haxton?"

"Information," Shya replied. "Mai is Jem's sister."

"I know who she is," Ronnie said, never taking his eyes off of Shya.

"She and Ryan are going to challenge Brock and Hayley for the Three Rivers Pack. We've heard that Tristan has been seen with them. We need to know what they're planning."

Ronnie let out a low whistle. "That's a big ask."

"I'm aware," she replied. "But it's one I'm willing to pay for."

Ronnie looked her over. "A favor," he said finally. "To be collected at a later date."

Mason bristled beside her. "Don't even fucking think about it."

She raised a hand. "I've done it before, Mason. And I'll do it again. Okay, Ronnie, terms. Nothing sexual. Nothing that requires me to remove my clothing. Nothing that will result in my death or serious injury. Nothing that puts the safety of my Pack or family at risk. Acceptable?"

Ronnie grinned. "Deal." Then his attention shifted to Ryan and me. "And you two, are you also willing to owe me a favor?" His voice was heavy with implication, the question hanging in the air like a loaded gun.

Ryan flashed his teeth at Ronnie. But we were in uncharted territory. We needed this information, and it was a price we had to pay.

"Same terms," I said, my voice firm. Ryan's jaw clenched. He knew I was right, but he didn't like it.

I felt uneasy agreeing to this deal, but the risk was necessary. We had to protect our Pack, avenge Jem's death, and challenge Brock and Hayley. Nothing else mattered right now.

"Alrighty, then," said Ronnie, and he leaned forward. "Brock and Hayley are sitting tight right now. They know you're in Bridgetown.

They can't personally attack yet, not without fucking up their plans with Tristan. But we're hearing whispers they've contracted out your removal. I don't know who, but someone outside the Pack is supposed to be on their way. If we find out who, I'll let you know. As for your boy Tristan, he's been cozying up to Brock and Hayley, just as you suspected," he continued, his gaze fixed on Shya. "They've got people on the inside of the Bridgetown Pack."

My eyes darted to Shya. It couldn't be easy knowing there were still traitors in her Pack.

"They're keeping a close eye on Michael and Camille. From what I hear, Tristan is planning to attack them during the trip to your regional Pack Meet in two days."

"You sure?" Shya asked, her voice strangled.

"You questioning my information, darlin'?"

Shya shook her head. "It's my parents, Ronnie. I need to be sure."

He stared at her for a moment, then nodded. "I guess I'd be the same. I'm sure, Shya. Tristan is out for blood. He's going to ambush them when they leave. He isn't planning on leaving anyone alive."

Mason reached out and placed his hand on Shya's shoulder. "We'll stop him."

She looked around at him, her face pale, then she nodded.

We had less than forty-eight hours to prevent this.

"Thank you, Ronnie." I locked eyes with him, making sure he saw the determination in mine. "We'll be in touch."

As we left Ronnie's office and began making our way back to the car, I couldn't help but wonder how Ronnie did it. How did he have access to this information? Ronnie was a man we were going to have to watch. If we got our Pack back, the last thing we needed was Ronnie knowing all our business.

"I hope you know what you're doing, Shya," Ronnie called out as we walked away. His voice carried a tone of finality, a goodbye and a caution wrapped up in one.

Shya turned around, a small, almost challenging smile on her face. "Always do," she shot back, her eyes twinkling with confidence.

"Well, you know where I am if you ever want to forget your troubles, Shya. I'll make them all go away for you." His voice was low and heated, full of promise.

Mason stiffened. "Hey," he snapped, striding toward to Ronnie. "Back the fuck off."

Shya placed a hand on Mason's arm, pulling him back.

"I can handle myself, Mason," she said, her voice calm but firm, as Ronnie laughed.

"We have to go," Ryan said, stepping between Ronnie and Mason. Mason stared at Ronnie for a moment longer, then nodded. He placed a hand on Shya's back and steered her to the car, keeping between her and Ronnie. Man, he had it bad.

We all piled into the car. Ryan behind the wheel, me in the passenger seat, and Shya, Mason, and Sam huddled in the back.

"Well, this is awkward." Sam was sitting in the middle between Mason and Shya and was glancing between them.

I didn't envy him. I could smell the anger rolling off both Mason and Shya.

"Shut up, bro," growled Mason.

Undeterred, Sam replied, "I mean, I get it. You're all broody and protective, and Shya's rocking the whole 'I'm a strong, independent woman' vibe."

"Don't make me shut your mouth for you, Sam Shaw!" Shya threatened.

Sam grinned at her. "I can see why Mason likes you so much. You're fun!"

Haxton disappeared behind us as we drove, replaced by the dull monotony of a deserted highway. Night began to fall, a cloak of darkness seeping across the sky, the last streaks of the sunset bleeding into the horizon.

"Ronnie might be a useful contact to have," I said.

"Are you kidding?" Ryan replied. "He's a human who knows way too much about our Packs and our business. Once this is over, we need to shut him down."

I turned to face Ryan. "You're right; he is a human who knows too much. That tells me he's resourceful, he has extensive contacts, and he knows how to leverage who and what he knows to find out things that we can't. We'll need to watch him closely, but he's useful, Ryan. We'll need people like him if we want to protect our Pack."

"He's human," Ryan repeated.

"And that means?"

"It means we should never forget that he isn't a werewolf. He doesn't understand our kind and shouldn't be involved in our business."

"I'm not asking him to join our Pack, Ryan. I'm suggesting we get information from him. He obviously has contacts and resources that we don't, and until we build those up, it would be stupid for us not to use him."

Ryan was silent as he drummed his fingers against the steering wheel.

"You're right. We need to use everyone at our disposal, no matter who or what they are. I'll deal with Ronnie in the future, though."

I knew it was the mating bond driving him to try to keep me away from any male, Shifter or human, and there was no point in arguing with him. Not right now.

Twenty minutes later, I was leaning my head against the cold glass window, the world outside blurring into a mix of inky skies and fleeting shadows. A deep sense of unease was creeping up on me, filling the pit of my stomach with dread. We had to stop Tristan, and we had to challenge Brock and Hayley. All in the next two days. Yet, we had no plan and weren't sure who was on our side and who wasn't.

The peace of the night was broken by a sudden roar of engines, the sharp, biting sound echoing through the otherwise quiet night. I jerked my head up and twisted around to look behind us.

Headlights, bright and blinding, were closing in fast, multiplying, until the road behind us was lit up like a runway. My breath hitched as I counted them. Six. Six cars.

"Ryan."

"I see them," he replied, speeding up.

"Ronnie?" I asked Shya.

"No," Shya replied. "He's strictly a bike guy. This isn't him."

An engine revved behind us. Ryan's eyes darted to the rearview mirror, and his knuckles whitened on the steering wheel. The car swerved as he jerked the wheel, trying to get out of the way of a car that was trying to ram us. The sudden maneuver threw us off balance. I could hear the panicked shouts of Shya from the back seat, the screeching tires, the snarling engines behind us.

Ryan swerved and dodged again, trying to throw them off, but they were persistent.

"Brace!" Ryan shouted, just as a deafening crash echoed through the car as one of the pursuing cars rammed into us, sending our car spinning. My head slammed into the window, the world tumbling around me. Ryan was trying to regain control of the vehicle, but it was too late. The world flipped, the car rolled, and everything went black.

Chapter Twenty-Four

Mai

My head felt like it was stuffed with razor wire, a sharp throbbing making me wince with each pulse. With an effort, I opened my eyes. The world was upside down, and I was hanging, suspended in the cool night air. The acrid scent of gasoline hit me first, followed closely by the coppery tang of blood. Pain, confusion, fear, and anger swirled around inside the car. My heart pounded in my chest, adrenaline coursing through my veins.

"Ryan?" I muttered, twisting my neck to get a glimpse of him. He was there, his eyes closed. I reached over, but my seatbelt yanked me back.

"Ryan!"

He stirred, his eyes fluttering open, a look of confusion in them. Then his face snapped into extremely pissed-off mode.

"Mai, you okay?"

"I think so."

Shya, Mason, and Sam were all stirring, too. They looked pale and shaken, but they were all alive. I felt a wave of relief so intense it almost made me black out again.

"They're not attacking," Sam said, his eyes searching the road . "But they've surrounded the car."

Unbuckling my seatbelt, I braced myself, pushing away from the crushed roof of the car. A rush of dizziness hit me as I fell, landing heavily on the shattered window.

"Dammit," I grunted, pushing myself to my knees. The metallic scent of blood filled my nose, and I swiped my hand across my lip, coming away with a smear of red.

"We have to get out of here," I whispered to the others, but they were already moving.

Crawling out from the wreckage, my gaze fell on a looming figure standing in the road, in the glare of the headlamps.

Korrin.

His broad shoulders were tense, his stance wide. He was waiting, a statue of patient revenge under the wash of the headlights.

Korrin was the outside contact. He had come for his retribution. I could almost taste it in the air. His son, Seth, had kidnapped me, beaten the shit out of me, and tried to sever my Three Rivers bond using illegal witch magic. Despite this, Korrin had loved Seth, had been grooming him to take over his Beta spot in the Cocrane Pack. I'd escaped from Seth, and when he came after me, Ryan and I had killed him. Isaac, Seth's best friend, had warned me that Korrin would look for payback. I just hadn't expected it so soon or that he would join forces with Brock and Hayley.

With my heart pounding in my chest, I staggered to my feet, my knees trembling. It felt as if the whole world had frozen over, the only movement being the slow swirl of dust and smoke around us.

I glanced back at Ryan, the fury and resolve in his eyes calming my racing heart as he strode toward me.

Gritting my teeth, I turned back to face Korrin as Mason, Shya, and Sam spread out behind me. Behind Korrin, I counted seven—no eight—werewolves. Some in human form, some as wolves.

"So here she is! The stupid bitch who thought she could murder my son and get away with it."

"Korrin, you don't want to do this," I stated, feeling the anger that had lain dormant in my chest for the last few days swell to life. My wolf had been quiet, too quiet, grieving in her own way, but now she was awake and alert and wanted blood. Fuck Seth!

Fuck Brock and Hayley! And fuck fucking Korrin!

I'd had enough of being pushed around, of being driven out, of being attacked. And now, the fucker thought he could attack my Pack, too.

Korrin laughed. "And now the bitch is telling me what I want and don't want. Didn't my son teach you any manners? Looks like I get to rectify his mistake."

"What the hell?" I heard Shya behind me.

"It's a long story," Sam replied to her. "But the short version is Mai was kidnapped by his son, Seth. Ryan and Mai then killed Seth. I'm pretty sure he's here for revenge."

If Korrin heard Sam, he showed no sign of it.

Shya was silent for a moment, taking it in. "Okay, then," she said, stretching her arms as if she was warming up. "I get the guys on the right."

Goddess, I really liked this girl.

"Ready?" Ryan asked beside me, a green sheen flaring in his eyes.

"Hell, yes."

The stillness of the night shattered as we sprang into action as one. Five against eight. I didn't care. I welcomed it. I yearned for blood and action, and these idiots just offered it to me on a plate.

Korrin and his werewolves charged like wild beasts.

"Stay close, Mai!" Ryan shouted over the chaos, but I didn't have time to respond. I headed for a Caucasian werewolf with a trimmed mustache who was running straight at me, his frame bulky with muscle. He lunged, a feral growl ripping from his throat.

Instinct and adrenaline kicked in, the primal part of my mind taking over. I dodged his attack, feeling the rush of air as his fist missed my face by a hair's breadth. I ducked under his grasp and kicked at the back of his knees. He stumbled forward, then crashed to the ground with a grunt. I knew he wasn't down for good, but as I spun around, I barely dodged a snapping wolf's jaws. The female wolf snarled at me, baring her teeth as she prepared to attack again. I didn't wait for her move; instead, I charged into her, putting my full weight behind it. She yelped in surprise as we tumbled to the ground, rolling in a tangled mess of fur and limbs.

"Get the fuck off her!" The male werewolf was back on his feet, roaring in fury as he grabbed at me. I twisted out of his grip, using the momentum to slam my elbow into his face. He fell back, blood pouring from his now broken nose.

"Surely you can do better than that?" I taunted him, adrenaline coursing through my veins. I knew I shouldn't provoke him, but I couldn't help it—I wanted them to know they couldn't break me.

The female wolf came at me again, her teeth snapping dangerously close to my flesh. I darted to the side, grabbing a fallen branch and swinging it hard against her skull. She collapsed. I turned to see the male werewolf charging straight for me, his eyes wild. I spun a roundhouse kick straight to his jaw. He went down, lights out.

I heard the fighting going on around me, the grunts, the snarls, the sounds of flesh hitting flesh. I didn't know if we were winning or not.

Just a few feet away, Ryan was locked in a battle with Korrin. I felt the pulse of his anxiety for me shoot along our bond. I sent a pulse back.

I'm fine, concentrate on Korrin.

I had no idea if Ryan would get the gist of it, but I hoped so. I needed to help the others. I was about to turn when I hesitated, then watched in horror as Korrin pulled a sword—a fucking sword—from a sheath on his back. I blinked. Korrin wasn't taking any chances with his revenge.

We were werewolves. We were our own weapons and tended to look down on those who needed knives or guns or fucking swords to win a fight. This blade was short, maybe twenty-one inches. It would make it more maneuverable, especially in close quarters. Korrin made circles in the air with it, warming up his wrist like he knew exactly what he was doing. I ran forward, but stopped when Ryan held out his hand to me.

"Mine," he growled, his eyes on Korrin.

Alrighty, then.

I'd give him some leeway, but if things looked like they weren't going his way, nothing was going to stop me from jumping in.

Korrin moved, swinging the sword fast toward Ryan. Ryan jumped back out of range, but Korrin went with him, swinging at Ryan's face. Ryan ducked under it and slammed his fist into the side of Korrin's head. I caught a glimpse of Ryan's face—a mask of grim determination, his eyes focused, the muscle in his jaw twitching with suppressed fury.

Korrin attacked again, a roar ripping from his throat. Ryan dashed in close to Korrin, blocked the swipe, grabbed his wrist, and twisted. I heard the pop of his broken wrist from where I stood. The sword fell to the ground, and Ryan kicked it away.

"Shya, watch out!" Mason's shout pulled my attention away from my mate. I turned to see Mason throw himself in front of Shya, taking the brunt of a vicious swipe from one of the wolves. Blood sprayed through the air, and Mason crumpled to the ground, clutching his side.

"Damn it, Mason!" Shya cried out as she rushed the wolf, jumped on its back, bore it to the ground, and smashed its skull against the floor until it went limp.

I ran over to Mason just as I heard a sickening crunch of bone and Korrin howl with pain. I looked back to see Korrin on the ground, clutching his leg, Ryan standing over him.

"Go! I've got Mason," Shya called to me.

I looked around. Korrin and his followers were all down; some conscious, some not. I didn't look too closely to see if any were dead. I brought my gaze back to Korrin; he was glaring at me, the hatred in his eyes clear.

I walked slowly over to him, then knelt beside him, my voice soft but firm. "I'm sorry about Seth," I said, meeting his glare unflinchingly. "I really am. But Seth's dead. He deserved what he got. You keep coming at us, and you'll get what you deserve, too."

"This isn't over," he growled, and I knew he was right. If he had a contract with Brock and Hayley, he wouldn't stop until we were dead.

I thought for a moment about killing him. He didn't just attack Ryan and me; he attacked our Pack. As Alpha, killing him before he could come at us again was the smart thing to do. But I knew I couldn't, not when he was beaten and defenseless. That wasn't the kind of Alpha I wanted to be.

Ryan placed a hand on my shoulder. He knew through the bond what I was feeling, just like I knew he disagreed with me, but that he'd respect my decision. I stood up as Ryan delivered a front kick to Korrin's head. He pulled it just enough to knock Korrin out, not to do any real damage. Ryan did a quick search of Korrin's pockets, pulling out a set of car keys.

"We need to move," Ryan called out, throwing a worried glance toward where Shya and Sam were helping Mason up. I nodded, standing up and leaving Korrin behind as I rushed toward a dark blue SUV parked a short distance away.

I opened the doors as Shya and Sam got Mason in the back seat, then jumped in the passenger side. Ryan started the car, and we sped away. Mason was struggling with his injuries, his face pale from the blood loss. Shya was beside him, her hand pushing against his wound, trying to stem the flood of blood, her face a mask of frustration and concern.

"You're an idiot, Mason Shaw," she said, her voice louder than she probably intended. "I can look after myself. I don't need you hovering over me like some overprotective bodyguard."

Mason met her fiery gaze, amusement glinting in his own eyes. "My apologies. I'll be sure to wait at least six feet away from you when you're fighting, lest you accuse me of hovering."

Shya let out an exasperated huff. "You know what I mean. I can handle myself."

"Of course. Though, perhaps you'd permit me to handle any attackers trying to sneak up on you before they get within striking distance? Only so you can properly handle yourself in the main fight, that is," Mason replied, lips quirking.

"You think you're so funny," Shya snapped, "but I'm telling you that if you ever get in the way of my fight again, it won't be my opponent you need to worry about."

"Er, guys?" Sam interrupted, his voice weak and shaky. "I think …" Sam slumped over into Shya's lap.

"Shit!"

"Pull over, Ryan," I ordered.

He swung the car left, and I jumped out, yanking open Sam's door. Ryan helped me get Sam out and on the ground. Ryan did a thorough search of Sam's body, trying to find where he was injured.

"Head wound. Probable broken ribs. Maybe internal bleeding."

We couldn't help Sam here. We needed to get him to a doctor.

"Put the back seats down; we can lie both Sam and Mason on that."

Ryan and Shya did what I ordered; we put the two men in the back, and we took off again. Sam's condition worsened with each passing minute, his breathing more and more labored. Ryan was driving with a grim determination, navigating the deserted roads back toward Bridgetown.

I squeezed his hand. "It'll be okay."

"We need to hurry," Shya called from the back, her voice tense. "They're both going downhill."

Chapter Twenty-Five

Mai

In the back, Mason was a grim statue of pain, his skin leeched of its usual healthy color. Next to him, Shya struggled to keep her composure, her usually fiery eyes now filled with worry and frustration. Her small hands pushed against Mason's wound, trying to stop the crimson flood staining his shirt, but the blood wouldn't stop.

The back of the SUV had been transformed into an impromptu field hospital. I was most worried about Sam, though. He was still out. His complexion was ghostly, and each of his breaths was now a wheezy struggle, the sound terrifyingly unnatural.

I pulled out my phone, finding Isaac's number. We needed information, and Isaac was the one who would have it. I hit dial, pressing the phone to my ear.

It rang once, twice. And then Isaac picked up.

"Mai." His voice was tired, worn.

"Isaac," I began, my voice sounding small in the confines of the car, "I just saw Korrin."

There was silence on the other end.

"He wasn't too happy to see me," I continued.

"Mai, I—"

"A heads up would have been nice, Isaac. He ambushed me and my Pack. We got away, but some were badly injured. Why didn't you call?"

"Mai, I'm sorry. I didn't know he was heading to you. After Seth … after Seth died, he lost it. I knew he was gone, but I thought he'd gone to clear his head."

"Is he here officially? Does he have the blessing of Ajak and Kara?"

I could hear the shuffling of sheets as Isaac moved. I guessed I'd woken him up.

"No. If Korrin is there, he's gone rogue."

Fuck.

"Mai, is he—?"

"We didn't kill him."

Isaac let out a sigh of relief. "Good. He might not be there with their blessing, but if you'd killed him, Ajak would want revenge."

"I'll be sure to bear that in mind next time he runs my car off the road and tries to kill me."

Isaac was silent for a moment. "I'm sorry, Mai. You don't deserve any of this."

I sighed. "Who does, Isaac? You'll let me know if you hear anything?"

"Sure," he agreed, and I hung up the phone.

"He's rogue?" Ryan asked, flicking his gaze to me before putting it back on the road.

"Yeah," I confirmed, my thoughts going to Tucker's grin as he'd swung on Ethan's biceps, trying to get Ethan to train with him. "We can't go back to Bridgetown."

"What?" Shya asked from the back. "We need to get Mason and Sam there. They need help now."

I twisted around to face her. "I know. But if Korrin was here officially from the Cocrane Pack, he wouldn't dare follow us to Bridgetown. It would be a declaration of war between the two Packs. Even though he badly wants revenge, he wouldn't put his Pack at risk. Korrin is rogue, though. It means he can do what the fuck he likes, and Ajak and Kara have plausible deniability. He can attack your home with no comeback on them. Korrin is like Seth in some ways. He can't take losing. He'll come back at us stronger next time. We can't risk your brothers, Shya. We can't put your Pack in danger like this."

Shya stared at me, her eyes wide and scared.

"Ryan, we need to turn around," I declared, but Ryan was already swinging the car around, the tires squealing against the asphalt. He and I were on the same page on this.

"Where can we go?" Shya asked.

"We'll go to Three Rivers," I said, my decision made. "We need to get to Thomas. He's our only chance now."

Chapter Twenty-Six

Mai

As night's cool cloak swathed the world, our SUV slipped quietly through the darkened country roads. Shadows and the soft outline of trees merged in a dance of camouflage, making us nothing more than a fleeting ghost against the quiet night.

We were a covert crew, Ryan at the wheel, his eyes focused like a hawk's on the uneven gravel path. I was in the back now, trying to keep both Sam and Mason alive. We'd dropped Shya off at the boundary between Bridgetown and the Three Rivers territories. She was needed there to stop Tristan and protect her family. She hadn't wanted to leave Mason, but I'd promised her I'd give her regular updates. Just before she got out of the car, Shya had leaned over Mason and then kissed him. His eyes had widened in shock, and she'd pulled back before he could kiss her back. Then she'd ordered, "Stay alive, Mason Shaw," and jumped out of the car.

I'd called Derek. Told him everything. He wasn't happy and was worried about his brothers, but he'd agreed he would be of better use in Bridgetown for the moment. He would warn Michael and Camille, then head out to pick up Shya.

Ahead, I could see the faint outline of Three Rivers. It was hostile ground now.

We drove for a while in silence until the vague shape of the town's outskirt buildings appeared, bathed in moonlight. We knew the main roads in were being watched, so we had taken an old track that Ryan knew about. He didn't think Brock had enough enforcers yet to cover this track as well as the others and keep guard on the Alpha compound. It was a risk, but we had to take it. The plan was for Ryan to drop us off near Thomas's house, help us in, and then go back and ditch the car.

Ryan pulled in a few streets away from Thomas's house. It was quiet. Sofia had texted that there was a curfew in place, which worked in our favor but meant anyone seeing us might report us as curfew breakers.

"Everyone out," Ryan ordered. "I'll carry Sam. Mai, you scout ahead. You see any trouble, you let us know. If it looks bad, make a run for it. We'll regroup behind the old Moorhead church."

My heart thudded in my chest as I nodded. This was risky. If we got caught, Brock and Hayley would kill us all.

Mason grunted as he got out of the car, and I knew he wouldn't make it as far as Thomas's on his own.

I reached out, putting my arm around him. "I got you."

Ryan looked at me, indecision clear on his face. He knew we just lost my role as a scout. It meant we'd have to move slower, when Sam was running out of time.

I felt the weight of Mason's body lean into mine. His breath hitched in pain, his usually strong frame trembling under my arm. Ryan's eyes met mine for a brief moment, a silent pact exchanged in that gaze. We would get them both through this. We had to.

"No time for second thoughts," I muttered, my voice barely a whisper against the hushed stillness of the night. I started to lead Mason down the shadowy alleyway, keeping close to the edge of the brick buildings, my senses on high alert. Every stray whisper of wind, every distant dog's bark sent a surge of adrenaline coursing through me.

Ryan followed, his larger frame a silhouette against the dim moonlight, Sam's limp body cradled in his arms. His movements were careful, calculated, every step a masterclass in silent prowling.

Mason stumbled, his grip on me tightening. I could feel the tremors racking his body, his determination battling against his injury.

"Not much further," I lied.

We were so slow. We were running out of time for both of them. The journey seemed to take forever as we moved deeper into the heart of Three Rivers.

The maze of alleyways led us to Thomas's place. The light from the windows was such a welcome sight that I almost cried. As we staggered up the rear pathway, the door swung open to reveal a surprised Thomas looming in the doorway with a bin bag in his hand.

"Wally!" he called, dropping the bag, rushing forward, and taking Mason from me.

Wally's slight frame appeared, his eyes wide with shock.

"Fucking hell!" he exclaimed, making way for us to enter. "I'll get the supplies."

Then suddenly, Sofia and Jase were there, grabbing us and hauling us inside. The door was shut and locked, and we were led into Thomas's office. Ryan placed Sam on the bed, and Jase helped Mason into a chair.

"Mason has a deep wound in his left side. We can't seem to stop the bleeding. Sam has a head wound and broken ribs. There may be internal bleeding. He's been out for over an hour," Ryan said, methodically listing what we knew, his voice steady and calm, even though I could feel how scared he was for his brothers.

Thomas nodded, then ordered, "Wally, cut the clothes off Sam; I need to see what I'm working with. Jase, clear the table and lie Mason down there. I'll need to clean the wound and sew it shut. Ryan, Mai, wait outside; there are too many people in here."

Sofia guided us out and sat us in the waiting room. "They'll be okay," she whispered. "They're strong, and Thomas is an awesome doctor."

I nodded, unable to say anything.

I was vaguely aware that Sofia left and sometime later, came back with hot drinks. She pushed one into my hand. "Drink this. It'll make you feel better."

We both sat there, Ryan and me, our bodies close, knees touching, the exhaustion of the night's events seeping into our bones. We didn't speak, just sat there and waited.

I don't know how long we stayed there. Time lost all meaning as I thought about Ryan's brothers and how it wasn't their fight. I'd brought them into this, and they were suffering because of it.

I didn't see him come in, but Thomas was suddenly there, standing in front of me.

"Mason lost a lot of blood, but I sewed the wound closed and gave him a transfusion. He'll be okay in a few hours. Sam is worse off. I've had to put him in a coma. It'll give his body a chance to heal. He should pull through, but it's going to be a couple of days before I can bring him out of the coma."

A weight lifted off me. They were both alive. They were going to be okay.

"What the hell happened?" Thomas's voice cut through my thoughts.

"Korrin attacked us," I explained. "He had friends with him."

"Tell us," Jase said.

So I did. I told them about the Bridgetown Pack, about Tristan being seen here, about Ronnie and what he knew, and finally about Korrin's attack.

"What?" Wally screeched after I was done. "You left me out of all the fun! I'm not missing any more. I want in. I want revenge. I'm part of this and not you," he pointed at Thomas, "and not you," he pointed at me, "and not even you, Ryan Shaw, are going to stop me!"

Thomas sighed and put his hand over his eyes. He looked tired, and I wondered how long he'd been working on Sam and Mason. "You are all mad," he said, sweeping his hand over his face.

"Mad? More like totally badass!" Wally retorted, his eyes gleaming with excitement. "Come on, Thomas, you can't expect me to sit on the sidelines while everyone else gets to be a hero."

Thomas groaned, shaking his head. "Wally, this isn't a game. People are getting hurt. It's dangerous."

"You think I don't know that? That's why they need me. I'm the tiny, gay werewolf that's married to the Pack doctor. I'm their secret weapon. Those assholes will never see me coming!"

As crazy as it sounded, Wally had a point, they wouldn't expect it from him. But I couldn't face putting anyone else in danger. Before I could dash his dreams, though, Sofia beamed at me. "Well, I'm just so glad you're back."

I smiled back at her. We were in enemy territory, Brock and Hayley were hunting us, Tristan was plotting to kill Shya's family, and Korrin was still out there, thirsting for revenge. Only Sofia would be happy that we'd just put a massive target on her back.

CHAPTER TWENTY-SEVEN

RYAN

The sun was barely peeking over the horizon when I found myself sitting at Thomas and Wally's weathered wooden table, sipping on a cup of coffee that had lost its heat some time ago. Across from me, Mai was lost in her thoughts, her brown eyes a pool of emotions I couldn't quite decipher. She'd had a deep cut on her hip from the broken glass when the car crashed, but Thomas had stitched her up last night, and it was mostly healed this morning.

Sam was still comatose. Mason was on the mend but far from fully recovered. I knew our position was dangerous, but I couldn't help but feel a sense of peace that we were back in the heart of Three Rivers. Back home where we belonged.

The clatter of cutlery and plates filled the quaint kitchen, breaking the silence. I looked up, my gaze meeting Mai's. Her dark hair was tousled, framing her face perfectly.

"We'll leave after breakfast. Can Sam and Mason stay until they've recovered?"

"Don't be silly. You're all staying here. I won't hear of any of you leaving," Thomas replied.

"Look, we appreciate the offer," I began, "really we do, but we can't stay here."

Wally rolled his eyes. "Yes, you can. It's easy-peasy. You just don't move your feet out the door."

"If we stay here, we're putting you in a lot of danger," Mai said, her tone serious. "Brock and Hayley want us dead. They'll stop at nothing to achieve that."

Wally got up then, his usual bubbly demeanor replaced by a hard look. "Enough, both of you." He leveled his gaze at us, his hands on his hips, the intensity in his eyes matching our own. "We're not going into this blind; we know the risks."

"But—" Mai started, only to be cut off again.

"But nothing, girlie. This is our Pack. We know who we're loyal to. We know who we support as our Alpha pair. We've got your back, whether you like it or not. This is our fight too."

I tried again. "We don't want to bring trouble to your doorstep—"

"And we don't want you out there, exposed and vulnerable," Thomas countered. "Wally and I have talked about it, and, although certain threats were made," Thomas raised one eyebrow at Wally, "he didn't need to remind me of where we've come from or what we're fighting for here. Wally's right; this isn't just about you. We are all fighting for this Pack. Our home is yours for as long as you need it, end of discussion."

I looked over at Mai, searching her face for her thoughts. She looked back at me, her eyes reflecting the same concern I felt. But through our bond, I got a ping of relief.

I opened my mouth to accept their offer, but Sofia beat me to it. "Of course, they're staying," she said, walking into the kitchen and pulling up a chair beside Mai. "Besides, we've got bigger problems." Sofia's gaze traveled from me to Mai and then settled on the mug in front of her. "Brock and Hayley. They're dismantling all the things Jem put in place."

Mai's fingers tightened around her cup, her knuckles turning white. "What do you mean?"

"They've imposed new rules. Only children from approved families can attend school. Every new job and every promotion must be approved by the Alphas. Any trip outside of the territory needs their consent."

"Clever," I said. "They can control the Pack that way. Any dissenting voices will shut up pretty quickly when they find their kids can't go to school, they can't leave, and they can't get a promotion or new job."

"A Pack isn't a prison," Mai said, her voice harsh. "They can't just dictate life like that."

"They can, and they are," Sofia countered, a touch of bitterness seeping into her voice. "They even tried to tell Thomas who he can treat, but he put his foot down. Told them he'd leave if they enforced that rule. They've relented, for now, but only because they need a Pack doctor."

The information hit my stomach like a lead weight. Brock and Hayley were destroying everything Jem and I had done since Oliver was defeated. We'd worked so hard to turn this Pack into a supportive community, one that Mai would be safe in. We couldn't let them continue.

"We have to do something," Mai muttered, meeting my gaze again.

"We need to start gathering our army," I said. "We have supporters.

We need to reach out to them. Quietly, without raising Brock and Hayley's suspicion."

Nods went around the table, a silent pact forming among us. We had to take back our Pack. For Jem. For the future of Three Rivers. No matter what.

⁂

I found Mason sitting up in the bed in Thomas's makeshift treatment room. The small space was at the back of the house and served as an exam room of sorts, with a couple of beds, some basic medical supplies and equipment, and a large window that let in ample natural light.

Mason was propped up against some pillows on the nearest bed. Some color had returned to his face, which I took as a positive sign after the blood loss he'd suffered. But there was a tension in the set of his shoulders and the furrow of his brow.

"How are you feeling?" I asked.

He blinked, focusing on me. "I'm doing okay. Just thinking through what happened."

I noticed a glass of water on the bedside table, untouched, and next to it a black ballpoint pen. Mason usually had something in his hands when he was thinking, and I'd seen him twirl pens through his fingers like a magician. It calmed him. It was not a good sign that was on the table and not in his hands.

"You should drink something," I said. "Doctor's orders, right?"

The corner of Mason's mouth quirked up, but the smile didn't quite reach his eyes. He reached for the glass with a slightly unsteady hand and took a few sips before setting it back down.

"I'm fine, really," he said. "I'm ready to get back out there."

I nodded. That desire for action, for resolution, was something we all felt. "Right now, you just need to focus on recovering."

Mason frowned but didn't argue. He lay back against the pillows, weariness etched across his features.

I considered him for a moment, debating how to approach this. "I saw what you did for Shya during the fight," I began. "Pushing her out of the way, taking that hit."

Mason's jaw tightened, his eyes dropping to the ground. "Someone had to protect her. She wasn't paying attention to her left side."

"Maybe," I conceded. "But she didn't exactly seem happy about it afterward."

Mason exhaled heavily, leaning forward to rest his elbows on his knees. "She's infuriating. She insists she doesn't need my help. That she can take care of herself."

"She's been raised to be an Alpha. You can't really blame her for being independent," I pointed out.

"I know," Mason replied, a hint of frustration in his tone. "Doesn't change my instincts, though. I want to wrap her in Kevlar and hide her in a bunker."

"I don't know Shya that well, but from what I've seen so far, I'm guessing she'd try and break out within five minutes."

Mason sighed, running a hand through his hair. "She would. And she'd probably succeed, too."

"She's stubborn and strong. Two traits that don't mix well with being protected. And, yes, I'm talking from experience here."

"Fucking tell me about it," he muttered. "Ever since I met Shya, I can't stop thinking about her or her safety. It's like this primal need to protect her, even though I know she doesn't want or need it. It's killing me that I'm here in bed while she's out there about to face down that fucker Tristan."

Understanding dawned on me. I recognized my own possessive feelings for Mai. The all-consuming need to safeguard my mate, to make her mine alone, was something I understood intimately.

"You think Shya is your mate?"

He scrubbed a hand over his face. "I don't know. Maybe? It feels different from anything I've experienced before."

"Have you talked to her about it?" I asked.

Mason shook his head. "And say what? 'Hey Shya, I know we just met, but how about you abdicate, come live with me, a PI from a rival Pack who lives with his three brothers, and we get down to mating for live'? After what Tristan has been doing to her, she'd laugh my ass out of the door."

"Maybe," I agreed. "Doesn't change what you're feeling, though. It's not just going to go away because it's inconvenient."

"Fuck," Mason muttered.

"Give it time. Get to know her first, outside of all this chaos. The bond will reveal itself when the time's right."

Mason nodded, though he still seemed conflicted. "I know she doesn't want me to step in and protect her, but I can't help it. Whether she likes it or not, keeping her safe is the only thing that's important."

"You'll figure it out. For now, just follow your instincts. Even if it annoys the hell out of her."

That drew a laugh from Mason. "Easier said than done. You might have noticed but she's not exactly the type to stay quiet when annoyed."

"All the more fun for us," I teased, clapping him on the back as I stood. Mason had always been the protector of our family; his utter dedication to those he cared about was an unwavering constant. His dry humor was reserved only for his inner circle. Others thought his imposing physique and no-nonsense demeanor made him seem aloof, but I knew beneath that tough exterior lay a deep empathy for others. He needed to be brought out of his shell. Shya was exactly the type of woman Mason needed to keep him on his toes.

CHAPTER TWENTY-EIGHT

MAI

The house seemed eerily quiet after Mason and Ryan left. Their lingering scent of determination and unwavering resolve mixed with the homely scent of pine and woodsmoke from Thomas and Wally's home. Jase and I were left in the relative safety of its walls, but I was worried about the rest of my renegade Pack.

Every tick of the clock echoed in the silence, each second a reminder of the dwindling time we had before the Pack Meet. We were running out of time.

Sofia had left after breakfast and gone to use her web of contacts in search of valuable information about Brock, Hayley, and Tristan's plans. She didn't want to use the phone—said many of them would only give up information if it was face-to-face and she was alone. I trusted her judgment, her ability to uncover the truth. But the lingering uncertainty gnawed at me. Was this what being an Alpha was? Learning to live with the worry and guilt when you sent others into danger?

Ryan and Mason were next, slipping out to find their enforcers. Mason was doing much better. He'd eaten more in one sitting than I could eat in a week, burped loudly, and declared he was ready. Thomas wasn't so sure, but Mason was as bull-headed as Ryan sometimes, and Ryan knew there was no stopping Mason from going with him.

They'd only been gone an hour when Thomas's cell rang. It was Martha, one of Brock's new enforcers. Thomas was needed up at the compound. Wally went with him to watch his back while Thomas dealt with whatever crisis was going on up there. I shivered at the thought, my gut churning. Thomas was needed to heal the wounded, but being in the Alpha compound with Brock and Hayley was risky. What if they knew that Thomas and Wally were helping us? I could only hope that with Wally at his side, they'd look out for each other and stay safe.

That had been ninety minutes ago. Since then, between checking on Sam, Jase and I busied ourselves around the house. I'd sat and watched Sam for a bit. His breathing was steady, and his color looked better. I couldn't tell that he was in a coma; he just looked like he was sleeping, except for the tubes running into his arms and the regular beep and whirr of the machines he was hooked up to.

I didn't stay long in the room. I kept moving methodically through the house, checking every window, every door, making sure they were securely barred. Jase was following me around like a lost puppy.

"What do you want to be, Jase?" I asked him, my tone playful, hoping to lighten the heavy atmosphere. When I left four years ago, Jase had been at the top of his class in every subject. "I somehow doubt it's being a delivery driver for Takymora for the next five years?"

His brow furrowed as he glanced my way. "I wanted to be an enforcer for Jem and Hayley. Jem brought in a new rule that you have to be twenty to apply. I've got another year to go, but now all I want is to be an enforcer for you and Ryan."

"You know, before you become the next werewolf Vin Diesel," I shot back, a smirk playing on my lips, "why don't you go see the world? Have some adventures?"

"My place is here, Mai. I don't want to be anywhere else. And I'll fight for it with my life if need be."

Okay, too serious.

I nudged him with my elbow. "Haven't you ever thought about it? Being anything else?"

He was quiet for a moment. "I guess ... I guess I've never really thought I had a choice."

"Choices are what we make them to be, Jase," I said softly. "Don't let the world decide what you become."

"But what if what the world wants me to be ... is what I want to be?" he challenged, turning his gaze toward me.

"Then, Jase," I said, "you make sure you're the grumpiest, stubbornest, most badass enforcer with a killer scowl that makes all the girls swoon this world has ever seen."

He laughed, and I sighed inwardly. It was a good sound to hear.

I was moving before I registered that I'd heard a noise. I don't know what alerted me. The birds going quiet, perhaps. But I was running before the clamor of a shattered window pierced the relative quiet of the house. We had to protect Sam. Jase drew level with me, his eyes wide in shock.

"Shit," he muttered, drawing in a sharp breath.

I grabbed Jase's arm, yanking him behind me as the first intruder barreled through the doorway. I positioned us back-to-back, Jase and me, as people—Brock's enforcers—flooded into the house from different directions. The first attacker lunged at me with a snarl, his eyes cold and merciless. I drove my foot into his midsection, sending him flying across the room. My hair whipped around my face as I spun to face the next assailant. I saw Jase throw an elbow into a man's stomach, forcing him to double over in pain, then Jase slammed his fist into the side of the man's head.

The next two jumped over their fallen colleagues. I kicked off the wall, gaining height, and brought my forearm down onto the first one's throat as he followed my move. I rammed into him, sending him falling into the man behind him.

I was furious that they'd come here, had attacked my little Pack and our safe haven, but there were more of them than of us, and they pushed us back until we were in the waiting room and the only thing standing between them and Sam, helpless in his coma.

"Get out of here, Mai!" Jase yelled, desperation creeping into his tone as he struggled to fend off two attackers simultaneously. "They'll kill you. You have to go!"

I ignored Jase and his idiotic suggestion. There was no way I was abandoning him or Sam. I would hold this line or die trying. One of the enforcers swung a right hook at me. I ducked, and he hit the wall instead. The sound of the bones in his hand breaking made me smile.

I saw the glint of a knife out of the corner of my eye as a woman stabbed toward Jase's unprotected back. I threw myself between them. Searing pain erupted in my shoulder as the blade sliced through flesh, but adrenaline drowned out the worst of it.

With a feral snarl, I rammed the heel of my hand into her nose. Blood spurted as cartilage crunched under the blow. I followed it up with a roundhouse kick to her ribs.

Rage boiled in my veins, fueling each punch and kick as I unleashed my fury.

My movements flowed seamlessly as I spun and twisted, dodging blows while landing my own in quick succession. The enforcers outnumbered us, but I was faster, fueled by the need to protect those I cared about. I just wasn't sure who would fail first: me running out of energy or them running out of enforcers to throw at us.

A short, stocky man with flaming red hair punched out, his fist connecting with my cheek, making my head spin. I staggered back, smelling my own blood. When he came at me again, I slammed my foot into his knee. He wobbled, and I curled my fingers into a ball and drove my knuckles into his chest. He crashed to the floor, and I followed up with a stomp to his sternum that had him gasping for air.

Finally, all the enforcers lay strewn around me, unconscious or groaning in pain. I stood in the center of the carnage, chest heaving, knuckles split and bleeding from a slash to my shoulder.

Jase stared at me with an odd look on his face. He'd seen me in school fights before, but never like this. Never with so much at stake.

I fell to my knees, my energy spent. He reached out, gripping my shoulder tightly. "Mai," he whispered, his voice filled with raw emotion, "you're one fuck of a badass."

"Stop swearing," I said automatically.

CHAPTER TWENTY-NINE

RYAN

Something was wrong. I could feel it in my bond with Mai—little spikes of fear and pain—but our bond was too new for me to know anything more than that. I'd cut short our last visit. We'd only just started trying to track down Ava, one of Jem's better enforcers, but she'd gone into hiding and we'd need to talk to her friends and colleagues to get an idea of where she might be. Instead of going to her workplace, I'd turned the car around and headed for Thomas' house.

The air was cool, the breeze carrying the faint scent of pine, but it was the coppery smell of blood that drew my attention as we neared the house. I stiffened, my senses heightened. Mason, ever alert, paused, following my gaze.

I moved, desperate now. As we ran in the back door, the sight was jarring. The familiar space was turned into a battlefield. Bodies of unconscious werewolves, most of whom I recognized as being followers of Brock's, were splayed around the room in an untidy sprawl like discarded dolls. Mai was kneeling in the midst of it all, Jase crouched down beside her.

I rushed over to Mai, my heart pounding as I took in her disheveled appearance. Her dark hair was wild, her brown eyes were glinting with a stubborn defiance, but it was the crimson stain on her shoulder that drew my immediate concern.

"How bad?"

"It's okay. No need to worry."

"Sam?"

"Still out. He's fine. The fight didn't get past this room," she replied.

"Let me see." I gently took her arm in my hands. I felt her wince. It wasn't deep, but it needed tending. "You need to stop getting injured."

"That would be nice."

"I mean it," I growled. I felt so fucking helpless. I was her mate; I was supposed to protect her. "Elise's attack, the car crash, and fucking Korrin. Now this. Enough. I have a safe house down south. I can send you there tonight—"

She touched my face with her fingertips. "Ryan, you were right. We're Alphas. We're going to take our Pack back. But to do that, we have to work as a team, you and me. You can't lock me away until this is all over. I have to do this. I have to fight for our family, our Pack. Yes, I'm going to get hurt, but I'll heal. Shutting me out of this fight is not something I will be able to get over, though."

"Jase, help me secure these fuckers," Mason growled, roughly picking up an unconscious man by his arm and dragging him across the floor, his head bumping along the ground in regular thumps.

Jase did as he was asked and went to grab another man.

I used a torn piece of cloth to bandage Mai's shoulder. I needed to stop the bleeding. I could feel her watching me, her gaze steady and unwavering.

"I didn't feel it through our bond. Just a sense of unease, small flashes that you were scared," I said, keeping my eyes on what I was doing. My wolf was fucking raging right now, wanting to kill all these fuckers here, but I didn't understand why I hadn't had a clear warning that my mate was in danger.

Mai tilted her head to one side. "The bond is still new. It's growing as we grow. We both have a lot to learn about the bond, as well as being Alphas."

It was taking all my effort just to keep my anger under control.

Once I wrapped the cloth tightly and told her to put pressure on it, I got Jase to sit down while I helped Mason with the rest of the group.

It had been close this time. Nowhere was safe anymore. We were being hunted, and next time, maybe we wouldn't be so lucky. Rage filled me. No one attacked my mate, my Pack.

"Ryan," Mai's voice cut through my thoughts. "We have to move. It's not safe here."

"I need to find out what they know first." I nodded to Brock's enforcers, now all tied up and thrown in a heap on the corner.

I strode toward them, my eyes scanning them, sizing them up. One of them, a burly guy with dark sideburns running down his cheeks, seemed less dazed than the rest.

"Bring him," I commanded. I knew if I touched any of them, they would not live.

Mason hauled him into the dining room and dumped him into one of the chairs. My wolf wanted to rip his head off. To kill them all for daring to touch my Mai. I agreed with him, but we needed information. I had to think about protecting Mai from further attacks.

The man glowered at us, his eyes a defiant shade of emerald, but I could smell his fear masked behind a facade of bravado.

I kept my voice calm. "It's Paulo, isn't it?"

He hesitated, then nodded.

"Jem got you that job at Sunny's hardware store. Sunny didn't want a werewolf working in the store, but Jem convinced him that you might look scary but you'd be a good worker. Sunny promoted you to manager last year, if I remember right?"

"Jem's dead, Ryan. It's no use being loyal to a dead man."

"No? How about his sister? How about his Beta? We're the true Alpha pair. We're here to take back what is rightfully ours."

"Rya—"

"Who sent you here?" I interrupted, my voice a low growl. I didn't want to hear his excuses.

He was silent.

I leaned in, my face mere inches from his. "You'll find it's in your best interests to tell me. Brock may be unhappy with you, but you're the one who just attacked my mate. Your one chance of getting out of here still breathing is to tell me what I want to know."

I don't know what Paulo saw in my eyes, but he started talking.

"I saw Sofia leaving here this morning. I was driving past on my way to the compound. Haven't seen her since Jem ... well ... you know. Figured it was worth mentioning in the morning briefing."

"And?" I leaned closer, my voice tinged with barely suppressed fury.

"There's a new wolf. Tristan. He's working with Brock. He was there." Paulo swallowed hard.

"Ah, Tristan," I sneered. "You sold out your own Pack members for a traitor from the Bridgetown Pack."

"My Alphas trust him."

"Your Alphas? You mean Brock and Hayley? And you say that with a straight face?"

"You weren't here, Ryan. You'd disappeared, Jem was dead, and Hayley was saying that Brock was the true Alpha, the pure one. I did what I had to so I could protect my family."

I stared at him, my anger curling around the room. Paulo's face paled. I'd get nowhere if I scared Paulo too much. I pulled my anger back before asking, "What did Tristan say about Sofia being here?"

Paulo hesitated before continuing, "He knew Brock had called Thomas to the compound. He saw it as an opportunity to order a raid to see who else might be hanging around here."

"You thought you'd find Sofia's pals? Her book club?" I challenged.

"We knew Sofia would be helping you. It's no secret she's Mai's best friend. We thought we could round up anyone else who was here, try to find out what they knew. We had no idea you or Mai would be here, I swear to the Goddess," he stammered. "Our sources had you both pegged for being in Bridgetown. If we'd known, we'd have sent a fuckload more people."

I gritted my teeth at the thought of how close we'd come to disaster.

"Look, man. There's stuff going on in the Pack. New rules, people getting roughed up if they don't fall into line. I gotta protect my family, Ryan."

I nodded. We weren't going to get anything else out of him. I slammed my fist into his head, knocking him out.

The door groaned on its hinges as I closed it behind me. My gaze slid across the living room before it anchored on Mai.

"They were looking for Sofia. They don't know about us being here. Not yet, anyway. But this place is compromised," I said, forcing the words out through gritted teeth. "You're right; we've got to get out of here."

Mai was up on her feet immediately, her dark eyes wide with a mix of fear and determination. "We can't move Sam without Thomas ..."

I gave a curt nod. "We'll secure this place as best we can and wait for Thomas. Sofia should be back any moment."

Mai glanced at the clock on the counter. "Anyone heard from Sofia? She should have been back a while ago." Mai's gaze darted between Mason and me, her concern clear.

The shake of our heads was answer enough. Mai's hand flew to her phone. I watched as she dialed, then waited for a response ... nothing.

"Something isn't right," she said, her voice barely more than a whisper.

A noise had me spinning for the door, but I backed off when I scented who it was. Thomas and Wally stumbled in, shock lining their faces as they took in the wrecked living room. But it was Thomas's grim expression that had me narrowing my eyes.

"They've got Sofia," he managed to get out. "Tristan tracked her down. She fought him but ..." Thomas trailed off.

I saw Jase freeze, his muscles bunched up in rage and fear for his sister. Sofia didn't stand a chance against Tristan, and we all knew it. She was a barista not a fighter.

"Where is she now?" I asked.

"Tristan took her up to the compound. I was there when she was brought in. I managed to stabilize her, she's not in any immediate danger from her wounds."

Then Thomas looked straight at Mai. "There's more," he began. "They don't know you're here yet, but Brock knows I can get in contact with you. He gave me an ultimatum to pass on. Ten hours to hand you over, Mai, or Sofia dies."

CHAPTER THIRTY

MAI

.

"Get it out of your head right now, Mai. It's not gonna happen," Ryan growled. His eyes were on me, their possessive stare practically a physical touch, a green sheen flaring in them.

"You need to deal with Derek first," I told him, my voice firm but my insides churning. "Then we'll talk."

Ryan's jaw tensed. He knew I was right.

He pulled out his phone, his movements slow and deliberate.

I turned away, but my acute hearing picked up every word.

"Michael, I have a request."

"What do you need?"

"Can you lock Derek down? Sofia's been taken hostage. We've received an ultimatum from Brock and Hayley. We hand over Mai, or Sofia will be killed."

"Dammit!"

"Can you do it? Derek will go nuts at the news. I know him; he'll charge over here without thinking and get himself killed."

"He's not going to like being locked down, Ryan."

"I don't give a fuck what he likes, Michael. I won't lose my brother. We are fighting fires on multiple fronts right now, and I don't need another complication. Can you help out or not?"

I heard Michael sigh. "I have some enforcers who will help me. We'll keep him locked down until he's calm."

"Thank you. Tell him I won't let anything happen to Sofia. I'll find a way to free her."

"Will do. Good luck."

Ryan ended the call and looked at me.

"We'll handle this," he said. "We'll find a way."

I wanted to believe him. I wanted to trust in his confidence. But the doubts were there, nagging at the edges of my mind.

Ryan's hand reached out, slipping round the back of my neck, his touch grounding and reassuring. "We're doing what we have to do. We're protecting our Pack, our family. We can't let Derek charge into a situation where he'll get himself killed."

I nodded. I knew he was right about Derek. Derek would lose his mind when he heard Sofia had been taken by Brock and Hayley. It felt wrong, though. Asking another Pack to lock him down. He should be here with us. He should be involved in whatever we decided to do. I looked around at the faces of my friends, our little renegade Pack. Jase, Thomas, Wally—all eyes were on Ryan and me, waiting for a decision, a plan.

"We've got ten hours," I said, my voice breaking through the silence, the words tasting bitter in my mouth. "That gives us maybe five hours to come up with a plan."

"We're not handing you over, Mai." Ryan's voice was strong, but I felt the ripples of fear coming from him through our bond.

"And what about Sofia?" Jase's voice was tinged with desperation. "We can't just abandon her."

"We won't," Ryan assured him. "But we can't play into Brock and Hayley's hands, either. No way will they release Sofia, even if we handed Mai over."

"The fuckers will want a public execution," Wally spat, anger and frustration evident in his tone. "They'll want to make an example out of Mai and Sofia at the Pack meeting."

I nodded. "Agreed. If I do hand myself over, I doubt they'll just let Sofia go, but I don't think they'll kill us right away. They'll want to talk first, and then, you're right, they'll want something public to send a message. The Pack Meet will be perfect for that."

"You can't know that they'll wait," Ryan replied harshly.

"You don't honestly believe that Brock is Hayley's mate, do you?"

Ryan stared at me for a moment, and I knew he wasn't sure where I was going with this. Then he shook his head.

"Jem was her true mate. Of that, I have no doubt. She killed him. Even as hard-hearted as that bitch is, there is no way she is not feeling the effects of having murdered her true mate. I'm Jem's sister, she'll want to talk to me. To absolve herself. To convince herself that she did the right thing. She'll keep me alive. Brock will want me dead at the Meet. If I hand myself over, it gives you time to come up with a plan. We don't have ten hours, we have twenty-four."

"I don't give a fuck if you kick me in the head. The answer is no, Mai. Absolutely no fucking way. We'll find another option."

"Okay, then. We could storm the compound. You went out this morning; how many people can we count on? We need them now. We'll need to go in the next few hours."

Ryan grimaced. "Not enough to take the compound. We need more time to gather our people. Maybe if we put out an alert, hope that enough people show up?"

"And trust Sofia's life to that? It would be suicide for us all. One last grand stand against Brock and Hayley. It's what they're hoping for, so they can kill all the rebels in one go. They'll have planned for it, Ryan. And as soon as we attack, they'll kill Sofia."

"You're not fucking doing it. End of discussion," Ryan growled, then he turned and walked out.

The cold, smooth sheets of the bed in Evelyn's cousin's guest room pressed against my skin. I was trying to rest, but my mind refused to quiet down, replaying the past few hours like a relentless movie reel. After Ryan refused to listen to me and walked out, I'd started planning our move from Thomas's. Ryan came back after half an hour, and we'd gone over the plan with him. Both Ryan and I had avoided the subject of me handing myself in, and we'd set things in motion.

I could still feel the tension that was in the air as we'd waited for Ryan, Mason, and Jase to scout around Thomas's house, taking out anyone who might have been sent to watch us. Thomas, Wally, and I had prepared Sam—still in a coma—for the move, working under Thomas's directions. The weight of Sam's limp body on the stretcher was a reminder of everything we had to lose.

Ryan and Mason had brought two cars around, and we'd bundled into them. They drove carefully, watching to see that we weren't followed, doubling back a few times to make sure. Then we'd headed to Evelyn's cousin's house. Ryan, Mason, and Jase had dropped us off to get Sam settled, then they'd headed back to collect all the enforcers still tied up at Thomas's house.

We couldn't kill them—that wasn't who we were—and we couldn't leave them there for Brock and Tristan to find. They would tell them that Ryan and I were back, and we still needed the element of surprise. Ryan knew one of his enforcers, one who hadn't been rounded up; a werewolf called Irina had a place where she could keep them secured until we decided what to do with them.

I'd sat with Sam for a while, watching his chest rise and fall.

"Everything will be okay, Sam," I'd whispered, my voice barely audible. "I promise."

Then I'd come up here to rest. Not that sleep was happening. As I lay there, the sound of the door creaking open broke into my thoughts. I turned to see Ryan walk into the room. He looked so tired.

"Any news?" I asked, sitting up and wrapping the sheet around me.

"Brock and Hayley have been rounding up our people," he stated. "We've been able to contact a few. But they're not just targeting our people. They're taking their families, too. My guess is they'll hold them until they are sure they can hold the Pack."

A lump formed in my throat, and I swallowed hard, struggling to keep my emotions in check. "They're destroying everything Jem worked so hard for."

"We'll get it back," he whispered, lying down next to me and stroking my hair. "We'll undo all the damage they've done. We'll make it ours, make it better for everyone."

I nodded, not trusting my words right now, and cuddled into him. The tension in my body began to ease. The warmth of his presence and the steady rhythm of his heartbeat lulled me into a state of calm. My mind wandered, unable to resist the magnetic pull of desire that sparked between us. In that moment, I craved nothing more than to be as close to him as possible.

"Ryan," I murmured, my voice thick with longing. He looked down at me, his blue eyes darkening with an intensity that sent shivers down my spine.

I didn't need to say anything more. He didn't hesitate. His lips found mine in a kiss that left us both breathless. Our bodies moved together slowly, exploring each other as if it was going to be our last time. Every touch was deliberate, every caress gentle yet possessive. It was tender and sensual, everything I needed right then. Ryan positioned himself between my legs, his hard length pressing against my entrance. My breath hitched as he slowly pushed inside me, filling me completely. We both gasped at the intense sensation, our bodies joining as one.

"You feel so perfect," Ryan whispered, his voice rough with desire.

With each slow, deliberate thrust, I felt waves of pleasure building within me. It was tantalizing; every nerve of mine was on fire. He was going to coax this orgasm from me, one stroke at a time.

"Ryan …" I moaned, my fingers digging into his broad shoulders as I clung to him.

"Shushhhhh," he murmured against my lips as he rolled his hips. Our bodies slick with sweat, I wrapped my legs around his waist, holding him close to me and giving him access to deeper parts of me. The pressure inside me grew, and I could feel my orgasm approaching, an unstoppable force threatening to consume me.

Ryan cupped my head with his hands, and I looked deep into his eyes, feeling the love he felt for me surround me and fill me up. I wanted this. I wanted this every fucking day. I had everything to fight for, and I intended to make sure it was me left standing, not Brock and not Hayley.

We moved together, taking our time, gradually increasing the pace. It felt amazing, this slow, relentless build-up that was making my whole body hum with pleasure. I never wanted it to stop, but my body had other ideas. It was like I had no control; Ryan's hard body was steering me toward the heights of bliss. My pussy tightened around his cock, milking him and sending me over the edge. I cried out as my orgasm hit me, just as Ryan shuddered with his own release.

Ryan collapsed on top of me, and I loved the feel of his weight bearing down on me. I wanted him to stay there forever so I could savor the intimacy and connection we shared. I wanted to shut out reality, but it was almost as if I could hear a clock ticking on our time together.

"We can do this, Mai. We'll find a way. Don't ever doubt that," Ryan said, kissing me gently.

I wished I could believe him. I really did.

Chapter Thirty-One

Mai

Ryan, Mason, Evelyn, and Jase had gotten up early this morning, heading out to track down more of our potential supporters. It was vital we rounded up as many as we could. They needed to go in person, as we couldn't be sure if Brock's enforcers were standing over anyone we called on the phone. Wally and Thomas were in with Sam. I'd stayed behind to help with Sam, but Thomas had ushered me out when he decided they were going to give him a sponge bath. Thomas thought we might be able to bring Sam out of the coma tomorrow.

I tiptoed into the kitchen, found a scrap piece of paper and a pen, and sat down to write.

He was going to be pissed, but I knew I was doing the right thing. I left the note on the table, addressed to Ryan. Then I opened the door, slipped outside, and ran straight into Jase and Mason.

I stared at them. They stared at me. Then Mason took out his wallet, removed a twenty, and handed it to Jase.

I lifted an eyebrow.

"I bet Mason that you'd go behind Ryan's back and try to hand yourself in."

"Did you now?" I asked, not amused. "Aren't you both supposed to be out helping Ryan?"

"We are. Evelyn asked us to pick up some food from the house. We can't trust the local stores not to snitch on us."

We'd decided everyone had to move in teams of two, especially with Brock's enforcers on the lookout for us.

I stepped to the side and gestured them past. "Don't let me keep you, then."

Mason grinned at me. "Not a chance. You need to turn around and get your booty back in the house."

Oh, really?

I showed him my teeth. "I'm your Alpha, Mason. You do what the fuck I say. Move. Before I kick your ass."

Mason narrowed his eyes at me, and I could see him thinking. "Mai—"

"No, Mason. Either I'm your Alpha—in which case, you're going to get the fuck out of my way—or I'm not your Alpha, Ryan is not your Alpha, and you better go and throw yourself on the benevolence of Brock and Hayley. Which I don't reckon they have much of. Your choice."

I could see the conflict in his eyes. Jase's face had gone pale. I knew this was unfair to them, but I had to do this, and there was no way they were going to stop me.

"Mai—" he tried again.

"Save it. You're either with me or not. Which is it?"

Mason sighed. "We're with you, Mai. Always. But this is a bad idea."

I nodded. "Your opinion has been noted. Now move the fuck out of the way."

He didn't move. Instead, he pulled me into a hug. "I'll drive you; just stay alive, Mai. No matter what you have to do, just stay alive until the Meet."

Mason parked the car over a block from the Alpha compound. I couldn't risk him dropping me off any closer and him getting taken as well. Jase nodded to me from the back seat, then opened the car door and slipped out into the cool morning air.

"Stay alert," Mason ordered.

"Look after Ryan for me," I said and got out before he could reply. Not looking back, I started walking.

This was the most dangerous part. People would recognize me; werewolves would scent me. This was the perfect opportunity if any of Brock and Hayley's followers wanted to gain favor with the new Alphas by attacking me, either to bring me in or to throw my dead body at their feet. My mind kept painting grotesque images of what might happen before I made it to the compound and the reception waiting for me.

The street ahead was soon filled with a restless energy. I could almost trace the whispers spreading like ripples in front of me. People emerged from the shadows, their curious eyes watching my progress. I could see the recognition flicker in their eyes, could hear my name on their lips, a ghostly chorus of judgment and speculation.

Out of the corner of my eye, I spotted a flash of movement, a swift shadow among the crowds. Jase. Then Mason. They moved like ghosts, unseen by the others but always there. A werewolf, in human form, ran at me from the left. Mason slammed into him, bearing him to the ground and stomping on his legs. A woman, knife whirling, darted in. Jase broke her wrist, then dislocated her shoulder, before melting back into the crowd. Maybe I was wrong. Jase was made for this. He already was a bad-ass enforcer. I just hoped we survived the next few days so I could tell him.

I saw the gates of the compound ahead and knew their protection would extend no further. This was my fight now.

The compound loomed before me, an intimidating fortress wrapped in shadows and silence. It had always been a place to fear when Oliver was Alpha, and I hadn't had time to banish those feelings when Jem was there. The gates, tall and forbidding, marked the line between me and the dangers that lurked within. Standing before them, I felt small, insignificant against the power that they represented.

As soon as I reached them, the gates swung open, and there was Brock, wearing a smug grin. I so wanted to kick that smile right off his face.

"Brock," I said, putting as much scorn into it as possible.

He laughed, a cruel sound that made my skin crawl. "I didn't think you'd be stupid enough to actually show up," he said, crossing his arms over his chest as he studied me with an appraising eye.

I squared my shoulders, meeting his gaze head-on. "Well, I'm here. Where's Sofia?" I demanded.

His smile widened, but there was no warmth in it, only a chilling sense of amusement. He leaned in, close enough that I could smell the stench of his breakfast cereal on his breath. "You didn't really think I was going to give her up, did you?"

He had lied. That was a big surprise.

"I did, actually." I raised my voice, wanting the Pack members around us to hear. "You want to be an Alpha. Alpha's keep their word."

"I don't want to be an Alpha. I am an Alpha. And I'll do what the fuck I please, and my Pack won't just accept it; they'll be happy they have me looking out for them." Arrogance oozed from him as he shrugged, the satisfaction plain on his face. "Besides, I think I'd rather keep Sofia close by for now. Keep you under control."

My fists clenched at my sides. Anger flared hot and fierce inside me, pushing back against the fear.

"You always were a fuckturd, Brock. I see that hasn't changed."

His laughter echoed around me, then before I could react, he lashed out with his fist, hitting the side of my head. I staggered back, but Brock wrapped his hand around my arm, his grip like a vise, as he punched me again and again. Stars danced across my vision. This was Brock making a statement in front of the Pack. I went down, the ground connecting painfully with my knees.

That was when I saw about fifteen enforcers emerge from the building behind Brock. They'd been lying in wait in case we'd hit the compound. Brock slammed his foot into my chest, sending me sprawling across the ground. As I tumbled, I saw Jase and Mason head toward me, murder in their eyes. I made sure I caught their eyes and shook my head. With his enforcers, Brock outnumbered Jase and Mason. There was no point in them dying here. Either Brock would kill me, or I was right, and he'd save it for a dramatic scene at the Pack Meet. Either way, I had to save Jase and Mason from a suicidal and futile attempt to save me now.

I saw Mason glance from me to Brock and then at his enforcers.

I clocked the moment he worked out there was nothing he could do. The pain and frustration on his face almost broke my heart. He reached out and grabbed Jase, holding him back. Then, I had other things to think about.

Brock strode forward, grabbed my hair, and started dragging me back into the compound. I kicked out, twisting to try to get to Brock, but then two of his enforcers joined in, catching my legs and slamming their knees and fists into my body. It hurt, fuck did it hurt. Their fists pounded into me, the dull thuds ringing in my ears. Sharp pain erupted in my ribs, my thigh, my chest, as their blows landed. I took the beating, trying not to cry out, and then everything went dark.

Chapter Thirty-Two

RYAN

I slammed Mason against the wall. "How could you?" I snarled, my face inches from his. "How could you let her walk out of here and straight into Brock's hands?"

Mason's eyes narrowed, a flicker of defiance igniting within them. "She's my Alpha, Ryan," he spat back, his voice laced with a stubborn loyalty that only infuriated me more. "We obeyed our Alpha. If you don't like it, take it up with your mate."

"My mate?" I said, my voice suddenly calm. I knew Mason realized this was even more dangerous than me yelling. "I would, except my mate is currently being held hostage by our enemies."

Jase, standing nearby, shifted uncomfortably. "We had no choice. She insisted. You know what Mai's like when she gets something into her head."

"That's not good enough. You knew it was a trap. You knew what Brock would do to her."

"It was her decision," Mason said quietly. "She made her choice, Ryan."

I stared at him, my breath ragged, my mind whirling. My heart was pounding with a fear I couldn't control. Mason was right, and yet it did nothing to quell the rage streaming through me. I stepped back, dropping Mason, as the door slammed open, and Derek stormed into the room. His eyes were furious, and they locked onto me with an intensity that matched my own.

"You! How dare you! Asking Michael to lock me down. Are you out of your fucking mind, Ryan? Never, and I mean it, bro, never try to lock me down when my mate is in danger," he growled, his voice low and threatening.

I snorted. "Your mate? Is that what you're calling her now, Derek? After all this time, you're finally ready to acknowledge her?"

His face twisted in anger, and he took a step toward me, fists clenched. "Don't question my feelings for her, Ryan. You know I've had my reasons. You had no right to try and keep me away."

I stared into his eyes. "No right? I'm your Alpha—or did you forget Sam's little speech about how Mai and I are the Pack's only hope? I did what is right for you and for the Pack. You're no good to us or to Sofia if your anger is clouding your judgment."

"Like you can talk!" Mason butted in, and I wanted to throttle him.

"Stay out of this," I ordered as I saw Jase backing away. He, at least, was being sensible and getting out of the way.

Mason moved between me and Derek. "You both think you're the only ones who care about Mai and Sofia? Neither of you is in a fit state to rescue them right now."

"Back off, Mason, before I put you down," Derek growled.

"That's enough!" Wally roared from the doorway. His voice cut through the room like a cold wind, instantly snapping us all to attention. His eyes swept over us, taking in the chaos, the anger, the fear.

"Enough of this infighting." His voice was tight with controlled frustration. "You're acting like pups squabbling over a bone, and it's time to grow up."

He stepped into the room, his presence filling the space.

"Mai and Sofia are in danger," Wally continued, his voice calmer now but no less commanding. "We don't have time for this. We need to be united, to be focused, and be ready to act."

Wally turned to me, his eyes filled with determination. "Ryan, we need a plan. I know you want to storm the compound, but Brock and Tristan will be expecting that. We need to be smart, to think ahead."

I sighed, taking a step back from my brothers and running a hand through my hair. "I want to run over there and rip all their heads off. But they'll kill Mai and Sofia as soon as I step foot inside the gates."

"Good. I'm glad you're finally seeing some sense. Here," he handed me a note, his eyes softening for just a moment, "I found this in the kitchen. Mai left it for you."

I took the note, my hands steady as I read Mai's handwriting.

I don't see another way. I can't just let Sofia die. This is what Alphas do, Ryan. We put ourselves on the line to protect our Pack. If you and I are going to make this work, if we are going to be together, then you have to trust me. You can't wrap me up in cotton wool. It would take longer, but it would kill me just the same as Hayley's knife would.

- Mai

Fuck!

She was right, and I hated that. Hated that she was there, in the compound with Brock and Hayley, and I couldn't reach her. Hated that if we were going to be the Alpha pair, she would need to repeatedly put her life on the line and there was nothing I could do about it. Not if I wanted her to stay with me.

"We need to gather our supporters," I ordered. "Brock and Hayley will take them to the Meet. We'll do whatever it takes to bring them back."

I looked around the room at the faces of our renegade Pack. Wally's whole stance screamed his determination to make us see sense. Jase was in the corner. He looked small and still held a guilty look in his eyes. He felt bad about letting Mai go, but right now, I didn't have it in me to forgive him. Not until I had her back in my arms, safe and unharmed. Mason stared at me, a look of pride on his face. Derek was a roiling bundle of rage, just waiting to explode. I could use that. I'd just need to make sure he was pointed in the right direction when he went off.

This was it. My Pack now. Our numbers were dwindling rapidly, but while there were still some of us alive and ready to fight, we'd keep going. We'd get Mai and Sofia back. We'd get justice for Jem. We'd rebuild what we lost. And then Mai and I were going to have a long, hard talk about her making decisions behind my back.

Chapter Thirty-Three

Mai

A sharp, metallic clang resounded as my eyes fluttered open, an unpleasant welcome back to consciousness. The stale, cold air and gray concrete beneath me were hints of where I found myself: trapped in a basement. Again. I turned my face, scenting the air. It was just me in here. No Sofia. Where the hell were they keeping her?

I pulled myself up into a sitting position, my ribs screaming at me and my head thumping. Brock had a mean right hook. Dried blood was crusted on my face. I traced the cut over my right eye with my fingertips and felt that it had closed. My muscles ached, and I felt stiff and sore and fucking angry.

I was in a cage, one of six in the room. I guessed this was in the cage room in Jem's house. No, not Jem's anymore. Hayley's and Brock's. Every Pack had one: a place to safely keep any werewolf who might harm others. This included those who were injured, grieving, or teenagers who were having a hard time controlling their wolves with all the hormones raging through them. It was the most secure place to put a werewolf, and I'd never heard of anyone escaping a cage before.

The thought turned my stomach, and for a moment, I thought

I was going to be sick. I shook my head, wincing at the pain the movement caused. If I was here, in the cage room, where were all Ryan's enforcers and their families who were swept up by Brock being kept?

I narrowed my eyes as the room door opened, the bright light hurting my head.

"Nice of you to join the land of the living, Parker," a voice echoed through the room.

"No thanks to you," I murmured, touching my head.

"Oh, please. I didn't really hurt you. Not the bad-ass, precious sister of Jem."

I frowned, realizing that Brock was still hung up about Jem beating Oliver to be Alpha. Brock's dad had been the Beta of the Pack under Oliver, and they both thought he would take over someday. Then Jem came along and challenged him for the Beta spot.

"You know, I could get used to seeing you like this," he said as he prowled closer. In school, Brock had been a lanky kid, but he'd filled out since then, and now he was a wall of pure muscle. His sandy hair fell in a tousled wave over his forehead, and his eyes raked over me, gleaming.

"Locked down here, waiting for me. Always wondered what Ryan saw in you. Maybe it's about time I had a taste myself."

I sighed. I'd been locked in a basement before, when Seth took me. I'd been there, done that. "Could you try not to be so predictable? Honestly, the creepy sex thing? It's not about sex or desire; it's just another way for you to show your power over me. You want to dominate, Brock, I get that. But be a bit original. You're going to have to try harder if you want me to be frightened by a pathetic little weasel like you."

His eyes flashed in anger, but I had to give it to him, he controlled it.

"Brave words from a caged shifter, Mai." He smirked, leaning on the bars of the cage. "You know, you're right. This isn't about sex. It's about power. Power that you've never respected." His voice softened as he leaned forward. "My dad was the rightful Beta of this Pack. He had power. Then Jem came along and took it from him. I don't know how—that's not important—but he cheated. Only Oliver was stronger than my dad, and Oliver was prepping him to take over. There's no way Jem could have won in a fair fight. The Three Rivers Pack was supposed to come to my dad. In time, it would have been mine. The succession was guaranteed. This Pack, Mai, this Pack was supposed to be mine." He stared at me, the hatred in his eyes obvious to see. "But then Jem and Ryan killed him."

"Oliver?" Hell, yes, they killed Oliver. Oliver was an asshole who should have given up the Alpha spot when his mate died. Instead, he clung on, becoming more bitter and sadistic each year.

"Not Oliver! My dad." Brock snarled. "Jem was the traitor! That's all he ever was, a cheat and a traitor. He murdered my dad, and stole the Pack from me."

I knew after Oliver died, there'd been a brutal battle between Oliver's enforcers and Jem and Hayley's supporters. I hadn't realized Brock's dad had been one of those who had died.

"I was on the cusp of being accepted into the enforcers. I trained with them; I hung out with them. I was made, Mai. Then Jem and Ryan took over and booted all of us out. Put in some stupid rule about being twenty before you could even apply. I had nothing. No dad, no job, no position. I had to beg for food; did you know that? Fucking Ryan found out about school. About me joshing you. You, Jem's precious little sister, who couldn't hack it and took off. That wasn't my fault. Ryan, your own mate, was the one who fucking rejected you. But he went out of his way to make sure I wasn't welcome here, that no one would give me work. I had to leave. But I didn't run away like you, Mai." Brock stood back, looking me up and down, contempt written all over his face. "No, I went to get stronger. To find allies. To learn so I could come back here and take what is rightfully mine. That's the power I'll have soon."

My body stiffened. Part of me felt sorry for Brock; I really did. I knew what it was like to feel that the whole Pack was against you. But that didn't justify what he'd done. He'd killed my brother out of some fucked up sense of entitlement. He hadn't done it to win the Pack so that he could help people, to make life better for everyone. He thought it was owed to him.

"You might have me, but we will stop you, Brock. There are too many in this Pack who see the real you. They won't let you be the Alpha of the Three Rivers."

His smirk grew wider, eyes sparkling with a dark glee. "You think too small, Mai. You always did. Maybe that's why you like Ryan so much. No, I mean real power. Not some fucking backwater Pack. You all deserve each other. Do you know how easy it was to convince Hayley to betray Jem? She was just begging for an excuse. And this is who they follow instead of Oliver? Instead of my dad? Nah, you're all fucked, and I'm going to make sure this Pack is destroyed. I'm going for real power, Mai. I'm going to unite all the Packs in North America under my leadership of the Wolf Council."

My heart pounded in my chest as that chilling thought echoed in my mind. Brock. Leading all of North America's shifters. The idea was horrifying, sending a wave of cold dread sweeping through my veins. I tried to keep my expression neutral, my surprise hidden, but from the smug satisfaction on Brock's face, I knew I hadn't succeeded.

"That's why you came back," I said, my voice a whisper as realization hit. "It wasn't about the Three Rivers Pack. It's about the Council seat."

Brock smiled. "Now you're getting it. Having the chance to destroy this Pack was just a bonus. The Alphas of the Three Rivers Pack get to choose who gets the next seat on the Council." He nodded, clearly enjoying my horror. "Didn't you know that, Mai? There was no way your brother would agree to it being me. Now, though, I can guarantee it. That seat is mine."

"What about Hayley? What about our Pack?"

"Fuck the Pack. After you and Ryan are dead, and I've got the seat, I'll make sure this Pack is decimated. A war with a local Pack might do it."

His words were like a punch to my gut. The war with the Bridgetown Pack. That's why he needed Tristan in charge. Tristan would make sure everyone in our Pack died or was subsumed under the Bridgetown one. Then Brock would be on the Council and could start his plan to rule over all North American Packs. He'd planned this for years.

Brock must have seen the realization hit my face because he laughed, then turned and walked out the door.

Chapter Thirty-Four

Mai

By my reckoning, it was another two hours before Hayley came to visit. She sauntered in, an insidious smile playing on her lips. I clenched my fists to stop myself from flying at the bars to try to get to her.

"Comfortable, Mai?" she purred, her eyes surveying me in my cage.

"Not really. Couldn't you have made up my room for me?"

She laughed, the sound echoing in the barren room and bouncing off the cold, concrete walls. "Well, I wanted to make sure you're safe. After all, that is what Jem would've wanted."

I clenched my teeth, swallowing the bitter taste of anger. "Jem would've never wanted this, and you know it."

"Maybe. But Jem isn't here anymore, is he?" Her voice was cold and callous, her eyes devoid of any sympathy. "Because of you."

I recoiled, her words hitting me harder than any punch. She was blaming me for Jem's death?

"You're the one who killed him, Hayley. The one who plunged a knife into his heart, not me."

She scoffed. "Semantics. If you hadn't come back, hadn't

interfered, if you hadn't tried to control everything, Jem would still be here."

I took a deep breath and let it out again. "You aren't honestly trying to say that you killed him because he wanted to spend some time with his sister? The one he hadn't seen in four years?"

"I was his mate!" she yelled, slapping her chest. "Me! That should have meant that I came first. In everything. But he always let his attention be swayed, first by idiotic little Pack disputes, with everyone always wanting us to be there to sort out their problems for them. Then you came back, and it was all, 'Mai this and Mai that.' He had no time left for me. Me, who was supposed to be his whole world." She shuddered, her eyes filling with tears. "I did what any mate would have done. I wasn't going to be treated like that."

"He was the Pack Alpha, Hayley. You both were. It was your duty to be there for the Pack."

"It was his duty to be there for me. It's the Pack's duty for all of them to be there for me!"

I always knew Hayley had an incessant need to be the center of Jem's attention, but the whole fucking Pack?

"You're not fit to be an Alpha," I snarled.

She stepped closer to the bars. I so wanted to grab her hair, and slam her head against the cage, but she stood just out of reach.

"And yet here I am. Still the Alpha after four years. I must be doing something right. Unlike you. You, Mai, will never be an Alpha. Never. You're going to come to the Pack Meet with us, you're going to renounce any ties you have to this Pack and any fucking claim you might think you have to the Alphahood, and if you do it right, I'll sever your bond with the Three Rivers and let you leave. You can find a new hole to hide in, as long as it's far away from here."

I laughed. I couldn't help it. Brock hadn't shared his glorious plans with Hayley. "You're delusional, Hayley! Brock has his own plans that have nothing to do with you. Didn't he tell you about his Wolf Council dreams?"

She frowned, a look of uncertainty quickly flashing across her face.

"Brock has no intention of letting me go. Just like he has no intention of sticking around and playing to your whims. You can't be this naïve, Hayley, not if you hope to survive."

"You don't know what you're talking about," she hissed. "Brock is good to me. He listens; he understands me in a way Jem never did. He gets me what I need."

I made my voice go soft. "Jem loved you. More than the Pack, more than me. Did you know he was giving it all up? He wanted to train me and Ryan, so we could take over. Then he was going to leave with you. Go someplace quiet where it was just you and him, and he could devote all his time and attention to you."

Her face paled. "You're lying!"

"He was going to give up everything, Hayley, just to find a way for you to be happy."

She stared at me for a moment, her eyes haunted, then she shook her head. "It doesn't matter now. The bond was impure, just like your bond with the Three Rivers is impure. The only way is to cut it out, sever it, for the sake of the Pack."

My hair stood on end. Impure? That was exactly what Seth had said to me when he'd kidnapped me, that my bond was impure and had to be broken. And Arabella had said something about feeling like she was only pure when she was on ripple.

I felt a cold shiver go through me.

"Are you using ripple, Hayley?"

She grabbed the bars, pulling herself up close to them. "At the Meet, just give up your claim. That's all you need to do, Mai. Then you'll be free."

I stepped toward her and asked again, "Hayley, are you on ripple?"

"It's magical, Mai," she whispered. "It lets me see the truth. It cuts out all the noise. All the doubts. I know what I have to do when I'm on it."

Fuck!

"Where are you getting it?"

She stared through me, not really seeing me. "Brock's so good to me. He takes care of me, Mai. Not like Jem. Brock sees the real me."

"Does Brock give you ripple, Hayley?"

Her eyes focused on me, and she looked so confused for a moment. Then she stepped back. "Give up your claim to the Three Rivers. You'll have the chance at the Meet. Take it. Break your bond. Or I'll do it for you."

Only a werewolf, or their Alphas, could break their bond with their Pack. Seth had tried to break my bond with the Three Rivers Pack. He'd used witch magic, though. Hayley was an Alpha. She had the power to break my bond, and now that she had me here, she could do it at any time. The thought sent ice skating down my spine, and I could feel panic trying to erupt from my chest. I had to distract her before she realized that she could sever my bond now and still take me to the Meet to banish me.

"You need that, don't you? The public spectacle?" I knew why Brock wanted it. It would be a powerful message if I renounced any claim, and then he could kill me for my insubordination. But I had a feeling it was different for Hayley. I stared at her, stoking my anger so I wouldn't feel the fear creeping along my limbs and she wouldn't smell it. "You always did need everyone to adore you, didn't you? Always wanted everyone's eyes on you, everyone whispering about how perfect and powerful Hayley is. You need me to renounce the bond in front of everyone so that they'll all know that you won. Do you honestly think it'll show them how powerful you are, and they'll love you for it?"

Her gaze faltered for a moment, but she quickly masked it.

"That was always your weakness, Hayley. It's why you could never truly be happy with Jem. Because you couldn't stand sharing him with anyone else, not even his own family." I stepped closer to the bars, making sure she felt the full weight of my words. "Even if he had taken you away, it wouldn't have made you happy, would it? Because deep down, you crave adoration; you need it like you need ripple. It's insatiable, your desire for validation. You want to be Alpha not for the good of the Pack but so that everyone will bow down to you, to constantly remind you of how cherished you are."

I tilted my head, my voice dripping with contempt. "That's what makes you such a shit Alpha. A true Alpha stands at the helm, not to be served but to serve. They lead to support and love their Pack, not the other way around."

Hayley's face contorted with rage, her hands clenching into fists.

I wasn't done. "If you truly believed in your cause, in your leadership, you wouldn't hide behind this facade. You'd face me at the Meet, a one-on-one challenge."

Her face was inches from the bars, her voice a venomous whisper.

"You think you're so smart, don't you? You're not going to goad me into fighting you, Mai. I'm not giving you any chance to wriggle out of this. You will renounce your claim in front of everyone at the Meet tomorrow, or the first person I execute will be Sofia."

Chapter Thirty-Five

Mai

The sensation of the cool leather seat pressed against my skin. My wrists and ankles chafed from the tight bindings that held me. The muffled rhythm of tires crunching on gravel played like a somber tune, filling the otherwise silent atmosphere of the moving car.

As they'd bundled me into the back of this car, I'd caught a glimpse of other vehicles. There seemed to be between ten and fifteen in total, all packed with enforcers. It was a show of force and unity and a reminder of the power Hayley and Brock now had.

I'd seen Hayley and Brock getting into one black SUV. And then I caught sight of Sofia. She had been bound just like me and thrown into the back of a third car. She was alive. I didn't know what they had in store for her, but if she was coming to the Meet as well, it probably wasn't a good sign.

It was just me and the driver in my car. I squinted, trying to make out his silhouette. He was unfamiliar—I couldn't place his face or his scent. He looked to be in his late thirties, with light-brown hair in a buzz cut, broad shoulders, and a bright red birthmark on the back of his neck. Maybe one of Brock's new recruits? Something told me he was no rookie, though, but someone used to doing tasks like this.

"Hey! Driver Guy! You got a name?"

Silence. He didn't even twitch.

"Hey! Dude, I'm talking to you."

Great. With nothing to distract me, this journey was going to suck.

"Look, Driver Guy—and unless you tell me your name, I'm going to have to keep calling you Driver Guy—I'm pretty sure you're driving me to my death, no? So, why don't you cut a girl a break? A little chitchat isn't going to cause problems."

Nope. Nothing.

Fabulous.

I pulled against my restraints for the hundredth time, but there was still no give in them. My mind wandered as I kept it up, yanking and twisting, trying to loosen the ropes. Was Ryan safe? Was he at the Meet already? Were we going to pull this off, or was I really driving to my death? I had so many questions, the butterflies in my stomach were doing loop-the-loops. What about Shya and the Bridgetown Pack? Were they under attack right now? Would they be able to defeat Tristan, knowing that he was coming? Were Henry and Tucker safe? I hoped they kicked Tristan's ass. The thought of losing more friends, more Pack members, hit me with the force of a bowling ball to the stomach.

I felt it when we left the Three Rivers territory. A flash of awareness ran along my Pack bonds. Huh. That was new.

The sensation was almost electric, like an invisible tether had snapped taut, pulling at the very core of my being. It was disorienting and comforting at the same time. Was it my bond with Ryan that gave me this awareness, or the fact that I was challenging for the Alpha pair of this territory? Did all Alphas feel this way when they left their territory?

I closed my eyes, concentrating on the lingering sensation. It was as if a part of me, an essential fragment of my soul, was being left behind. I wondered if Ryan felt it too, this sudden stretching of our Pack bond, like a rubber band stretched to its limits but not breaking.

For a moment, my mind filled with images of him—the laser focus in his eyes when he looked at me like I was the only thing in the world; the strength in his arms when he lifted me up like I weighed nothing; the feel of his lips against my skin.

I shook my head, snapping back to reality. Now wasn't the time to get lost in thought. I had to get out of this mess.

Regional Meets to announce a new Alpha pair were always on neutral territory, so no one Pack held the advantage. Each Pack would send a team a couple of days ahead of the Meet to secure the area and make sure that no other Packs were planning something nefarious. Derek had let us know that this Meet was due to be held in Knowlton. The Packs had hired an old camping ground there, giving us seclusion from the human world but plenty of modern facilities.

My thoughts shattered when the car veered off sharply to the left and headed down a side road. I twisted around, looking back to see the rest of the convoy continuing straight on. Panic spiked. What the hell was going on?

"Hey! Driver Guy! You missed the road!" I yelled.

Still no answer. Okay, then. I drew my bound legs up to my chest, then slammed them into the back of the driver's seat. "Where are you taking me? Answer me, you dickhead!"

The dickhead remained silent, his eyes fixed on the road. I kicked again, and again, and again, watching with some satisfaction as his body jumped forward with every strike.

Outside, the woods were growing denser, and the road narrowed. A thousand thoughts raced through my mind, each one more terrifying than the last. Was this part of the plan? Was this a betrayal? Was I being taken somewhere to be killed or rescued? Surely, if it was a rescue, he'd have talked to me by now?

I continued to kick and yell, trying to distract him or get him to talk. "Tell me." Kick. "Where." Kick. "We're going!" Kick. "You owe me that much!"

The driver's silence was a wall I wasn't breaking through. The sense of desperation grew, clawing at my throat, choking me. I knew I had to keep it together, had to find a way out of this. But the uncertainty, the fear, suddenly felt overwhelming. I could only hope that Ryan was safe, that the others were okay. Would Ryan's mate bond tell him where I'd gone? Would he be able to track me here? I couldn't rely on that. I had to trust that they would handle things on their end, trust that I could get myself out of this. Because one thing was clear to me. I was on my own.

The car's sudden stop jolted me forward. I scanned out the window to see an old, secluded cabin surrounded by gnarled trees. The driver turned in his seat to look at me. He was handsome in a classic sense, with a strong jaw and a straight nose, but his eyes were cold and calculating.

"My name is not Driver Guy," he said, his voice calm and low.

"Hallelujah, Driver Guy speaks!"

"I'm Carl. I'm your executioner for today."

Okay. The way he said it left me in no doubt that he meant it and sent spikes of fear along my spine.

"Brock asked me to pass on a message."

"Yeah?"

"As you might have realized by now, you're not going to the Pack Meet," he continued in his calm voice that was starting to really get on my nerves. Somehow, this was worse: the calm, everyday conversation we were having. He just told me he planned to kill me. It should have some emotion behind it, anger or vengeance or justice. But this? This was just another chore for him, like changing a car tire.

"Brock decided that Sofia's execution at the Meet will serve just as good a warning as yours. So, you are no longer needed. You and Ryan have to challenge for leadership of the Three Rivers by the end of the Meet. Given that, he couldn't risk taking you there, not when Ryan likely has a plan to release you and give you the opportunity to make that challenge. Brock wanted a way to make sure neither of you was there."

My breath caught in my throat as the reality of the situation hit me. They were using the mate bond as a trap, betting that Ryan would come to rescue me rather than go to the Meet.

"You think Ryan will fall for this?"

Carl responded by pulling out a gun, the cold metal gleaming in the dim light. He brandished it with a smirk, the sinister glint in his eyes a promise of a deadly confrontation. "Yes. And when he does, I'll be here, waiting for him."

I stared at the gun, my heart pounding in my chest, my mind

reeling. This was more than a threat; it was a challenge, a dare. They were playing with our lives, manipulating our bond, and all I could do was hope that Ryan would see through it.

Carl got out, opened my door, and grabbed me. I fought. There was nothing else I could do, so I kicked and screamed and threw my body around. Carl just sighed, like I was a puppy who'd peed on the floor. Then he punched me in the stomach. I doubled over, the wind knocked out of me, as Carl picked me up and carried me into the cabin.

He left me tied to a chair in the middle of the cabin, the door slamming shut behind him.

This was not good. I was petrified. Not just for myself, but for Ryan, for the Pack, for the future we were trying to build. This wasn't just a battle for leadership; it was a fight for the very soul of our Pack, and we were losing.

My mind went back to Sofia, to the horror that awaited her at the Meet. And for what? To serve as a twisted warning? The injustice of it all gnawed at me, the rage and despair intertwining until I felt like I was drowning in it.

I was so angry with Brock and Hayley. Their treachery, their manipulations, their willingness to destroy everything we held dear, all for power and control. How had it come to this? How had we let them win?

For the first time, I felt truly defeated. The ropes binding my wrists were tight, but they were nothing compared to the sick sensation of helplessness that squeezed my entire body.

I pulled at my bonds, the frustration boiling over, but they held fast. Tears stung my eyes, but there was no way I was letting them fall. I wasn't going to break, not now.

I rocked the chair to the left and the right, then the left again, tipping myself over onto the ground with a dull thud. I froze, waiting to see if Carl would come in. Nothing. Probably out there lying in wait for Ryan, the prick.

My legs were strapped to the chair. I wriggled and thrashed. And didn't move a fucking inch of the bonds. Sure, tip the chair over so I can lie on the dusty, cold floor.

Great bloody idea, Mai.

CHAPTER THIRTY-SIX

RYAN

I stood still, the forest around me a cacophony of nature's whispers, but I only focused on the soft padding of Derek, Mason, Ivan, , and a select few others from the Bridgetown Pack. All of them were in wolf form, muscles taut, eyes alert, noses sniffing the earth and the wind. Only the ones we really trusted were with us. Tristan had spies in the Bridgetown Pack, eyes that were tracking every move Michael and Camille made, ready to inform him of their movements and actions.

We had to be careful, so damn careful. Michael and Camille had been forced to playact their normal routine, putting on a show as if everything was fine, hiding the truth that we knew what Tristan was planning. Now, it was our turn. We were hunting Tristan and his men, and I was hoping to get to him before he could attack. Michael had asked me to be in charge of this operation. I knew he was worried that there were still people in his Pack who were working with Tristan. He was putting the lives of himself, his mate, and his daughter in my hands, and I wasn't going to let him down.

A sudden halt in movement from Derek caught my eye. His wolf form, massive and alert, was frozen like a statue, ears forward. Mason, too, stopped in his tracks, his body a tense line of anticipation.

I crept ahead, and then, through the veil of leaves and shadows, I saw it. Tristan's ambush. His men were stationed beside the road, hidden by the thick underbrush. A truck was parked on the road, and a tree had been felled so it landed across the truck. The convoy from Bridgetown would have to stop to remove the tree and the truck before they could go on, and while they did so, Tristan and his men could attack.

I signaled to the others, telling them to stop, my gestures conveying the need for caution and precision.

I inched closer. We were upwind; they wouldn't be able to smell us coming just yet. We were ready for this. Eager for the fight. I couldn't see Tristan, and most of his team were pretty well hidden from a first glance. If you looked closer, though, you could see the telltale signs. A piece of clothing to the left, the tip of a boot poking out from under leaves. I counted six on the other side of the road and five on our side.

I crept back to the others, but a rustle in the foliage behind them caught my attention. My body tensed, my senses sharpening as I turned.

Tucker.

He stepped out from behind a tree, his human form looking out of place among the stealthy wolf forms of Derek, Mason, Ivan, and the others.

He crossed his arms and glared at me. "I'm not leaving!"

"What are you doing here?" I hissed, my voice a mix of disbelief and anger. This was no place for Tucker; his presence could jeopardize everything.

"I came to protect my family," Tucker asserted, his voice resolute but with a slight tremble to it. "I couldn't just stay at home and wait for them to be attacked. It's my parents, my sister. I had to do something."

I opened my mouth, but before I could respond, another figure arrived. Henry, also in human form, and he was about as mad as I was.

"Tucker, you're in deep shit! You're supposed to be back at the Alpha House!" Henry snapped, his eyes locked on his brother.

I turned to Henry. "What happened?"

"We're supposed to lie low at home. They're ready for an attack on the Alpha House, just in case this is a trick. I know you talked to my dad about this. But bright spark over here snuck out. I saw him escape from the top-floor window. I knew the others wouldn't be able to track him. Only my parents, Shya, and I have been able to catch him since he was four. I followed him here, and I intend to drag his sorry ass back home."

The situation was spiraling, the appearance of Tucker and Henry complicating our mission, adding a layer of risk that we didn't need. My mind raced, weighing the options, calculating the best course of action.

I glared at Tucker, my voice cutting like a knife. "You've put us all at risk. What if you were caught by Tristan? He would kill you without a second thought. You led your brother here. Henry could have been taken instead of you, Tucker. I get that you want to help, but you'll help by keeping yourself and your brother safe and making sure the rest of us don't have to worry about you. Henry, take him back to the Alpha House. Now. Derek, go with them. Make sure they get back okay."

I could see the protest in Tucker's eyes, the desire to argue, to fight for his place here. Then he hung his head low. "I just wanted to help."

"I don—"

I stopped talking. A sound at the edge of my hearing stopped me. A distant rumble, growing louder, the unmistakable sound of the convoy approaching.

Fuck!

The plan changed in an instant. There was no time for Tucker and Henry to leave, no time for anything but action.

"Henry, protect Tucker. Do not let him out of your sight. Tucker, you will stay here, right here, you understand? You will not move, you will not twitch a tail until I come back, no matter what happens, no matter what you hear."

Tucker looked up at me, his eyes wide.

"I'll look after him," promised Henry as he grabbed his brother and forced him to sit down. Fuck, Henry was barely more than a child himself.

There was nothing for it. If we wanted to save Michael, Camille, and Shya, we had to act now.

CHAPTER THIRTY-SEVEN

RYAN

Derek, Mason, and I sprang into action, our bodies moving with a purpose honed through years of training. I motioned to Ivan and the Bridgetown Pack to circle in from the west, and they set off, a shadowy force moving quickly and stealthily through the forest.

My brothers and I came from the east just as the convoy halted, the car engines dying. The sudden silence reverberated through the forest. A moment passed, then another. The tension in the air was a tangible thing, a force that pressed down on us, urging us into action.

I watched Danni get out of the first car with Ethan. Danni's hair was pulled back into a tight ponytail, and she moved with a grace that was deceptive, a fluidity that hinted at a power and explosiveness she could unleash in an instant. As she moved closer to the truck, her nose twitched, scenting the air, searching for any sign of the enemy. Her hands were steady, her movements controlled. Every part of her screamed competence and readiness.

She approached the truck alongside Ethan, and I could see them exchanging a quick, knowing glance. They were ready, and so were we. The trap was set, and we just had to spring it. It was vital that we made sure we had all of Tristan's men, made sure there were no extra surprises for us waiting in the shadows.

I glanced at our team, checking we were all in place, when Tristan's men exploded into action. I caught sight of Danni and Ethan, both prepared for the attack. Three of Tristan's men lunged at them, their movements coordinated and fast. They were a well-trained team, and Danni and Ethan would have their work cut out.

I sprinted forward with Derek and Mason, heading to intercept the attackers.

Ethan blocked a blow with his arm, then spun and landed a kick to his assailant's chest. Danni was right beside him, her movements swift and deadly. They fought back-to-back, the sound of fists and feet hitting flesh filling the air. I reached the fray just as one of the attackers leaped at Danni. I tackled him, my shoulder slamming into his midsection, and we both went down. The impact jarred, but I rolled to my feet and kicked his face just as he was getting up.

I blinked as Mason jumped on two attackers, his claws and teeth doing significant damage. His movements were savage and powerful, leaving his attackers no time to defend themselves. Derek's jaws closed around the throat of another man, ripping it out. The man went down in a spray of blood.

To my right, Danni knocked out a man with a roundhouse kick to his head.

She grinned at me, her eyes shining with adrenaline.

"That was fun," she said.

I couldn't help but grin back at her. Then I noticed the car. It was the third car out of the convoy of five. That's where Michael and Camille were supposed to be, and four of Tristan's men were heading straight for it.

The men approached the car, their faces set in grim lines, weapons at the ready. My legs were already moving, and I knew Derek and Mason were right behind me.

Before they could get the door open, I flew straight at the two on the right, my eyes narrowing to a single point of focus. One of them swung at me, a wild arc that I easily dodged. The other came at me from the side. I moved fast, kicked off the car, sailed over him, and rammed my knee into his back on the way down. I landed on them, dragging them both to the ground, and slammed the first man's head into the asphalt. He went limp under me, and I twisted, missing the kick that the second man had aimed at my head. I leaped and drove my elbow into the other one's throat. He choked, clutching his neck.

The air was filled with the sounds of shouts and snarls. On the opposite side of the car, Derek and Mason had taken care of the other attackers.

I turned as Shya jumped out of the car. I could hear Michael shouting at her to get back inside. I guess Tucker wasn't the only one in her family who was stubborn and reckless; neither of them wanted to stay on the sidelines. Mason saw her, too, and he veered off, heading straight toward her.

I scanned the road, looking for Tristan. There, at the edge of the woods. He was watching, waiting, calculating. His eyes locked onto mine, a brief moment of understanding passing over him that he had lost. Then he was gone, melting into the shadows of the forest.

I surged forward, propelled by a need to catch him, to end this. The forest was a blur, trees and shadows melding into one as I ran. My legs were aching, my breath ragged, but I pressed on, my focus narrowed on the figure sprinting ahead of me.

My wolf was tugging at me, trying to get my attention. Something was off. A rustle to my right, a faint scent in the air.

Fuck! It was Tucker! That kid could not stay out of trouble.

I pushed even harder, my eyes widening as I watched, helpless, as Tucker sprang from the bushes, his tiny body aiming straight for Tristan. Time seemed to freeze as he crashed into Tristan, sending them both flying in a tangle of limbs and snarls.

CHAPTER THIRTY-EIGHT

RYAN

I sprinted forward, every muscle tensed, a growl building in my throat. My eyes were fixed on Tristan, whose hand was now clasped around Tucker's neck, his fingers digging into flesh. Tucker's face was twisted in pain, his body writhing, his legs kicking as he struggled to break free.

"Come any closer, and I'll snap his neck."

I stopped, my breath caught in my throat, my body aching to move but frozen by Tristan's threat. Would he do it? I didn't know enough about him to judge, and that meant I had to play on the side of caution.

"Let me go!" Tucker yelled as he fought to get free from Tristan's grip.

"Tucker," I called. "Tucker, look at me."

The boy stilled and brought his eyes to mine. There was frustration there, frustration and anger. He wasn't scared. Good.

"It's going to be alright, Tucker."

"Of course it is, Ryan," Tucker replied, ignoring Tristan now and still staring straight at me. "I'm going to kick Tristan's ass. I just need a minute to get out of—"

"Oh, my fucking Goddess, Tucker. Aren't you delightful?" Tristan laughed. "You have your sister's sass. Unfortunately, it ain't gonna help you here."

The wind shifted, and I caught the scent of Shya's fear, sharp and acrid. She burst through the trees, her eyes wide, her body trembling. She was on the verge of Shifting, her control fraying at the edges.

"You fucker! Let my brother go!"

"Uh-uh. You know I don't like you using that language, Shya. Tone it down."

Shya growled, and for a moment, I thought she was going to Shift. Her body hunched over, and her eyes flashed. Then she took a deep breath and straightened.

"That's a good girl," Tristan said.

"Fuck you!"

Tristan grinned at her. "That was the idea, yes. But you had to keep turning me down, didn't you. Never mind. We'll get there soon enough."

"Let go of Tucker," Shya insisted.

"I don't think so. He's the only thing stopping Ryan from attacking me. How about this? Shya, you come with me, and when we're far enough away, I'll let the boy go."

Tucker's face turned a shade redder, his eyes bulging, as he tried to twist around and kick Tristan. "Don't even think about it, Shya!" Tucker yelled.

Tristan shook the boy like a badly behaved puppy, then tightened his grip. I could see the flash of pain on Tucker's face.

Shya took a step forward. "Let him go, Tristan. You don't need him," she said, her voice tinged with desperation.

I didn't like how this was playing out. Out of the corner of my eye, I saw Mason slip through the trees, tracking around behind Tristan.

Tristan backed away, dragging Tucker with him. "Come on, sweetheart. Just you and me. Let's make a trade."

"Shya, don't!" Tucker screamed, his voice breaking. "Run! Get out of here!"

But Shya was already moving, following Tristan, her eyes never leaving her brother.

I watched, feeling helpless, as Tristan let Shya inch closer to him and Tucker. She stopped about a foot from them both.

"I'm here. I'll go with you. Just let Tucker go," Shya tried again to bargain with him, but I knew he'd never go for it. Instead, I saw his lips move but couldn't make out what he was saying to Shya. Whatever he said, it made her stiffen.

Then, with a swift laugh, Tristan tucked Tucker under his arm like some damn football and bolted into the forest.

I glanced at where I knew Mason was, but he was too far away to intercept them. "Fuck!" I snarled, sprinting after Tristan and Tucker, Shya and Mason with me.

I motioned with my hands for Mason to flank left. Shya went right and hounded after Tristan, driving him onward.

The forest was a blur as we ran, my wolf close to the surface, urging me faster. Every snapped twig, every rustle of leaves amplified a thousand times in my head. What was Tristan's plan? Would he hurt Tucker to get at Michael and Camille? Would he try to grab Shya if we gave him the chance? The questions gnawed at me as we pushed through the underbrush.

We burst out of the forest, and there he was—Tristan, standing at the edge of a cliff, Tucker squirming in his grasp, his feet dangling over the abyss.

Tristan looked at each of us in turn and grinned. "This ain't the end, you know." His voice was strong and confident. This was not a man who had run out of options.

"Tristan. You drop my brother, and I'll—"

"You'll what, Shya? Nothing. The only thing in store for you is to be my mate. That I promise you. You'll get to watch from my bed while I undo all the damage your fucking parents have done to the werewolves pretending that we are less than we are. You'll see me reset the balance of power so humans know where they really stand."

Mason growled and stalked toward him. Shya motioned with her hand, and Mason stopped.

Tristan ignored my brother; just continued to stare at Shya with a knowing look in his eyes. "This is just the beginning, darlin'."

Then he let go, dropping Tucker off the cliff.

I sprang forward, but too late. Tucker disappeared off the edge, and Tristan jumped after him.

"No!" Shya collapsed, her knees buckling. Mason rushed to her, nuzzling against her as she sobbed. I sprinted to the cliff's edge, peering down, my heart in my throat.

There. A rocky ledge about twenty feet down, sprinkled with weeds ... and amidst them was Tucker, unconscious but breathing.

"Tucker's alive," I called as I scanned around for Tristan. Thirty feet below the ledge ran the Coldbrook River. Further east, it weaved into our territory and, along with the Westfall and the Whispering Willow rivers, made up the three rivers that our Pack name came from. An animal trail snaked alongside the flowing waters of the Coldbrook, and Tristan was sprinting flat out along it.

Dammit.

Shya scrambled over to the edge, her scent a bloom of relief as she caught sight of Tucker.

"Thank the Goddess," she whispered.

This was far from over. But for now, Tucker was alive, and that had to be enough.

I turned back to Mason, my voice tinged with a mixture of relief and a promise of the reckoning that was to come. "We need to get Tucker. And then we need to end this."

Mason looked up, his eyes meeting mine. In that moment, I saw it—the same fierce determination that fueled me—and I knew he was going to kill Tristan.

Chapter Thirty-Nine

MAI

My wrists ached where I'd rubbed the skin away, trying to get out of the ropes that bound them. I could taste the dust in my mouth, feel it clogging my throat. Panic scratched at the edges of my mind, but I pushed it away. I had to think, had to find a way out.

My eyes swept around the dim room, assessing every shadow, every crevice. A rusty nail protruded from the wall. Was it sharp enough to cut the ropes? Could I get myself over there? I strained against my bonds, feeling for any give. Nothing.

The door creaked open, and Carl walked in. He raised an eyebrow at my position on the floor. Then my heart stopped as he dragged in an unconscious figure. Jase. What the hell was he doing here?

"Found this pup snooping around," Carl said, his voice dripping with contempt. He looked at me, his eyes cold, calculating. "You know him?"

My mind raced. If I admitted to knowing Jase, would Carl kill him on the spot? If I lied, would he believe me? My heart pounded in my ears, but my voice was steady when I looked Carl in the eyes, shrugged, and answered, "Never seen him before."

Carl's eyes narrowed. "I think you're lying." There was no hesitation in his movement as he grabbed Jase's leg, positioned Jase's ankle between his legs, and, with a methodical twist, broke it.

My stomach dropped in horror as Jase's scream tore through the room. I screamed with him. It was like I could feel the echo of the pain in my own bones.

"You bastard!" I yelled, my voice breaking as I thrashed against my ropes. "Get the fuck away from him!"

Carl looked at me, his face impassive. Then he picked up Jase's other foot and broke it with the same clinical precision. I closed my eyes, bile rising in my throat as Jase screamed again.

When I opened them again, Carl was watching me, his expression unreadable. "Don't lie to me again," he said quietly, and then he turned and left the cabin, leaving me alone with Jase's ragged sobs.

I glanced around the room for the millionth time. Jase had slumped into unconsciousness about fifteen minutes ago. The pain was too much, and his mind shut down. It was a blessing. Awake, he was in too much pain. He needed to Shift. It would start the process of mending his ankles, enough perhaps that he could limp out of here. But to Shift, he needed to be awake. It would be agony Shifting with those broken bones. Normally, after an injury like this, a werewolf would Shift with the help of the Pack doctor. They'd talk them through it, give them painkillers if needed, and guide the bones into the right place so that they would heal properly. We didn't have Thomas here. If Jase wanted to survive, we were going to have to wing it.

My mind was working overtime. There had to be a way to escape, a way to save Jase and myself. I could feel the panic rising again, threatening to overwhelm me. The room seemed to close in on me, the walls pressing down, the air thick with the smell of dust and sweat, pain and fear. It came in waves, this feeling of helplessness. That we were both going to die here. It was taking me longer each time to push it back. To remember that I had to be strong, had to be focused. Carl was a killer, a man who would follow Brock's orders without question. There was no negotiating with him. He would kill us both if I didn't find a way out.

I was not going to die here. Not like this. I was going to get back to Ryan, and we were going to have mind-blowing sex three times a day for the next seventy years. I would get Jase out of here and watch him grow to be a bad-ass enforcer who was sulky and possessive and made all the girls and boys swoon when he walked past.

I scanned the room for the millionth time. The rusty nail? Still out of reach. The window? Too small, and it was barred, even if I could get free and reach it. If I Shifted, given my arms were bound behind my back, my forelegs would break, and I would be useless. Time was running out. Every second that ticked by was a second closer to Carl's return.

My anger flared, hot and fierce. Who the fuck was Carl that he'd become so twisted, so ruthless? I wanted to scream, to rage against the injustice of it all.

I looked at Jase again, his face pale and glazed with sweat. I had to find a way. I had to.

"Jase," I hissed, my voice colored with desperation. "Jase, wake the hell up!"

His eyes flickered, then slowly opened. The pain was a living thing in them, murky and intense.

"Mai?" He groaned, trying to adjust to his grim reality. "Fuck, it hurts!"

"I know. I'm so sorry, Jase. I will get you out of this, I promise. But you need to Shift."

"I ... I don't know if I can, Mai. My wolf, he's not there. I shut him away when that fucker broke my ankle the first time."

I felt my wolf surge inside of me at Jase's words. She was doing something that I didn't understand. She yanked on my bond with Ryan, drawing energy from it, holding it, and then she pulled on a different bond.

What the fuck?

I closed my eyes and tried to follow what my wolf was doing. She was pulling on my Three Rivers bond, but she was searching among it for Jase's Pack bonds. Finally, I saw it along with Sam's and Derek's, Mason's and Sofia's, Thomas's and Wally's. I don't know how I could recognize each one, but I was sure of it. They were all there: our renegade Pack. This would only be possible if all of them really did see me as their Alpha. They believed in me. Trusted me to look out for them, to protect them, no matter what.

With a nudge from my wolf, I reached inside myself and drew on those bonds. Then I redirected the energy along the thread that was Jase. His eyes widened in shock, but I could feel his pain receding.

"Now, Jase. Shift now!" I ordered.

He gritted his teeth, his body tensing. And then he Shifted. His bones cracked, snapping and reshaping with gut-wrenching brutality. Fur sprouted from his skin like wildfire, his face elongating into a snout. I could hear his stifled whimpers as his broken ankles realigned themselves. Then it was over, and he lay there, a dappled gray and black wolf, panting heavily.

"Well done. I'm proud of you," I murmured, even though my heart was pounding like a drum solo.

After a moment, Jase braced his forelegs and tried to stand. His back legs collapsed immediately.

Shit!

Jase didn't stay there. Instead, he started to pull himself forward, crawling slowly but surely over to me.

"You're amazing, you know that?" I whispered when he reached my side. I couldn't imagine the pain he must be in. Jase grunted quietly at me; then his jaws closed firmly around the ropes binding my wrists. He tugged and gnawed while I kept my eyes on the door. I was sure Carl was going to appear any second.

Finally, after what felt like days, the ropes gave way, snapping apart, and my hands were free. The blood rushed back into my numb hands, making them sting. I massaged them, trying to get some feeling back. We had to get out of here, if only my fingers would start working. The feeling came back slowly, so damned slowly. When I could move them, I leaned forward and went to work on the bindings around my feet. They came loose easier, and I stood up. Ignoring all the pains and aches in my legs, my ribs, my arms, I slipped over to the door. My ear pressed against the cold wood as I listened for any sign of Carl. Silence. That bastard could be anywhere.

I looked back at Jase, his wolf eyes meeting mine with an intensity that shook me to my core. He shook his head. I knew what he was trying to say. That he couldn't walk. That he would slow me down.

That I should leave him.

"Not a fucking chance, Jase. I'm getting us out of here," I promised, my voice a low growl that left no room for doubt.

And with that, my fingers closed around the door handle, ready to crack it open and face whatever hell awaited us on the other side.

CHAPTER FORTY

RYAN

The old camping ground was alive with tension. All twenty-one Packs from the northeast were here. They all knew about Jem's demise and were here to witness the crowning of Brock and Hayley as the new Alpha Pair of the Three Rivers Pack. The other Alphas weren't stupid, though. They all had their equivalent of Derek. They knew about Mai and me and were waiting to see what would happen.

A central fire pit lay at the heart of the camping site, a relic of countless human and Shifter ceremonies. At the moment, it lay cold and dormant, waiting for the spark that would set the night ablaze.

I scanned the perimeter, spotting my enforcers hidden in the shadows. Mason was poised like the predator he was, muscles taut and ready.

I went over the plan in my head. Every step had to be perfect, every movement synchronized. Mai's life depended on it, and I couldn't allow anything to go wrong. The image of her face, determined to save Sofia, to be a good Alpha, haunted my thoughts. I couldn't fail her.

Derek's footsteps crunched behind me, snapping me back to reality.

"They'll be coming from the south-western road," he said. "Brock and Hayley should be here in the next ten minutes."

"Any news from Jase?"

Derek shook his head. I'd sent Jase to follow the convoy of cars leaving Three Rivers. He was supposed to track them here and then meet up with us.

My gut twisted with a growing sense of unease. "Everyone's ready, right?"

Derek's steely gaze met mine. "Relax, brother. We have everyone here. All our supporters, even Wally and Thomas."

I glanced at him sharply. "Who's watching Sam?"

Thomas had brought Sam out of his coma last night. He was weak, but he was going to be okay.

Derek shrugged, looking out over the campsite. "I couldn't keep him away. You know what he's like."

Shit. Sam was in no state for this fight.

"Mason will look out for him. Ryan, we've done everything we could. Now we have to let it all play out."

I nodded, knowing he was right. Derek wanted Sofia back just as much as I needed Mai.

It was time to act, not doubt.

Derek's hand landed on my shoulder. "We won't make any mistakes. We've got this."

His confidence should have reassured me, but instead, it gnawed at me, feeding my anxiety. Something felt off, a nagging doubt that I couldn't shake.

I glanced back at the old camping ground, the ghosts of the past whispering in the wind.

I had to trust in the plan, in Derek, in myself. But most of all, I had to trust that Mai was still alive.

My heart pounded restlessly as I turned away from Derek. The bond between Mai and me, once a comforting warmth, now felt like a cold, tight knot in my chest. I reached out to it, trying to feel her, to check she was still alive.

The connection was there, distant and faint but undeniably present. It told me nothing, though, not how she was or where she was, just that she was still alive. I'd been obsessively checking the bond since she gave herself up, each time fearing the worst, each time relieved to feel her still there.

The ache in my chest deepened, a longing for her that was both painful and fierce. I wanted her safe, back by my side, where she belonged.

Derek's words echoed in my head, a reassurance and a challenge. "We've got this."

I took a deep breath, steeling myself for what lay ahead. We had to succeed. We had no other choice.

A convoy of cars appeared on the south-western road, kicking up dust as they drew nearer. This was it. I grinned in anticipation. Derek and I both had an overdue appointment with Brock.

The cars came to a halt. The doors opened, and one by one, they emerged. Brock's smug smile, Hayley's cold eyes. Then, Sofia, hauled out of another car, disheveled but alive.

But no Mai.

My breath caught, a sharp stab of panic slicing through me.

"Mai's not there," I muttered. "She's not with them."

Derek's eyes scanned the cars. "Are you sure?"

I reached for the bond, desperate this time. It was there; she was still alive, but it was faint. She wasn't here, wasn't anywhere near here. "I'm sure," I snapped, anger and fear rising in a deadly mix.

Derek looked at me. "All our plans were based on rescuing Mai and Sofia, then challenging Brock and Hayley for the Alpha pair."

I knew what he was asking. I had to make a decision, one that could change everything. Trust that Mai was okay, that she would get herself out of whatever situation she found herself in, and stay here and challenge for the Alpha pair? Or follow my instincts and find Mai?

There was no choice. The thought of Mai in danger overpowered everything else. I had to find her, to protect her. She was my mate, my responsibility.

Derek's voice broke through my thoughts. "What about the Meet? What about the challenge?" He already knew the decision I would make.

"I trust you to handle it, Derek," I said, my voice firm. "You have to stall them; buy us as much time as you can. We'll be back before the end of the Meet."

"Ryan—" he began, but I cut him off.

"Just get it done."

And with that, I turned. I knew what I had to do.

Chapter Forty-One

MAI

I heaved Jase onto my shoulders, my muscles straining under his weight. His wolf form was heavier than his human one, but I had werewolf strength, and I'd be able to carry him for a few miles before I needed a break. His forelegs draped limply over my shoulder, and I gripped them tight. There was no sign of Carl as we slipped out of the cabin, but that didn't mean he wasn't close. My eyes scanned the dusk, the dimness casting shadows across the yard, my ears straining for any sound that wasn't the forest whispering its secrets. Carl's SUV was parked a few feet away.

I tiptoed down the steps, cursing every creak of the wood as my feet touched them. I looked around one last time. Still no movement, no sound, no recent scent of Carl.

Where was he?

I realized I didn't care as long as he wasn't near here. I crept closer to the car. Could we break in and use it to escape? I had no idea how to hot-wire a car, so unless ... My eyes squinted as I focused on the keys lying on the dashboard. Jase's phone was right there on the passenger seat.

No bad guy in sight, an open car with the keys inside and a phone to boot. How convenient.

"It's a trap," I muttered. "He's baiting us."

I put Jase gently on the ground and scanned the area. Seeing nothing, I fished out Jase's phone from the car, pushed in Ryan's number, then hesitated. What did Carl want? Was this the plan? That I would call Ryan and tell him to come rescue me? Carl could shoot him as he arrived. Even if I told Ryan not to come here but to meet me somewhere, Carl could shoot me and Jase as we were leaving, then wait for Ryan to realize we weren't coming, track Jase's phone, and come here—where Carl could pick him off too.

There were no good options. I hit the green button.

Ryan picked up on the first ring. "Jase? Talk to me? You got Mai?"

"It's me."

"Mai." The relief was clear in his voice. "You okay? Where are you?"

"Ryan, listen. I've got Jase. We're okay. Brock ordered some guy called Carl to take me to a cabin in the woods. It's a trap designed to lure you here so he can take us both out."

"Carl Utson?"

"I don't know. Got a birthmark on his neck. He's a complete dickhead. He broke Jase's ankles. He's calm, Ryan, methodical. No emotions."

"Yeah, that's Carl Utson. He joined the Pack while you were gone, did some work for Jem, but we saw what he was like and kicked him out about a year ago."

"Well, he's working for Brock now. You can't come here, Ryan. I'll find a way out of this—"

"No fucking way, Mai. I don't care if it's a trap. Just tell me where you are."

I paused. "No. I can't risk—"

"I can track Jase's phone. I'm coming for you."

"No, Ryan. We can't—"

"I'm coming, Mai. End of discussion."

The line went dead.

Great. Fucking wonderful.

If I got out of this, he and I were going to have a talk about him listening to me. We had to stop playing into our enemies' hands.

I opened the glove box of the SUV, rifling through it. A stack of old receipts and an engraved metal lighter. Nice. I stuffed the crumpled papers into the gas tank, struck the lighter, and set them ablaze. I didn't wait to see if it worked. Grabbing Jase, I hoisted him back onto my shoulders and sprinted toward the woods.

The night erupted behind me, a deafening explosion that tore through the silence, followed by a wave of heat that singed the ends of my hair as I ran. The SUV was now a fireball, lighting up the night sky, and if that didn't distract Carl, I didn't know what would.

I ran for half an hour. I had to put Jase down twice. Once to check the route across a small river and again to clear a path through thick bushes. Both times, he'd whimpered quietly when I picked him up. He needed to Shift again to accelerate the healing, but I wanted to get us somewhere safer first.

My legs pumped, every muscle screaming in protest, every pain from my injuries shooting through me as I wove through the trees. Branches snagged at my clothes, roots tried to trip me up, but I kept going, aware that Carl would be tracking us.

The forest thinned gradually, and then, all at once, we broke through into an open space. The meadow was surreal, bathed in the silvery light of the moon. Wildflowers dotted the landscape, their colors muted in the darkness but still painting a serene picture. For a moment, I allowed myself to take it all in—the crisp air filling my lungs, the soft rustle of the leaves, the distant chirping of nocturnal insects. But then reality snapped back.

I set Jase down, my muscles grateful for the reprieve. As beautiful as this meadow was, it was also a killing field. Open, exposed. If Carl followed us, we'd be sitting ducks; he could shoot us at his leisure while we crossed it.

My eyes scanned the tall grasses, the clusters of trees that bordered the meadow, and the sky above. No sign of Carl, but that didn't mean anything. My nostrils flared, trying to catch a scent on the wind, but all I got was the sweet aroma of blooming flowers and the damp earthiness of the soil. Should we go through the meadow or waste time tracking around it?

I was about to bend down and lift Jase back onto my shoulders when a voice came from upwind, slicing through the night's stillness like a knife.

"Hard choice, isn't it?"

My head snapped up, my nostrils flaring as I tried to catch the intruder's scent. My fingers itched, my body coiling, ready to tear into whoever this was.

A figure stepped out of the tree line, his silhouette framed by the moonlight. He was tall, at least six four, and broad-shouldered with muscles that bulged. He had dark blond hair that was evenly cut close to his head but a rough beard that hadn't been trimmed in at least a couple of weeks. His eyes were a deep brown, almost black in the dark, but they held a haunted look. Despite his height and bulk, there was a calmness about this man. A measured stillness that hinted that it was important to him that he was controlled and thoughtful in everything he did.

"You're Carl's backup?" I guessed.

He inclined his head. "I'm AJ."

The wind shifted, and I finally caught his scent. It was faint but unmistakable. My eyes narrowed. "You're the fucking bear who attacked Tucker! He's a child! What the hell were you thinking?"

His face twisted, a grimace of what seemed like genuine regret. "I'm sorry about that. I hope the boy is okay."

"You could have killed him!"

He glanced out at the meadow. "I'm not like other Shifters," he said softly. "My family wronged a powerful witch, and she took her revenge on our animal forms. My bear is insane. When he takes over, I have no control. And he … he just wants blood. Doesn't matter whose—adult, child, Shifter, human."

Fantastic. As if we needed more complications. But still, his words unsettled me. There seemed to be genuine sorrow in his voice, a weight and a burden that he carried. Didn't mean I'd trust him, though.

"I try to stay away from others as much as possible. The encounter with the boy was … unintentional."

I snorted. "You were on Bridgetown Pack lands. You were bound to encounter someone sooner or later. Why risk it? Why were you there?"

AJ hesitated, as if he was considering how much to tell me. "Tristan. He has my mate. He knows I'll do anything to ensure she's not harmed." He shrugged. "So, I now follow his orders."

I was getting an uneasy feeling about this. "And what exactly are your orders?"

His eyes met mine, and for a moment, I saw a flicker of something—desperation, perhaps, or maybe it was just the reflection of the moonlight.

"I'm sorry," he said. "I truly am. If there was any other way ... but I have no choices anymore." He paused, looking straight at me. "I've been told to kill you."

Chapter Forty-Two

MAI

Before I had time to react, AJ's eyes glazed over, turning a shade of primal gold. His muscles expanded, bones contorting and snapping with sickening cracks, fur sprouting from his skin. Where AJ had stood a moment before, a monstrous bear now crouched, its form almost surreal in the moonlight. I couldn't believe how quickly he'd Shifted. Was this a bear shifter thing or an AJ thing? I didn't know enough about bear shifters to know. A scent—musky, wild, tinged with an underlying note of madness—wafted toward me, causing my nostrils to flare and my senses to sharpen. My mind took in all the little details that would freak me the hell out later, like the fact that AJ's paws were massive, each one the size of a dinner plate. Claws, longer than my fingers and seemingly honed to razor-sharp points, extended from his paws like deadly talons. A growl, so deep and bone-chilling that it seemed to echo from the depths of the earth itself, reverberated through the night air, setting every nerve in my body on edge.

Holy fuck!

Every instinct I had told me to run. I'd fought AJ before, but I'd had the help of my Pack then. This time, it was just me and Jase.

The bear grunted, swinging his body to the left and right, sussing me out. AJ said he didn't have any control when his bear took over, but I briefly wondered if the bear remembered what AJ knew. My wolf and I were one; she knew what I knew and vice versa, but this bear seemed surprised to see me and Jase here.

I took a step back toward Jase. I didn't have time to Shift. I was going to have to fight AJ while in my human form.

Fan-flipping-tastic.

I took another step back, hoping I could make it to Jase, maybe pick him up and slink out of here. The bear had other ideas. He charged at me. I dodged to the right, but his claws caught the edge of my jacket, shredding it like paper.

I had to stay away from those claws. One swipe, and he could disembowel me.

I ran right, and the bear followed me. Out of the corner of my eye, I saw Jase dragging himself forward. What the fuck was he doing?

Was he seriously trying to distract AJ? What was he going to do? Offer himself up as a chew toy?

AJ turned. He'd seen Jase, too, and lumbered straight toward him.

I picked up a stone and threw it at AJ. The stone flew through the air and hit him right above his nose.

Goal!

The bear swiped at his face, then roared at me. The sound shook my whole body. And I got a good look at his killer teeth, saliva dripping down them.

Alrighty, then.

I sprinted left this time, trying to draw him away from Jase. The idiot boy started snarling and crawled after us. I wanted to hug Jase and shake him silly at the same time.

"Hey, AJ, over here, you oversized furball! Bet you can't catch me! Too slow and dumb, huh? Come on, try to keep up."

The bear swung his head around to me and barreled forward. Jase growled loudly, trying to get AJ to concentrate on him.

AJ veered around, distracted by Jase's growls. I picked up another stone and another, throwing them at the bear. I'd been great at stone skimming as a kid, always beating Jem and my parents. To my surprise, I hadn't forgotten those skills and put all my strength into sending the stones like little missiles toward AJ's head.

He wasn't buying it, though. The bear had caught sight of prey, injured and weak, and was going to take the easy win. He swiped at Jase, his claws punching through the skin on Jase's side. The scent of fresh blood filled my senses as Jase let out an agonized whine.

That was it. I'd had enough. Jase wasn't going to die. Not on my watch. I ran straight at AJ, jumped onto his back, and wrapped my arms around his massive neck, squeezing with all I had. The smell was overpowering. The musky, wild odor of the bear filled my nostrils, and for a moment, I was lost in it, the sheer power and ferocity of AJ's beast form almost overwhelming.

I tightened my grip on his neck, digging my fingers into his thick fur. He roared in response, thrashing wildly beneath me, trying to shake me off. But I held on, yelling in pain as his claws raked across my back. I could feel something hot and wet run down my back and sides.

Jase's eyes were on me, and I saw his jaws move, but the sounds were lost in the raging storm of fury around me. All that mattered now was me and AJ. His muscles bulged and flexed beneath me with each swing of his body as he tried to violently shake me off.

He reared up. I let go with one arm and drove my fist into his jaw. It was like punching a wall, but AJ staggered back, momentarily disoriented.

This was my chance. My fist became a blur, connecting with AJ's skull once, twice, three times.

AJ flailed, his claws digging trenches in the ground, but I put both arms around his neck again and squeezed. Little by little, his movements slowed until he finally slumped to the ground, unconscious but alive.

I jumped off AJ and looked down at his massive body. I stood there, catching my breath, and realized that I'd faced down a cursed berserker bear Shifter and walked away. If I could do this. I could do anything. I glanced across at Jase.

He was panting in exertion.

"I've had enough of this shit, Jase. We're going to finish it."

Brock and Hayley's reign was coming to an end, and I was going to be the one to end it.

Chapter Forty-Three

RYAN

My nostrils flared as I picked up Carl's scent, mingling with the earthy aroma of damp soil and decaying leaves. I could smell Mai and Jase, too, but it was Carl's scent that I locked onto—a combination of faint sweat and anticipation. He was always methodical and calm in his work, but he could never hide his joy, his satisfaction when he hurt someone, from other werewolves. That was why Jem kicked him out and was probably why Brock recruited him.

Flashbacks of the chaotic scene I'd discovered earlier flickered through my mind. The empty cabin, stinking of Jase's pain and fear, of Mai's frustration and despair. The car nearby, still smoking. I couldn't help but grin, feeling a surge of pride. Mai had blown up the damn car. Trust her to pull a stunt like that.

I'd tracked Jase's phone. The signal had led to the cabin and then into the woods. I could follow his scent and Mai's. But it wasn't theirs I was interested in right now. Mai had disrupted whatever plan Carl had, and he'd taken off to track her and Jase.

I closed my eyes for a moment, focusing solely on Carl's scent. The acrid stench of his anticipation was growing stronger, which meant he was close. My wolf growled softly, eager to hunt anyone who had touched Mai.

I picked up the pace, my movements a blend of human agility and wolf-like reflexes. My ears caught the distant sound of footsteps. He was hurrying, not taking his usual care to cover his tracks. He wanted to take out Mai and Jase quickly before coming back for me, and it was making him sloppy.

I had to be quick but careful. Carl might be many things—cruel, sadistic—but he was not a fool. He was a sophisticated killer and was cool-headed even when the odds were against him. My wolf understood the predator in Carl, respected it even though we both loathed the man.

I sped forward, my feet flying over the ground, my senses fully on alert. I could hear the steady rhythm of Carl's heartbeat, the soft exhale of his breath. I could smell his sweat and the faint whiff of a metal weapon he carried. Then I saw him, up head and to the right, scurrying between the tall trees.

Carl paused, his head tilting slightly, as if sensing something amiss. I froze, still too far away, my body taut as a bowstring, my muscles quivering with the effort of staying still. My wolf was yelling at me to move, to end this, but my human side urged caution. This was a man who was skilled in the art of death. I needed to be sure, absolutely sure, before I attacked.

Seconds felt like hours. Sweat trickled down my forehead, but I dared not wipe it away. And then, as if the Goddess had decided to favor me, a sudden gust of wind rustled the leaves, and Carl moved again, dismissing whatever warning his instincts had given him.

It was the opening I needed.

With a surge of speed that only a werewolf could muster, I darted forward, closing the distance between us. Carl turned, bringing the gun up. I slammed into him, my shoulder connecting with his chest, sending him sprawling to the ground. His weapon skittered out of his hand and into the underbrush.

Carl rolled to his feet, a blade appearing in his hand as if by magic. I was on him before he could fully rise, my fist colliding with his jaw. The sound of bone meeting bone echoed in the quiet night.

Carl snarled, slashing with his knife. I twisted, avoiding the edge, and my foot shot out, jabbing into his hip. Carl stumbled, grimacing in pain.

We circled each other. My eyes were locked onto his, reading every flicker of emotion, every hint of movement. His gaze was icy, devoid of emotion, but I could smell it—the first faint whiff of fear.

"You're out of your league, Ryan," Carl said, twirling his blade in a fancy figure of eight.

I ignored him. He was trying to distract me, and I was too seasoned to fall for it. I feinted left and then moved right, my fist striking his temple. Carl staggered, disoriented.

I don't know what he saw in my face, but his pulse quickened, and his eyes widened.

"I ... I can help you, you know," he gasped, catching his breath.

"Not interested."

"Ryan, be sensible. Every Pack needs someone like me. I take care of the inconvenient problems that no one else has the stomach for. Brock saw my potential. Saw the advantages I could bring. I could do that for you instead. Let me prove myself, hmmm? You need Brock gone. I can do that. I'll phone him right now, tell him you and Mai are dead and that we need to meet. I'll have his head on a plate for you by sunup."

I looked at Carl and swallowed down the bile threatening to come up. He was right; lots of Packs had someone like Carl. But not *my* Pack. That wasn't the sort of Pack that Mai and I were going to build. He was clever, though, offering to take care of Brock for me. Plenty of Alphas would take him up on that offer. It was how men like Carl got you. They offered something big, something almost impossible, something you really wanted. They showed how easy it was to just click our fingers, and they'd do all the dirty work. And each time, they dug a little deeper in, making themselves indispensable. Until one day, you woke up and found your Pack was built on the back of a man like Carl. And they wanted something. Perhaps a bigger cut, perhaps greater freedom, perhaps a child or two. That wasn't going to happen. Not while I was still breathing.

"Thank you for the offer, Carl, but I'll take care of Brock myself."

I sailed forward and drove my fist into his chest, right over his heart, using all the supernatural strength I possessed. There was a sickening thud, a gasp, and then Carl crumpled, his eyes wide with shock and disbelief as he hit the ground, lifeless.

I was still catching my breath, the adrenaline slowly ebbing away, when the rustle of footsteps caught my attention. I turned, my body tensed for another fight, but it wasn't another threat. Mai and Jase burst through the foliage. Mai was carrying Jase on her back. She was alive. Bloodied, looking exhausted and angry but alive.

My bond with Mai thrummed with need. I had to have her in my arms. Now. "Mai," I breathed out her name like a prayer of thanks to every deity I'd ever heard of. She lowered Jase gently to the ground, and in three strides, I closed the distance between us, sweeping her into my arms. My wolf was going mad, wanting to touch and lick Mai all over to make sure she was okay. I captured her lips in a kiss that was fierce and tender, a mingle of relief, joy, and a dozen other emotions I couldn't begin to name coursing through me.

"I was so worried about you," she whispered against my lips, her hands clutching at my back as if she'd never let go.

"Me? What about you? Blowing up cars, running off into the woods."

"We ran into the bear Shifter."

I stiffened. I could smell her blood. "You okay?" I asked as I subtly started patting her down, checking her out for injuries.

"What are you doing?" She smiled up at me. "Are you checking me out?"

Okay, so not so subtle.

"Yes. What's sore? Anything broken?" I kept moving my hands over her, not wanting to stop touching her.

Mai pushed me back. "I'm okay. Really. His claws got my back and side but I think the wounds have closed."

I turned her round, ignoring her protests, and lifted up her shirt. Then crouched down, inspecting the gashes. Most had closed already, but there was a deep one on her side that Thomas might need to look at.

"Really, Ryan, I'm okay," she had turned her head to watch what I was doing. "That one is deeper than than the others but it'll close."

Thank the Goddess.

I stood up to face her. She was okay. Relief hit me like a dam breaking, flooding every inch of me. I took a deep breath. "What the hell were you thinking? Just walking into the Alpha compound like that? I thought we agreed you weren't going to do that!"

"No," Mai glared at me, pulling down her shirt, "you agreed. And you can talk! Why are you even here? I told you not to come."

"Of course I was coming." I was yelling now. Not able to help myself.

"You never listen to me, Ryan!"

"I never listen? Mai, you're the one who took off without talking to me! You left me a note, Mai. A fucking note!"

We were face to face, our noses almost touching, the tension and worry of the past hours spilling over in a torrent of words and emotions. It was chaotic, it was heated, and it was the most "us" thing that could have happened.

Just then, a loud cough interrupted us. We both turned to find Jase, now in human form, standing awkwardly, blood from a wound in his side leaking down his leg and his modesty barely covered by some strategically placed foliage.

"You know, if you two are done yelling at each other, I could really use some clothes before I freeze my cute-as-hell ass off out here."

CHAPTER FORTY-FOUR

MAI

Ryan's car was back at the cabin. He carried Jase, who was none too pleased about it. Jase was still in a lot of pain, though he was trying hard not to show it.

"Hey, you're gonna be okay," I assured him.

He grimaced as Ryan jumped, as carefully as possible, over a fallen log.

By the time we got back to the car, Jase's face was a mask of fatigue. Two Shifts in such a short amount of time, plus all the healing his body was trying to do, was really taking it out of him.

Together, Ryan and I gently laid Jase on the back seat of the car.

"Damn it," Jase hissed as he lowered himself down, the muscles in his face taut with pain.

I shot Ryan a worried look. He placed a hand on Jase's shoulder, and a ripple of energy seemed to pass between them. Jase's face softened as the pain visibly drained away.

"You're easing his pain."

The Alpha power cascading off of Ryan left me almost lightheaded.

"How did you do that?" I looked up at Ryan.

Ryan shrugged, his eyes meeting mine. "I don't know, to be honest. My wolf knew; it was instinctual to him. He saw a member of his Pack in pain and wanted to take some of it away for him."

"It sounds similar to something I did in the cabin before. I think I forced him to Shift."

Ryan looked at me thoughtfully. "I don't think that would have worked if Jase hadn't acknowledged us as his Alphas."

"I thought the same thing." I nodded. "Proper Alphas, huh? Aren't we full of surprises?"

Ryan's lips curled into a quick, flirtatious smirk before he got back into the driver's seat. "You have no idea what surprises I have in store for you."

"Oh really?" I raised an eyebrow. "Care to give me a hint?"

"Hell no! I'm going to have a fuckload of fun showing you all the surprises I've got planned."

"I'm not exactly known for my patience, Ryan."

Ryan grinned wickedly at me. "And that just makes it more fun for me."

"Can you two not flirt while I'm bleeding out here?" Jase said from the back seat.

Ryan winked at me. Jase was going to be okay.

"Hang tight, Jase," Ryan declared, and we sped off into the night.

As Ryan navigated the winding roads, I filled him in on what Carl had told me about Brock's plans. "He said Brock and Hayley were taking Sofia to the Meet. They're going to execute her in front of everyone as a warning to the rest of the Pack."

"We know. Derek and Mason have got this. If anyone can get Sofia free, it's those two. We need to get ready. As soon as the Meet is over at midnight, we can't challenge Brock or Hayley for a year. Derek said he'll stall as much as he can, but it's gonna be tight."

Ryan maneuvered the car around a bend at full speed.

"I hate this. I hate being stuck here when our family is out there fighting. We should be there, fighting with them."

"I know." Ryan reached over and twined his fingers in mine. "We'll make it. We'll stop Brock and Hayley, and we'll spend the next fifty years making the Three Rivers Pack a place where everyone is supported and protected."

"You promise?"

"Absolutely."

Jase snorted from the back seat. "Fifty years of marital bliss leading a Pack? You two planning on the white picket fence and two point five pups too?"

"The half pup is a bit concerning," I said, glancing at Ryan with a teasing smile.

Ryan shot me a playful look, his eyes twinkling. "Well, the point five is just there to keep us on our toes, you know? Never a dull moment in an Alpha household."

"Sounds chaotic. I like it," I replied, my eyes meeting his. For a brief moment, the car dropped away, and it was just Ryan and me and the promise of hours and hours of fun making pups.

Ryan glanced over at me, his eyes softening. "Do you want to talk about what happened back at the compound?"

"Do I want to? Not particularly. Do I need to? Probably," I

answered, chewing on my lower lip.

He sighed, his grip tightening around the wheel. "Mai, I was scared out of my mind when I found out you walked right into their lair. Don't ever do something like that again, or I swear, I'll put you over my knee."

I grinned at the image, my eyes twinkling with mischief. "Promises, promises."

Jase groaned theatrically from the back. "Ugh, get a room, you two."

"Oh, we will, after this is all done," Ryan promised, his voice dark and seductive.

Jase was right, though. We had to focus right now; it was just that I thought I wouldn't ever see Ryan again. I'd been so scared, and now he was here. I wanted to lighten the mood, to take a moment, breathe in the scent of him, and steady myself for what was to come. It sucked, but we didn't have time.

"I think Hayley's on ripple."

Ryan's eyebrows shot up. "What? How do you figure?"

"After Seth kidnapped me, there was a witch at the house he kept me in. He was working with this witch to try to break my bond with the Three Rivers Pack. Seth said my bond was 'impure' and that the witch had helped him see it."

The car veered sharply to the left before Ryan corrected it. "What the fuck, Mai? Why didn't you tell me?"

"We've been bouncing around from one disaster to the next. It didn't seem important. Seth was dead. I figured we wouldn't see the witch ever again. But then Arabella said that when she was on ripple, she felt 'pure.' I didn't think anything of it at the time, but Hayley came to see me in the compound. She wanted me to go to the Meet and give up my claim and bond to our Pack. She said, and I quote, 'Your bond with the Three Rivers is impure.'"

"It could be a coincidence," Jase said from the back seat.

I shook my head. "Hayley all but admitted that she was taking ripple. She implied that Brock had been giving it to her."

Ryan tilted his head to one side. It was his thinking pose. "It might explain her personality change. Why she killed Jem. If Brock's been keeping Hayley on ripple for a while now, there is no telling what effects it's having on her."

Jase chimed in with a sarcastic tone, "Ah, the circle of life. Witches, drugs, and impure bonds. What's next? Zombies?"

Ignoring Jase's comment, Ryan looked serious, his eyes searching mine. "Once this is over, we're digging into this, Mai. Ripple, witches, the whole nine yards."

The sincerity in his voice melted away some of the tension I'd been carrying. "I have a feeling this is important. Something bigger is going on here, and if it involves the witches and this drug, then it's bad news for all werewolves."

Ryan swung the car round a corner. He was pushing it, taking it to the limits of what the car could do, and I was so grateful. He would get us there in time, I had to believe that.

"You killed Brock's father."

Ryan glanced at me. "Yes, I did. And I loved every fucking second of it."

Okay then.

"You know, I think he's been planning this ever since then."

Ryan's jaw clenched. "The thought had occurred to me."

"You could apologize," I suggested.

Ryan looked at me for a moment, then we both started laughing.

"I've got a much better idea," Ryan said, as his face turned serious and he let a bit of the rage he was feeling escape along our bond. "Let's go and rip his fucking head off."

Chapter Forty-Five

Mai

We heard the sounds of fighting from over a mile away.

"Derek," Ryan growled, putting his foot on the accelerator. Jase was passed out in the back seat; it was a healing sleep and probably not one he was going to wake from any time soon.

The moment Ryan and I entered the camping ground, we were swallowed by an atmosphere thick with primal energy and conflict. Ryan slammed on the brakes, and we both jumped out. Fighting was all around us. I ran. Two wolves, a snarling ball of teeth, claws, and blood, came from my right. I dodged as they tumbled past me. Ducking under arms and pushing against fighting bodies, I fought my way toward the fire pit at the center of the camping ground. It roared; its flickering light painted a chaotic tapestry on the faces of those nearby who were locked in combat, casting shadows that seemed to dance in rhythm with their strikes.

Derek, Mason, Wally, Thomas, even Sam, looking slim and pale but utterly furious, were in the thick of it, a whirlwind of fur and fangs, fighting with the kind of ferocious abandon that left no question about their will to protect what was theirs. Against them were some of Jem's old enforcers, now Brock and Hayley's. Some were in human form, but most had managed to Shift, and their snarls were meeting snarls, claws clashing against claws.

Amongst them, Sofia stood like a warrior queen, her eyes ablaze, her body a blur of motion as she fought back-to-back with Derek. There was a synchrony in their movements, a unity that was beautiful to watch. Emotions crashed through me—relief that Sofia had escaped, gratitude to Derek for getting her free, pride in both of them and a burning desire to join them and finally, finally, get justice for Jem.

Werewolves from other Packs formed a wary perimeter around the battlefield. They watched with eyes narrowed, caution lacing their stances. They were watching carefully, but not getting involved. They'd wait to see who would emerge the winners. The Bridgetown wolves were there, and I saw Michael, Camille, Danni, Ivan, even Ethan. They couldn't interfere in an internal Pack war, not during an official Meet. We were on our own in this fight. Camille nodded sharply at me, as if to say that we could do this.

My eyes met Ryan's, and in that brief moment of connection, our thoughts were one. We had to find Brock and Hayley. Now.

We pushed forward, our bodies weaving through the chaos. Around us, the fight raged on.

Derek glanced in our direction and shouted, "Now, Ryan! You have to do it now!"

My ears picked up a subtle shift in the howls and growls—a change in pitch that signaled a retreat. My eyes darted, searching, until they locked onto a pair of figures racing toward the edge of the clearing. Brock and Hayley. If they left the Meet, we'd be locked out of challenging for the Alpha pair for a year, a delay I couldn't allow.

There was no way we could catch them in time. I broke into a run, Ryan keeping pace with me, dodging fists and sharp teeth. My eyes were locked on the platform near the fire pit.

"Mai!" Ryan shouted, and I veered toward him, took two steps, and leaped. Ryan caught me, spun, and threw me in one fluid movement as if we had trained this maneuver hundreds of times. I flew through the air, tucked my legs, and landed in a crouch on the platform.

Around me, the din of battle seemed to fade into a distant roar, drowned out by the pounding of my own heart. I had one shot at this.

I howled, my voice rising above the snarls and growls, the clash of bodies, and the breaking of bones. I was acutely aware of every eye turning to me, of the sudden hush that seemed to descend upon the clearing. This was it—the point of no return.

"I, Mai Parker, and my mate Ryan Shaw challenge Brock Madden and Hayley Parker for the Alpha pair of the Three Rivers Pack!"

From my vantage point on the platform, I saw Brock and Hayley freeze at the edge of the clearing, then exchange a rapid, hushed conversation. Brock was frowning, while Hayley's face was twisted, arms gesticulating. She did not want to fight.

Michael and Camille broke from the crowd and marched toward them.

"The challenge has been issued," Michael said, his voice clear and authoritative, cutting through the noise like a knife through butter. "According to the Laws of the Packs, you must accept. Refusal is not an option unless you're willing to abdicate right here, right now."

Brock looked at Hayley for a long moment, his sandy hair falling over his forehead as he tilted his head in a question. They seemed to reach a consensus, their body language shifting subtly, and I could see his muscles straining under his shirt.

Hayley, on the other hand, looked almost frail. Her long blond hair cascaded down her back, framing a face that had grown gaunt. Her green eyes, which always reminded me of a cat stalking its prey, were clouded with a grief she couldn't hide. Yesterday, in the cage room, I hadn't clocked how skinny she'd become. But it was clear now. It was as if the stress had eaten away at her, both physically and emotionally.

Brock looked over the crowd. With a nod, he began moving toward the platform. There was a cocky tilt to his chin and a swagger in his stride as he came toward us.

Hayley followed him, her eyes darting to meet mine. There was no mistaking the venom in her glare. She hated me for this.

Werewolves from various Packs, who had been watching the fight, drew back, giving Brock and Hayley room to pass.

Brock and Hayley finally reached the platform, stepping up to stand opposite us.

"It's fitting your lives should end here like this," Brock sneered, his voice dripping with disdain.

Ryan chuckled, a low, dangerous sound. "You always were a fan of theatrics, Brock. Let's see who dies, shall we?"

"Says the man who's so desperate he just threw his girlfriend onto a platform."

"I'm surprised you saw that while you were running away, your tail between your legs. Just like your dad."

I knew what Ryan was doing, baiting Brock, trying to get him angry enough to make mistakes in the coming fight.

"My father was not a coward," Brock ground out between clenched teeth.

Hayley's eyes locked onto mine, her voice icy. "This is your last chance, Mai. Walk away. You don't have to die for him."

I shook my head, meeting her gaze squarely. "I'm not running anymore, Hayley."

Her lips tightened, and I could see her hands clenching into fists. "You've always been too stubborn for your own good."

"And you've always underestimated me."

Ryan stepped closer to Brock, his voice low but carrying enough to reach every ear. "We challenged you according to the Laws of the Packs. You can either fight or surrender your claim to the Alpha pair. Choose."

Brock looked at Hayley one last time, as if seeking confirmation. She gave a nearly imperceptible nod, her eyes never leaving mine.

"Very well," Brock said, rolling his shoulders back as if preparing for a physical feat. "We accept your challenge."

The crowd erupted, the tension snapping to a new level of intensity. This was it—the point of no return.

Chapter Forty-Six

Mai

Brock and Hayley stepped back, putting a little distance between us. Ryan and I did the same, our eyes locking for a brief second—I sent a pulse of my love through our bond. *If we don't make it out of this, I love you. I always did.*

Ryan growled a warning at me. *Not gonna happen. We're gonna win this thing.*

I smiled softly at him, then Brock lunged. His body was a blur of motion as he aimed a punch at Ryan.

I dived at Hayley as Ryan parried Brock's blow, then snapped his forehead into Brock's nose. Brock staggered back, anger flashing across his features as blood poured down his face.

I collided with Hayley with a thud that sent both of us flying off the platform. Landing on top of her, I wasn't quick enough, and she scissored her legs around my waist and twisted. We flipped, me slamming into the ground with Hayley on top. I punched out, and she reared back, a snarl escaping her lips.

"Stupid, Mai!" she hissed, wiping a trickle of blood from her lips. "Just like your brother. He didn't see it coming either."

Hayley started raining blows to my head, face, and chest. I threw my arms up to block her, then bridged up sharply. She flew over my head, rolling as she landed, then charged at me before I could get to my feet. Her foot smacked into my chest, knocking the wind out of me. I fell back, gasping, my ribs screeching at me.

From the corner of my eye, I saw across the platform that Ryan had Brock in a headlock. Brock's face was red, his eyes bulging as he struggled for breath. Hayley had seen it, too. With lightning speed, she leaped and hammered her elbow into Ryan's face.

Ryan's grip loosened for a split second—enough for Brock to break free, slamming his fist into Ryan's abdomen again and again. Hayley twirled around to face me. I wanted to go to Ryan, but I couldn't. I had to trust that he could handle Brock. My fight was in front of me.

The crowd's excitement reached a fever pitch, their roars and cheers mingling with the grunts and snarls on the platform. The noise pounded against my eardrums. I shut it out, concentrating only on Hayley. Every nerve in my body was humming. This was it—the moment I'd been waiting for. It was either Hayley or me.

She came at me, her fingernails sharpened into talons, aiming for my throat. I saw what she intended to do, saw the bloodlust in her crazed eyes. I dodged her, but she was fast—too fast, and her nails slashed along my skin. If I'd been a second slower, she would have ripped my throat out. The pain was sharp, fire erupting under my skin, and I could feel my hot blood soaking into my top.

"Is that all you've got?" I spat through gritted teeth. "I expected more from someone who killed their own mate."

Her eyes narrowed to slits. "You've got no fucking clue what I've been through. Someone like you could never understand my pain. But bring your skanky little ass over here, and I'll show you what pain is really like."

My wolf growled within me, hungry for justice, for retribution, for blood. I whirled around, grabbed her arm, and punched with my other hand. Her joint popped out of its socket. Then I brought my knee up and slammed it into her midsection. She doubled over as the air was forced from her lungs. I stepped closer, ready to finish her off, but she came up swinging with her good arm, pounding her fist into my face. My head snapped back, stars exploding behind my eyes. The metallic taste of blood filled my mouth where I'd bitten my tongue. She followed it up with a strike to my temple that rattled my skull. The platform tilted. I blinked, trying to clear the dark spots swimming in my vision. Then, somehow, I was kneeling on the ground.

Fuck.

How did that happen?

I looked up. Hayley loomed above me, her foot coming straight for my face. I rolled, and her foot swept past. I threw myself forward and grabbed at her legs. She hit the ground hard. I didn't hesitate, jumping on top of her, using my body weight to pin her down. I wasn't going to let her get back up. My wolf screamed inside me, clawing for me to end it, to snap her neck and tear her apart. The crowd was a distant roar, but in that moment, I could feel their eyes on me, their anticipation of her death.

I reached around and clutched Hayley's neck and head. I had her, and she knew it. She started to buck wildly, trying to throw me off, but I held on. All my rage—at losing Jem, at his betrayal by his true mate, all the frustration I felt for not being there to stop it or to prevent Brock and Hayley from decimating the Pack that Jem had worked so hard to create—it all came pouring out of me. I tightened my grip, ready to twist and end it all. I felt the fight go out of Hayley. She sobbed once, then stilled, waiting for the end.

I hesitated. I don't know why. I could end it, end her, right here. The dark part of me, the part still raging with pain over losing Jem, desperately wanted it. Wanted vengeance. Wanted blood. But as I looked down at Hayley, broken and defeated, I realized I didn't need to do this. Killing her, as satisfying as it might feel in the moment, wouldn't bring back Jem. And I knew in my heart he wouldn't want this—wouldn't want me to kill his mate.

"You murdered my brother," I said, my voice low and cold. "I'll never forgive you for that, Hayley. Leave. Leave our Pack and our lands and never come back."

I dropped her, stood, and took a step forward, feeling a strange sense of finality wash over me.

That's when I felt it—a sudden spike of danger prickling my bonds. I turned just in time to see Hayley lunging at me, her eyes filled with a crazed desperation, her sharpened nails aimed straight for my heart.

There was no time to think, only react. I twisted my body to the side on pure instinct, and as she stumbled past me, carried by her own momentum, my hand shot out. Only it wasn't a hand any longer. Razor-sharp claws swiped at her.

Huh. That was new.

Unlike Hayley, I wasn't on ripple, but I was an Alpha. I could Shift and partially Shift.

Hayley's eyes widened as she clutched at her throat, blood spilling between her fingers. She stared at me with a look almost of relief on her face. She wanted this. She wanted to die, to finally pay for what she'd done. She wanted to let go and be with Jem again. With a final sigh, she fell to her knees, then collapsed onto the ground.

274

CHAPTER FORTY-SEVEN

MAI

I looked up, searching for Ryan. My eyes found him just as Brock landed a roundhouse kick to Ryan's head.

Should have ducked, baby.

Ryan stumbled back; Brock saw his advantage and dashed in with a forward kick. Ryan had been waiting for it, had baited Brock. He caught Brock's leg, twisted to the side, and drove his fist into Brock's thigh. It took a tremendous amount of force, even for a werewolf, to break the femur bone, but everyone heard the bone snap. Brock's face turned pale and gaunt. Good. I looked Ryan up and down, trying to gauge how badly he was hurt. His shirt was torn and bloody, and he was favoring his left leg. Blood spattered his face, but his eyes were aflame with a feral mix of determination and something wild.

Brock sailed forward far more quickly than anyone with a broken thigh bone should be able to, jabbing at Ryan's chest. Ryan swerved to the left and slammed his fist into the back of Brock's head.

"Stop!" I shouted. "Hayley's dead. You're finished, Brock."

Brock spun around, seeking out Hayley. His eyes rested on her body for a moment. I didn't see any grief there, only annoyance. He'd used Hayley to get what he wanted, and she had let him down. My wolf snapped at him from inside me, appalled by his cavalier use of another werewolf.

Brock glanced up at me and panted. "It doesn't matter. I'll run the Pack alone. Oliver did it after his mate died. I claim the right to govern solo."

Fuck!

I had hoped that with Hayley dead, the fight would be called off. One werewolf couldn't be announced as the Alpha of a Pack; it always had to be an Alpha pair. But Brock was right; some Packs only had one Alpha. Usually, that Alpha would continue in their role after their mate had died. That was how Oliver had stayed in power after his mate passed away. Brock and Hayley had already announced themselves as the Alpha pair of the Three Rivers Pack. So, technically, if Brock won this fight, he could rule solo.

Brock surged forward, soaring off the platform, and slammed into me. We hit the ground with a jarring thud and rolled. Before we'd stopped, Brock grabbed my wrist and twisted. I heard the pop a split second before a sharp rush of pain flooded me.

Ryan Shifted in an instant. One second, there was a man sprinting toward me, the next, a massive wolf was flying through the air. I'd never seen anyone Shift so quickly. Ryan hit Brock like a missile, and they both tumbled past me.

I cradled my broken wrist. It hurt like hell, the pain a knife stabbing my brain. I had to get up. I had to help Ryan. I got to my feet and stumbled toward them. Ryan had his jaws around Brock's shoulder. He must have gone for Brock's neck, but Brock had managed to twist away. Ryan was working Brock's shoulder, yanking the muscle. Brock yelled out when Ryan's teeth hit bone, then drove his elbow into the side of Ryan's head. Once, twice, three times.

Brock broke loose, and I rushed toward them, stomping on Brock's shoulder where Ryan had bitten him. He turned and jabbed his fist into my solar plexus. Air disappeared. I couldn't breathe. Ryan was suddenly there between us. Brock smashed into Ryan, their momentum carrying them straight into me. We all flew across the ground, tumbling over and over, my broken wrist a blaze of white-hot pain. Everything ached, and my limbs felt heavy as I pushed myself up. The crowd hushed; they knew it was almost over. Brock grinned at me, swiping away blood from his still-bleeding nose.

"Last chance, Mai. Save your boy and walk away. Or I'll kill you both."

I ignored him and stalked to the left. Ryan went right. Brock swung from Ryan to me, not sure who to face or where the attack would come from first. A flash of uncertainty crossed Brock's face. He knew he couldn't take us. I rocked on the balls of my feet, ready to end this, when a flash of fur streaked past me, and a wolf barreled into Ryan, taking him down. A familiar scent reached my nose.

Korrin.

Fucking hell.

Could he have worse timing? Korrin and Ryan were a rolling ball of chaos, snarling, darting in to attack each other, then dashing out of range. Ryan could take care of Korrin. I glanced back at Brock. He was gone. He'd used the distraction to melt into the crowd.

Shit!

Before I could go after him, Michael and Camille were there.

"Interfering in an Alpha challenge is against the law. Mai and Ryan are hereby declared winners and the new Alphas of the Three River Pack," Michael said, his voice raised so everyone could hear.

Then he moved. Michael leaped on Korrin's back, taking him by surprise, and clamped an arm around Korrin's neck.

"You bite my mate, and I'll bring the full force of our Pack down on you and yours, Korrin. I don't care if you've gone rogue or not, your whole Pack will burn," Camille said calmly.

Korrin froze, and that was all it took. It was over.

Chapter Forty-Eight

Mai

Ryan and I stood on the platform, our eyes meeting for a heartbeat. Even amidst the chaos, that connection felt like an anchor. My broken wrist already felt better. Ryan had insisted I take the super-strong painkillers Thomas had brought with him, then I'd done another partial Shift with it. By the time it had Shifted back into a human hand, Thomas had felt along it and declared the bones were probably fixed, though he wanted to do a proper check-up as soon as we got back to Three Rivers. I'd been shocked at how fast the bones had healed, but as Thomas pointed out, there were definitely some upsides to being an Alpha.

Ryan was next to me, his face a mosaic of bruises and scrapes, his eyes a blazing blue inferno. He was angry that Korrin had interfered, furious that Brock had gotten away. I agreed. Leaving them both alive meant they would come back at us in the future. We'd have to watch our backs until they'd been taken care of.

I looked into the crowd. Derek was there, his left arm held at an odd angle. He was hovering near Sofia. Her face was pale, her fiery red hair a mess, but she was staring at me with a look of excitement on her face. With everything that had happened with Sam and then her getting taken, I hadn't had time to tell her that she was wrong about Derek and Shya. Although, from the possessive looks that Derek was giving her, I was pretty sure she'd find out soon enough.

Wally was next to Sofia, blood seeping from a cut on his head. Thomas was trying to stem the blood, but Wally waved Thomas off, flicked the blood away, then gave me a grin and a thumbs up.

Mason had told me that Shya had gone back to Bridgetown after Tristan's attack on their convoy to guard her brothers. Mason was huddled in a group of about fifteen werewolves. I recognized them as some of Jem's enforcers and I was guessing these were the people who fought on our side, who never joined Brock's crew. Most of them looked worn out and beaten up, but they were all standing. I memorized their faces. I owed them. They believed in us, put their lives on the line for me and Ryan. I would do everything I could to make sure they were safe, and I would protect them with my life.

Camille and Michael jumped onto the platform beside us. Michael nodded to us both, while Camille grinned at me.

"You did good," she whispered above the restless murmurs of the crowd.

I inclined my head to her. "You supported us, offered us sanctuary when we most needed it. We owe you a debt."

"Perhaps," Camille paused, looking out over the people waiting in front of the platform, her eyes coming to rest on Mason. "This is just the start, though. I'm quite sure there will be plenty of opportunities for you to repay the favor."

I got the uneasy feeling that she knew about Mason's feelings for Shya, and wondered for a moment if she was going to ask us to keep

Mason away from her daughter. I followed Camille's gaze to where Mason was chatting with the enforcers. He glanced up at me, his face full of pride, and I knew no matter what Camille asked for, I would have Mason's back.

"Are you ready?" Michael's question cut through my thoughts.

I glanced at Ryan. He was looking down at me with such a look of love of his face that I had a sudden urge to jump him right here.

Ryan knew what I was thinking, and his grin turned wicked. "Patience, Mai."

I narrowed my eyes at him, then nodded at Michael. "We're ready."

A hush came over the crowd. They knew what was coming. Butterflies started swarming in my stomach.

Michael turned to face everyone. "By the laws that bind us and the traditions that guide us, the Alphas of the Bridgetown Pack recognize Ryan Shaw and Mai Parker as the new Alphas of the Three Rivers Pack. Are there any here who would challenge our word?"

I held my breath.

It was only a moment, though it felt like a year, before Camille declared, "Ryan Shaw and Mai Parker, you are hereby recognized by Pack laws as the new Alpha pair of the Three Rivers Pack. Guide your family well."

The crowd erupted into howls and cheers, a wave of sound that washed over me. I grinned as Michael grabbed my good hand, and one of Ryan's, and held them up in the air. I felt it in my blood, in my soul, and through our bond. This was right. This was meant to be.

CHAPTER FORTY-NINE

MAI

My eyes filled with tears as our renegade Pack rushed toward us. Wally got to us first, sweeping me up in a hug.

"You did it!"

"We did it!" I replied, as Sofia and Thomas joined our hug.

I let their scents envelope me. It grounded me, connected me to . They were my family, and after everything we had been through, I just wanted to enjoy this.

"You, girly, are going to make an awesome Alpha!" Wally said, as he put me down.

He must have seen the panic on my face as the idea of actually being an Alpha, of running the Three Rivers Pack and being responsible for over four hundred Shifters, hit me. Wally laughed. "That's a challenge for another day, Mai."

Sofia leaned in for another hug. Wally was right. I'd face that challenge tomorrow. Today was for celebrating and recuperating.

I felt Sofia sob quietly on my shoulder. I was so happy that she was alive I didn't want to let go. She smelled of blood and exhaustion but also of elation and relief.

"You okay?" I whispered. "I was so scared for you."

She nodded. "Me? I thought for sure that Brock had killed you. And then you had to go through that challenge. Fucking hell, Mai! Having to watch and not help in any way, it was worse than when Tristan took me."

I squeezed her tight. "I saw you fighting. You and Derek moved like you were one person. You guys did amazing!"

I felt Sofia shrug as she stepped back. "I'm guess I'm not just your friendly barista anymore; I've picked up a few things. Besides, I'd fight back to back with daemons if it meant getting you free."

I looked at her and grinned. "Comparing Derek to a daemon?"

"No. That would be unkind to daemons."

I guess them fighting together hadn't thawed Sofia's heart. I opened my mouth to tell her that she'd been wrong all this time and there was nothing between Derek and Shya, when Wally said, "We've sent out a call. The whole Pack is coming here. We're going to have a cookout and celebrate properly."

"In that case," Ryan said, as he grabbed me from behind and lifted me up into his arms. "I want some alone time with my Alpha before the hordes arrive."

I giggled as Ryan set off towards the forest. "What are you doing?"

"Taking you somewhere where it will just be us." He growled, holding me so close that I could feel his heart pounding against my chest.

A bolt of desire shot right to my core.

"Ryan," I whispered, my voice husky.

"Nearly there."

He stopped in a small clearing at exactly the point where I judged no one would be able to hear us. He put me down on a bed of soft moss, but I was determined to have control this time.

His expression changed as I unbuttoned his pants and pushed them down his thighs until they fell away to the ground. He wasn't wearing underwear, and his huge cock sprang free. My fingers traced the length of him, from root to tip. He felt solid in my hand, warmth seeping into my palm as I worked him, teasing him with my touch. I lowered my mouth onto him then—savoring the heady flavor of him as the flared crown pushed past my lips and onto my tongue. One hand palmed the thick base, while my tongue worked the top that was just as hard and hot. The saltiness heightened the sweetness of his skin and left a burning trail on my tongue as he pulsed against my lips and tongue.

Ryan moaned when I took another inch of him between my lips, sucking lightly at the rigid flesh throbbing against the back of my throat.

His hips bucked beneath me, meeting every flick of my tongue with a groan.

I lost myself in his pleasure, basking in his panting moans.

"Mai," he warned, his voice low and gruff, as I took more of him into my mouth and sucked. "Fuck!"

That was it. He hauled me up and dropped us both to the ground, his arms snaking around me to protect me from the fall.

I grinned up at Ryan. "Feeling impatient, are we?"

He thrust my legs apart, settling between them. The hard length of him pressed against me, eliciting a throaty moan.

One hand slid under my panties, teasing me with swirls of his finger. His fingers brushed my core, circling but never entering.

"Ryan!" I cried out in frustration.

Laughter rumbled in his chest.

I fisted his shirt, glaring at him. "Now."

He kissed me, and then finally gave me what I craved. Three fingers thrust deep inside me. I broke the kiss, throwing my head back in a strangled gasp. He pumped into me, curling his fingers with each stroke.

The pleasure was almost too much as he increased his pace. Sensation shot from my core, spreading throughout my body.

"Come for me, Mai," he ordered, his eyes locked onto my face. "I want to watch you come."

The coil in my belly snapped, pleasure flooding my veins. My muscles clenched around him as my orgasm ripped through me. I shuddered, crying out his name.

"That's my girl."

He kissed me softly, gently easing his fingers free. I whimpered at the loss, still wanting more.

He knew I wasn't done and grinned wickedly at me. Then he hauled me up and turned me, so I was facing a tree.

"Hold on," he ordered.

A growl rumbled in his chest as he positioned himself behind me. In one hard thrust, he buried himself to the hilt inside me.

I cried out, nearly collapsing at the sensation of being so utterly filled by him.

Ryan's fingers dug into my hips, holding me in place. "You feel so damn good." He pulled back slowly before pounding into me again.

I rocked back to meet his thrusts. This was what life was about. We'd fought for our lives, we'd finally gotten justice for Jem, we were both alive and there was nowhere else I wanted to be. Our bond flared to life, desire and pleasure swirling between us. He pounded into me, each slap of his hips pushing me closer and closer to the edge. Our bond was flooded with sensations. Not just the feel of him against my inner walls, filling me up, stretching me with such pleasure, again and again but I could feel what he was feeling, could feel his raw desire to fill me up with his cum, to make me scream his name.

"Ryan," I gasped.

"That's it, Mai." One hand slid around my hip, fingers finding my clit.

He rubbed tight circles over the sensitive nub and my vision went white. Pleasure erupted through me as I came.

"Fuck, Mai!" Ryan surged into me once, twice more, before stiffening behind me. Warmth flooded my core as he found his release.

My arms shook, threatening to collapse under me. Ryan wrapped an arm around my waist, easing us onto the ground without breaking our connection.

I sighed, snuggling back into his embrace. Our hearts pounded as one, breaths mingling in the cool forest air.

"I love you," he murmured against my neck.

I smiled, lacing my fingers through his against my stomach. "And I love you."

Chapter Fifty

Mai

The rustling leaves and chirping birds formed a soothing lullaby. I traced lazy circles over Ryan's knuckles, content in a way I'd never known before him.

"I partially Shifted. Twice." I said, softly.

"I saw."

"I didn't plan to. Not during the fight with Hayley. It was instinct, like my body just knew what was needed and did it."

"It's part of being an Alpha. You not only had access to the Pack bonds but you could draw energy from them. They gave you the power to control each part of your body, to partially Shift just some of it."

I was silent for a moment, thinking it through. "It felt like our renegade Pack truly believed in us. That we were, are, their Alphas. They gave me the strength to do it."

Ryan nodded slowly. "I've heard rumors about Packs that have lost faith in their Alphas, and their Alphas are weak, unable to partially Shift anymore. It's never been clear if the Pack lost their faith because the Alphas became weak. Or if the Alphas became weak because the

Pack lost faith in them and this weakened the Pack bonds to the extent that the Alphas couldn't draw on the power in them."

"So, if a Pack loses faith in their Alphas, they become easier to defeat?"

"Maybe. It's certainly an interesting theory. I'll need to do some digging."

"Why don't we know already? Why don't Packs know about this stuff?"

Ryan shrugged. "If it's true, there could be a number of reasons. Packs tend to keep to themselves. This is not the sort of information that gets passed around Alphas. Plus, most Alphas have challenged for the position. Not many are trained up by the previous Alphas to take over. They go into it just as blind as we are and learn about things like this on the job, as it were."

"It's wrong. Everyone should know about this. It's part of who we all are."

I fell silent, thinking it all over. I needed to talk to Camille. See what she knew about it.

After a time, Ryan pressed a soft kiss to my shoulder. "We should head back."

I sighed, not wanting this moment of just being us, to end. But he was right. We had responsibilities waiting for us.

We dressed slowly, stealing kisses and caresses along the way. By the time we emerged from the forest, my lips were swollen, and a pleasant ache had settled between my thighs.

Ryan wrapped an arm around my waist, pressing a kiss to my temple. "I don't know about you, but I'm starving."

I laughed, leaning into his side. "You certainly worked up an appetite."

"Only for you, beautiful."

My wolf sighed in contentment.

The sounds of laughter and conversation met us as we approached the campsite. Our Pack, those who fought and were battered and bloody, and those who had come after they heard we had won, milled about, grilling food, and enjoying each other's company, seemingly without a care in the world.

I smiled up at Ryan, love and determination burning in my chest. Today we'd cemented our claim on each other and the Three Rivers. And anyone who challenged that would soon regret it.

The scent of smoked meat reached my nose, and my stomach rumbled in response. Ryan chuckled, giving me a little squeeze. "Let's get you fed."

We made our way over to the grills, where Derek was flipping burgers and bacon. One arm was in a sling, but he was doing a good job with his other one. He glanced up as we approached, a grin splitting his face. "Well, don't you two look properly ravished?"

Heat flooded to my cheeks. Beside me, Ryan growled.

Derek's grin got wider.

"How's your arm?" I asked, nodding to his sling.

"It'll be fine. Thomas patched me up. I'll need to Shift when we get back but I'm on Thomas' painkillers so I don't feel a thing right now."

Ryan nodded, and I caught a quick spike of relief through our bond. He'd been worried about his brothers.

"What about everyone else? Any serious injuries?"

"No deaths. A few serious wounds but Thomas has been working his magic. They'll all live."

It was my turn to feel relief. I knew Ryan felt it through our bond when he stroked the back of my hand.

Sofia arrived carrying an empty tray. "They sure scoffed those quickly!" she said to me, pointedly ignoring Derek. Derek only had eyes for her though, tracking her every move.

"You know, you had some pretty fierce skills out there, Sofia," Derek said, oh so casually. "You been training?"

I exchanged a glance with Ryan. We both knew Derek was really trying to find out if Sofia had been training with someone and if so, who.

Sofia wasn't falling for it. "If I have, it's none of your business. Besides, someone had to pick up the slack while you were busy getting your arm broken."

"Ouch, that hurts." Derek placed his good hand over his heart in mock offense. "And here I thought you'd be impressed by my battle scars."

Sofia scoffed. "Please, I've seen paper cuts more impressive than that."

Derek leaned forward slightly, his voice deep and smooth. "I could show you things more impressive than that. You just have to ask, Sofia."

"Not interested, Derek," Sofia said, holding his gaze and putting down her tray. "I'll never be interested." And with that, she turned and walked away, Derek's eyes trailing after her.

I wondered if I was the only one who knew she was full of shit.

"You're going to have to work a hell of a lot harder than that, bro," Ryan laughed. "You've got a fuckload of groveling to do, if you're finally ready to admit she's your mate."

"Yeah ..." Derek trailed off, his expression dark.

"What about Brock's enforcers?" I asked, pulling Derek's attention back from wherever he'd gone to in his head.

Derek grimaced. "Most of them escaped. They'll be helping Brock but we know who they are. The rest of them are being guarded by our enforcers."

My stomach rumbled loudly. Ryan glanced at me and smiled.

"We'll deal with that later, Derek. Right now—"

"Right now, you both need food. Before you two starve," Derek said as he passed us two plates loaded with food.

I dug in gratefully, the first bite of juicy burger melting in my mouth. A blissful moan escaped me as I chewed; I hadn't realized just how hungry I was.

After we'd eaten, I curled up in Ryan's lap, basking in the warmth of the fire and my Pack's presence. Apart from those with serious injuries, everyone who had fought for us that day sat around the fire, silent, protective. I felt safe and happy. Ryan's arms came around me, holding me close as he rested his chin on the top of my head.

"We should get some rest. We'll need to head back soon, announce ourselves again at Three Rivers. It's important we do it on our territory as well," he said softly, though he made no effort to shift me from his lap.

"In a minute," I murmured.

Ryan pressed a kiss to the top of my head, his lips curving into a smile against my hair. "As long as I have you in my arms, I'm in no hurry to go anywhere."

Warmth flooded me at his words, my heart swelling with love for this man who had turned my whole world upside down. I tipped my head back to meet his gaze, drowning in the depths of his blue eyes.

My contentment dimmed when a sleek black SUV rolled to a stop about twenty feet from us.

What now?

The driver's side door opened, and a statuesque woman stepped out. Her skin was a rich shade of ebony, glowing in the morning light, and her piercing amber eyes seemed to take everything in at once. She wore a tailored white pantsuit that screamed authority, with a lavender silk blouse peeking out underneath. A silver wolf-head pin adorned her lapel. I didn't recognize her, but power radiated off her in waves.

The woman glanced around, her eyes settling on me and Ryan, then headed straight for us. She moved like she was someone who knew how to fight and was confident they were the baddest person in the area. "Alpha Mai Parker and Alpha Ryan Shaw?"

I lifted my chin. "Yes."

She nodded, her lips curling in a half-smile that was both pleased and predatory. "Excellent. I'm Talia Johnson. I work for the Wolf Council, and I'm here to commend you both for how you handled the Brock Harris and Hayley Parker situation."

I blinked, confused. How did they know? Was someone keeping them informed? And was it usual for the Council to send a representative to congratulate all new Alphas? I didn't think so. The Council only usually turned up when there was trouble, and she'd missed that boat by a few hours.

Her voice was velvety, but with a steel undertone as she continued, "The Council has been notably impressed with your resilience and your strength in the face of threats to your authority. You both have proven yourselves worthy Alphas for the Three Rivers."

"Thank you," Ryan said, his tone icy. He didn't like her sudden appearance any more than I did. "We appreciate the Council's vote of confidence."

Talia's eyes twinkled, and her smile widened just a bit, revealing a row of impeccable teeth. "You're guarded. That's understandable. I assure you, I'm here to help."

Help? I took a guess at her real motives. "Are you here about ripple? Or about the witches?"

She swung her eyes to me. I felt like an ant who'd just ridden a tiny unicycle in front of a human. I'd done something surprising, and now she was assessing me.

"Both actually."

"So, you think they're linked, too?"

She inclined her head. "I can see that we have a lot to talk about, Mai Parker. However, my primary role here today is to remind you that the Three Rivers Pack is due to nominate a new Council member in five days."

"I'm aware of the nomination," Ryan interjected, clearly unimpressed. "And if you really wanted to remind us of it, a phone call would have sufficed."

"Well, you're currently a Pack of particular interest to the Council, and this will be a special nomination. These are turbulent times. Your nominee will wield extraordinary power and their vote could be vital in swaying the Council's decisions one way or another. You need to be sure of who you nominate."

Of particular interest to the Council? That did not sound good. My phone rang in my pocket, the sound loud and jarring.

"I'll let you get on with your new roles. Congratulations on becoming the Alpha pair. I'm sure we'll see each other soon," Talia said, before turning on her heel and striding back to the car.

Well, that wasn't ominous at all.

I watched her get into the back seat before pulling out my phone and answering it.

"Yes?"

"You and your fucking family," Brock panted. "You always screw things up. No matter. I always have a Plan B."

Ryan looked sharply at me and held out his hand for the phone. I didn't think so.

"You sound out of breath. Are you running, Brock? Or hobbling with your broken leg? You better run, because we're coming for you."

"I don't need to run, Mai. You're going to welcome me back with open arms, and in five days, you're going to nominate me to the Wolf Council."

I laughed. "Did Ryan pummel your head so much that you have a head injury? You need to find a doctor, Brock, to put you out of our misery before we do."

"Laugh all you want. It's going to happen."

"What makes you think we're going to do anything other than kill you?"

He paused, and for a moment I wondered if he had hung up. "Because Jem isn't dead, and I'm the only one who knows where he is."

Can Mai and Ryan can find Jem in time? Find out in *The Resolute*

Mate – Book 3 in the Shifters of the Three Rivers series.

Want to know what happened on Derek and Sofia's hot and dangerous first date? Sign up to my newsletter at www.kiranightingale.com for a *free* prequel novella!

FREE BOOK! COME JOIN US IN THE SHIFTER REALM!

Kira Nightingale
Mystically Dark, Wildly Romantic...

Sign up to my newsletter and get Fairground Fling, a free prequel short story about Derek and Sofia's first date!

As an author, I write paranormal romance books that are mystically dark and wildly romantic. I send out my newsletter every week, and in it you can get exclusive content and snippets from my current work-in-progress, news about what I'm up to, and sometimes even photos of my clumsy cat, Scout. You can sign up to my newsletter at www.kiranightingale.com

Fairground Fling, Shifters of the Three Rivers 0.5

No way will I let fate decide my destiny, but Derek Shaw is back and

proving impossible to resist.

Sofia

All I wanted was to run my coffee shop in peace, avoid my fated mate, and forget about our Shifter bond. Is that too much to ask for?

Apparently it is, because Derek Shaw just walked back into my life, all rippling muscles and piercing eyes. The man sets my blood on fire, but there's no way I'm giving in. I've seen what happens when "fated mates" are torn apart, and I won't let that happen to me.

Derek left to join the military, turning his back on our bond. Now he's back in the Three Rivers Pack, determined to win me over. But I've built walls around my heart that even an Alpha wolf can't break through. At least, that's what I keep telling myself...

Derek

I left Three Rivers to serve my country, but I never forgot Sofia. Every day, her fiery hair and captivating scent haunted my thoughts.

Now I'm back, and the pull towards Sofia is stronger than ever. My wolf won't rest until I claim what's mine. But Sofia's determined to keep her distance. That's okay, though. I'm a Shaw, and we never back down from a challenge.

ALSO BY KIRA NIGHTINGALE

Shifters of the Three Rivers series

The Runaway Mate

The Renegade Mate

The Resolute Mate

The Rescued Mate

The Reluctant Mate(coming 2025)

The Relentless Mate (coming 2025)

A Three Rivers Holiday Tale: A Shifters of the Three Rivers Novella

Boxsets

Shifters of the Three Rivers, Omnibus of Books 1-3 (ebook only)

Mai and Ryan's story with *an exclusive epilogue!*

Audiobooks

The Runaway Mate (available on Audible and Amazon)

Coming Soon

The Renegade Mate
The Resolute Mate

THE RESOLUTE MATE

The Resolute Mate

Their bond is undeniable, but the challenges they face could tear them apart forever...

Mai

Just when I thought Ryan and I had finally got our revenge, our world is thrown into chaos once more. A deadly drug is wreaking havoc among the Packs, and to make matters worse, Brock is blackmailing us to nominate him for a seat on the Wolf Council. If he wins, it's not just us that he'll be coming after—he wants every Shifter community under his control.

But this Alpha gig is not proving easy, and if Ryan and I can't work out how to rule together, we could lose everything.

Ryan

Protecting Mai is a constant battle; my mate has made some dangerous enemies. With my wolf demanding I stop at nothing, and

Mai fighting my every move, I have to navigate our new situation with care—something I'm not exactly good at. Only now we're in a race against time, and if I don't get this right, it could destroy all Shifters. But I'll do anything to protect my mate, my pack, my family.

Filled with heart-pounding action, sizzling romance, and unexpected twists, The Resolute Mate is a breathtaking conclusion to Mai and Ryan's epic journey in the Shifters of the Three Rivers series. Will their love withstand the ultimate test, or will the shadows of their past destroy everything they hold dear?

ABOUT KIRA NIGHTINGALE

Kira Nightingale is a Scot living in Canada. She has always wanted to be a writer, and can't believe how lucky she is to finally be able to write romance stories all day long. She lives with her husband, her two children and a massive cat called Scout. Kira loves to drink tea (her favorite is Long Island Iced Tea, but unfortunately she only gets to drink this occasionally) and likes to dunk cookies in it (yes, even the Long Island kind.)

Acknowledgements

Putting together a book for publication is no small project and involves many steps after the author has written 'The End.' Once again I'd like to thank my wonderful editor, Brigitte Billings. Any mistakes are mine. The awesome cover was created by 100 Covers – thank you Jamie Ty for all your help and support.

9 781738 283835